JOHNNY HAZZARD

GO THERE.
OTHER TITLES AVAILABLE FROM PUSH

JOHNNY HAZZARD

EDDIE DE OLIVEIRA

PUSH

SCHOLASTIC INC.

NEW YORK   TORONTO   LONDON   AUCKLAND   SYDNEY

MEXICO CITY   NEW DELHI   HONG KONG   BUENOS AIRES

ISBN 0-439-67362-3

Copyright © 2005 by Eddie de Oliveira

All rights reserved. Published by PUSH, an imprint of Scholastic Inc., 557 Broadway, New York, NY 10012.

SCHOLASTIC and associated logos are trademarks and/or registered trademarks of Scholastic Inc.

12 11 10 9 8 7 6 5 4 3 2 1   6 7 8 9 10 11/0

Printed in the U.S.A.   40

First PUSH paperback printing, November 2006

To my friends

America is a large, friendly dog in a very small room.
Every time it wags its tail it knocks over a chair.
— Arnold Toynbee, British historian

Oh my God, it's a mirage. I'm telling y'all, it's sabotage.
— Beastie Boys

JOHNNY HAZZARD

ONE

It takes precisely thirty-three minutes from number twelve Olfman Drive to Austin-Bergstrom International airport.

Johnny Hazzard (grade-A average at math, always tall for his age, the greenest eyes) remembers two journeys taking a little longer, and one in particular being dangerously stretched, after a four-car pile-up. But thirty-three minutes is how long it should take, providing Mrs. Hazzard doesn't drive too cautiously. (Her driving is not known for excessive vigilance.)

Every May for the past six years, Mrs. Hazzard has driven her son Johnny and daughter Lydia (slight of frame, ever so sensible, ever so clever) to catch the connection to George Bush Intercontinental in Houston. From George Bush, it's a hefty flight to London Gatwick.

The car journey from London Gatwick to Flat 4, Mountview Mansions, Maida Vale, takes approximately seventy-five minutes.

A more specific figure is impossible to ascertain, as London traffic can be as temperamental and unreliable as its weather.

Houston to London: The in-flight food will be a choice of two hot dinners (usually a vegetarian option and/or fish, as well as reliable white meat) followed by a damp and uninspiring dessert. On many occasions, possibly four but certainly three, this has been a fruit salad accompanied by a dollop of allegedly fresh, off-white cream. After a brief and uncomfortable economy class snooze (provoked by the airline's screenings of Hollywood fare, documentaries on Alaska, and ancient situation comedies), a cooked breakfast is always served approximately one and a half hours before landing. This morning meal is a mixture of the British and the continental, often depending on which airline Johnny and Lydia Hazzard are flying. Over the years, sausages, pancakes, strawberry jam, raspberry jam, chewy bacon, waxy cheese, crunchy cereal, and sugary doughnuts have all played their part.

Johnny Hazzard has always loathed the car journey to Austin-Bergstrom International. On this occasion, he consoles himself with the thought that for five of the previous summers he has dreaded the trip, then found his time in London to be occasionally lonesome, but largely agreeable. Since his parents divorced, some seven years ago, London has been his second home. The entire summer vacation, from May to mid-August, is spent in Mr. Hazzard's central London apartment. And, with the exception of the first summer six years back, when Johnny Hazzard was just nine and tears were not uncommon, the trips have turned out to be far more enjoyable than he initially thought. But still, the drive to the airport remains difficult. Although he

2

could never admit it to either parent, Johnny prefers his mother's company to his father's.

Traditionally, Johnny has always thought he'd miss his high school friends as well. Especially his closest pals: Jack (short, keen to please, fast becoming a chain smoker), Kade (young for his years, stout yet debonair, possessed of an unhealthy interest in TV detective shows of the seventies and eighties), and David (baby-faced, acerbic, sardonic, sarcastic, eats too much fudge). But, without fail, he would forget about them after a week or two in London and move on to the dizzying heights of online video game contests, DVD and video marathons, heavy reading, and Internet chatroom shenanigans. This year's feeling is different. In the past few months, Johnny had felt some changes going on in his friendships with Jack, Kade, and David. Quite quickly, and quite naturally, there had been a shift in conversation subjects, and in manner; Johnny Hazzard had been happy to tell himself that, at long last, they had all "matured."

Physically, Johnny had always been a step ahead of his classmates. His voice dropped when he was just twelve, and he began shaving twice a week at fourteen. This made him the envy of the boys who hadn't started shaving twice a week. Johnny preferred a wet shave, as it gave him a sense of control over his face. But when it came to girls, Johnny had been just as retarded as Jack, Kade, and David. Until recently.

Kade has been "seeing" Natalie Perez, the lovely cheerleader, for three weeks now. Johnny has been regularly convincing himself he isn't jealous. Natalie, he has deduced, is a nymphomaniac who uses and abuses boys. Johnny is not interested in a girl so superficial. Besides, they have been going steady for three weeks, and Kade has yet to take the plunge and get a hold of her tits. "It just doesn't feel right yet," Kade has said. Johnny has told him Natalie is manipulative, shallow, inane, weak-willed, dumb, and easy.

Jack hasn't even kissed a girl, and David is much too rude to get very far. More than one grown-up has told David he has a future in literature. And more than one girl has told David to never call her again. Johnny Hazzard figures that David can't help but be offensive, and that this flaw might cost him dear in the "getting laid" stakes.

Like his three best friends, Johnny Hazzard is a virgin. The urgency that has crept into conversation recently has made him uncomfortable. Sex has become the mission, the quest, the whole point of being alive. And with Kade having a regular girl, it seems he will reach the Holy Grail first. This is pissing Johnny Hazzard off slightly. After all, he was the first to properly kiss a girl, when he was just eight years old. Tongue hockey at eight is a messy business, but Johnny Hazzard struggled through. He opened and closed his mouth like a fish, imitating what he had seen on *Dawson's Creek*. Saliva dribbled down his chin and dripped onto his hand. The memory of his first kiss is forever marred by the news, when he came home that evening, that his parents were divorcing.

Then there was his first grope, some four years later. Johnny first felt a pair of breasts in his bedroom, while his mother hosted a

New Year's Eve party in the living room directly below. Jessica Travis (not slim, happy-go-lucky, unacceptable breath) lay down on Johnny's Porsche duvet (present from Mr. Hazzard, unwanted, now disposed of). As party music and dozens of voices filtered up through his floor, Johnny Hazzard lay next to Jessica Travis and stroked her hair. Without a word being shared, he began moving his hand downward, hovering it in midair before gently cupping her right breast and moving his lips close to hers, kissing her gently, considerately. As the kiss became more intense, so did the hand movements. In mid-grope, Johnny couldn't help but think how cool the whole incident was, and how desperate he was to tell his friends about it at the first available opportunity. After just five minutes of fun, Jessica Travis decided she had had enough, and the young couple descended the stairs to rejoin the party. Johnny never really talked to her again. The boys ensured that word spread throughout the school. Johnny is not a jock, he is not an idol, he is not a pinup. But for three days at least, Johnny Hazzard was *the* boy.

So it is perfectly understandable that Johnny Hazzard is peeved at his predicament. He deserves to lose his virginity, dammit. While the friends have not been pressuring each other, they have still all managed to be haunted by a spirit-crushing sense that time is running out (all except Jack, who just assumes sex won't happen to him until at least twenty-one). Sixteenth birthdays are approaching, and the boys know something has to be done. (So long as they love the girl, of course. Slutty cheerleaders won't do. Kade has justified himself by claiming that although Natalie Perez *is* a cheerleader, she is a good Catholic and far from slutty.)

All this is preying on Johnny's mind. It is unfair and unjust to leave Austin just two months after Mrs. Hazzard has bought him a bottle of expensive aftershave for his fifteenth birthday. Johnny loves his dad, sure, but he's beginning to feel put upon. As he passes the sights he won't see for a third of a year, he thinks about London, where he will not have a single friend to call or hang out with. It was tolerable while he was a kid, but not now. Now it's just punishment.

"You look like shit," Johnny Hazzard's older sister Lydia says from the front passenger seat, interrupting a lengthy silence.

"Fuck off," Johnny Hazzard replies.

"Johnny . . ." Mrs. Hazzard speaks with the weariness of a mother who's heard it all before.

Lydia is probably right. Johnny Hazzard looks miserable. The sixth car journey, the sixth flight, the sixth damp dessert, the sixth meeting with his father since the divorce, the sixth summer of rain, gray days, and the occasional humid heat wave, the sixth summer of watching Lydia have a better time — the full weight of this hits Johnny Hazzard, and he is sure he has never had such a feeling before.

TWO

"Did you pack the bag yourself, sir?"

It is not often that Johnny Hazzard is called sir. The man at the check-in desk is either naturally polite or hideously sarcastic, using "sir" in the same way police officers do — twirling a term of respect into a vile and condescending sneer. Johnny sides with the former possibility, satisfied to be considered an adult even if the check-in guy has his passport and knows full well he's only fifteen.

"Actually, I packed it," says Mrs. Hazzard, destroying any illusion the check-in guy might have that Johnny is his own man.

Mrs. Hazzard has insisted the Hazzard clan arrive at the airport check-in very early, in order to give time for the numerous checks that have been commonplace since September 11, 2001. Mrs. Hazzard takes the kids, as she always does, to the coffee shop for hot chocolate. Conversation is thin. Mrs. Hazzard hates this day as much as Johnny does. Each time she accidentally reminds herself of the loneliness of summer, she tries to cover it up by asking a question. Johnny and Lydia give one-word answers. Then the silence returns. Then Mrs. Hazzard is saddened by the memories of summer again, so she asks another question, and so on. Johnny knows his mom is sad, and that makes him feel worse. Lydia puts on her headphones and listens to some music. Other people in the coffee shop laugh loudly and kiss slowly, while the Hazzards couldn't look more disparate. It's as though the three of them are three silent strangers in the same family. It's easier not to show too much warmth and fondness because it will only make the parting that much harder.

Ten minutes later, they walk, slowly and without great enthusiasm, to the departure point. Mrs. Hazzard hugs Lydia, then Johnny. She straightens Johnny's shirt collar and strokes her daughter's hair. A tear trickles out of her left eye. She dabs at it with a handkerchief and kisses each child on the cheek. She realized some time ago that although they're still her children, they're no longer children.

"Have fun. And be careful. Make sure you call, okay?" Mrs. Hazzard asks.

"Sure," replies Lydia, wearily.

"Don't let your brother get bored," orders Mrs. Hazzard, which she has never said before.

Without really thinking, Johnny Hazzard leans in and gives his mother a second hug. The tears really start sliding from Mrs. Hazzard's eyes now.

"Bye, Mom," says Johnny. "Don't cry."

Lydia and Mrs. Hazzard say bye-bye, and the siblings walk down the aisle to departures. As is the tradition, Mrs. Hazzard stands perfectly still and waves until her children, having shown their passports and boarding passes, turn back and wave before disappearing behind a screen, ready for their security checks.

Johnny Hazzard begins to feel a little empty in his stomach. It just doesn't feel right leaving Mom all by herself for so long. A small puddle of tears seeps into his eyes, but he won't let himself cry.

"Could you remove your shoes please, sir?"

There it is again. "Sir." Johnny is disturbed from his melancholy, delighted as he is to take off his sneakers and pass them through the X-ray machine for the man who called him sir. He walks through the metal detector. No Klaxons sound. All clear. Lydia follows behind. Klaxons abound. Three security men approach, realize she's a woman, and summon the only female security guard on duty. This, of course, is no straightforward matter. Somebody radios somebody else, who calls somebody else, who ends up radioing the guard who radioed first, to inform him that nobody seems able to find the only female security guard. Lydia is left waiting for a few minutes, until a rotund young woman with a face that takes no prisoners arrives driving a buggy for disabled passengers.

Lydia tries to explain that it might be her tongue-piercing that is setting the machine off. The rotund security woman insists on running a thorough metal detector search across her body, as well as frisking her. Lydia doesn't help herself by rolling her eyes, huffing, and puffing.

"We take security very seriously, young lady," is the security woman's response. Johnny Hazzard smiles. *Young lady*, he thinks to himself. *Awesome. I get a "sir," she gets a "young lady."*

The departure lounge is filled with businessmen and business-women, screaming babies, young European travelers, and nondescript folks you'd never even notice. He's interested in the small clique of European travelers. Spanish? Portuguese? Italian, perhaps. Long dreadlocks on some, neat side-partings on others. What the hell attracted them to Austin? How do they know it exists? Are they a band? Johnny often wonders if his fellow passengers are in massively successful and hip European bands he ought to have heard of. The one thing foreigners might know about Austin is that it is a beehive of musical activity. Virtually everybody there has something to do with a band or singer. Live music pours out of the bars and clubs of downtown to form an eclectic wave that passes over wandering pedestrians. And once a year, the South by Southwest Music and Film Festival provides the city with a huge influx of visitors. Musicians and filmmakers come from all over the world. For a week or so, Austin's where it's at.

The flight is delayed by twenty minutes. Johnny Hazzard begins reading his Michael Moore book. Johnny saw *Bowling for Columbine*, and bought all of Moore's books the following day. But it was *Fahrenheit 9/11* that had the most profound effect. He saw it at the movies with friends, and was embarrassed to be a little tearful in places, shocked at the gung-ho, almost deranged enthusiasm of some of the US troops, and embarrassed that his government's actions had killed so many people. It was a curious mixture of embarrassment and pity that made him cry. Johnny pitied the kids seduced by the army at shopping malls — he himself had sat in a classroom listening to the bullshit spouted by recruitment officers. But he *knew* it was bullshit, and for Johnny, and the boys, being a soldier was a choice not a necessity. *Fahrenheit 9/11* was a horrific eye-opener.

At last, the gate opens. Johnny and Lydia Hazzard board the plane. And just as he steps into the gate tunnel, he suddenly feels as though something — though he has no idea what — is about to happen. One of the flight attendants, no older than twenty-five, smiles and welcomes him aboard. He is stirred out of his stupor and thanks her. Lydia grabs the window seat. Johnny folds his jacket neatly and places it in the overhead compartment, takes his seat next to Lydia, and moments later is joined to his left by a lanky and eagle-nosed white man in a sober blue suit.

As the passengers come aboard, Johnny takes out a chocolate bar and begins to munch. The young female flight attendant walks down the aisle and definitely stares and smiles at him. Not the "ah, you poor little thing, flying by yourself" sort of smile he's used to. Nor the "isn't he sweet" smile, which Lydia's friends occasionally give him.

I must've smeared some chocolate across my mouth, thinks Johnny Hazzard. But no.

This smile is serious. It means business. A shy-but-certain smile, the kind Johnny Hazzard has seen in movies. Johnny enjoys the fact Lydia has missed out on this personal moment. He turns in his seat, catches the eye of the eagle-nosed white man in the sober blue suit, and twists his neck further around to find the flight attendant again. She's leaning in to help a small boy fasten his seat belt. She straightens, looks up, and catches Johnny's eye again. Her mouth cracks into a closed half-smile, the left tip of her lips stabbing her left cheek. She's not the flawless type of beautiful you see in models. She's the real type of beautiful you see in wait-resses, hot moms, and, well, flight attendants. His heart thumping, feeling more than a little nervous and more than a little excited, Johnny imitates her, offering a crooked closed smile in reply.

He turns back around and sits up straight in his seat. All bleak thoughts about a summer away from his pals melt away, albeit briefly. Then the self-satisfaction is interrupted —

"She's way too old for you."

"Fuck off, Lydia."

And Johnny Hazzard is reminded of the way he felt so good the New Year's Eve that Jessica Travis allowed him to touch her.

THREE

Johnny Hazzard is woken from his sleep by the captain's voice.

"Ladies and gentlemen, British Summer Time is seven thirty A.M., the temperature is fifteen degrees centigrade, and the weather is overcast."

If it's overcast, it must be London. The changeover at George Bush had been relatively painless, but the flight from Houston to London was the usual — too long, too hot, and too cramped (despite the plane being only half full). Lydia sleeps on as Johnny stretches in his seat, wipes the gunk from his eyes, and tries to get a look out of the window by the seat in front. The plane has yet to begin its descent. Johnny Hazzard tries hard to remember what his dream was about, but fails and returns to his book.

Following a surprisingly tasty British breakfast of high cholesterol and weak tea, the plane arrives at London Gatwick ten minutes ahead of schedule. After a lengthy queue at passport control,

Johnny and Lydia wait around at baggage claim for even longer. They collect their suitcases, Johnny waits a few more minutes for his skateboard, and they head out to find their dad. Johnny Hazzard finds himself looking forward to seeing the old guy. They last met at Christmastime, when Mr. Hazzard headed out to Austin, alone, and Mrs. Hazzard allowed him to stay in the spare room for a week. The festive season wasn't quite as fa la la la la as it ought to have been, but then it's never going to be easy when a divorced couple are brought together again at precisely the time of year when everyone hopes for happiness, then unwraps to find misery. Johnny respects his parents enormously. Their split was inevitable and undramatic — a conflict of philosophies and ennui. The conflict was the inevitable conclusion to a marriage between a hippie and a quasi-hippie. Mr. Hazzard wanted to branch out and make big bucks, while Mrs. Hazzard thoroughly disapproved. They had married young; both were just twenty and Lydia was born two years later. The family home had always been somewhere in or around Austin, and some of Johnny's earliest memories include front doors left wide open and assorted friends and distant family popping in for cake and shoulder-crying. Music (folk, soft rock, Bob Dylan and Willie Nelson, naturally) was a fixture of the home. Johnny remembers both his parents being very popular and apparently very understanding. He remembers a transvestite couple who used to drop in every Saturday, in full garb, for Mrs. Hazzard's delicious low-fat pizza. He also remembers his mother and her mother having long arguments about how best to bring up Johnny and Lydia. Mrs. Hazzard always won.

* * *

Johnny's early childhood had been colorful and inconsistent, but always happy. His parents ran a restaurant together, until Mr. Hazzard wanted more, and they had become bored with each other. And so it was that Johnny's father moved to London.

Standing behind a metal barrier, waiting for his children, Mr. Hazzard is wearing blue dungarees, a bright yellow T-shirt, and flip-flops. Despite this, Johnny and Lydia smile broadly and speed over to hug their dad. Johnny has always thought the airport arrivals catwalk a bit too much of a stage, with people on either side watching you, some of them clutching signs reading MR. BAXTER, MRS. GOLDBERG, or PARADISO HOLIDAYS. He doesn't like the feeling of a dozen or more people observing him in a tender moment with his dad.

"You get any taller and I'll start to bang your head down with a hammer," jokes Mr. Hazzard, for the third consecutive year. Johnny laughs. He is pleased to see him. Lydia kisses him on one cheek and Mr. Hazzard offers Johnny his other. Johnny feels self-conscious, but kisses. Mr. Hazzard takes over control of the baggage cart and they head to the parking lot.

The drive to Maida Vale is a long one. Heavy rush-hour traffic isn't helped by a bomb scare at the Great Portland Street underground station, which has resulted in road closures and diversions. Mr. Hazzard puts on a jazz radio station quietly and asks, as ever, to be filled in on the previous six months' events. Lydia kicks things off with a detailed description of her final months of high school, of graduation, and the prom. Johnny Hazzard feels a little

15

distant this time. He talks, but isn't fully switched on. The sagging clouds impose on the buildings beneath them and on Johnny Hazzard, too. It is the dismal nothingness of overcast weather — neither sunny nor raining, just gray. Johnny is beginning to really miss Olfman Drive. This could have been the summer like in all those growing-up movies — the summer when he and his buddies would go on a camping trip, find a dead body, and jump across a leach-infested quagmire into adulthood. He *is* happy to see his father, but he tells himself he should have put his foot down and demanded an Austin summer for once.

"I got A's in math, science, and history," Johnny reports now, somewhat proudly.

"Well done," says Mr. Hazzard. "How about English?"

"B."

"One better than last time!" says Mr. Hazzard, as enthusiastic as he usually is on these long car journeys.

Lydia is the first to ask after Siska. Siska is Mr. Hazzard's new wife. They married three years ago. Johnny and Lydia were best man and bridesmaid, respectively. She is originally from Belgium, but moved to London to teach art at one of the universities, which serves as a neat supplement to the income she makes from selling paintings. Siska's abstract works sell for four-figure sums, despite Johnny having absolutely no idea what any of them mean.

"Oh, you know, she's fine," says Mr. Hazzard.

"Sold any more paintings?" Johnny asks.

"Another three just this week, to a collector from Ireland." Mr. Hazzard beams. And then the car journey is over, and they have arrived at the underground garage beneath the twelve-story apartment block where Mr. Hazzard and Siska have made their new home.

Mr. Hazzard helps Johnny carry the suitcases into the elevator. Fifth floor. *Too many mirrors*, thinks Johnny Hazzard, not for the first time. The walls are indeed covered in oblong, overlarge mirrors that make the place look like something out of *The Shining* rather than a home sweet home. Too many mirrors damage self-confidence.

Johnny Hazzard notices a new couch on the fifth floor, located between flat four and flat five. The hallway is spacious, its carpet fluffy, and, Johnny suspects, probably fun to roll on naked.

Before Lydia has a chance to open the front door, Siska is there, her sky-blue blouse flapping in the breeze against her thin frame, her reading glasses perched on the edge of her nose like a car balanced precariously over a cliff. Her dark blond hair is tied up with a series of hairbands, elastic bands, and clips, so that it sits on her head looking a bit like a wedding cake. She opens her arms wide, her left hand clutching a half-empty bag of tobacco.

"Dah-lings!" she screams, almost unnervingly loud, in what most think is a French accent, but which is in fact pure Brussels.

17

"Hey, Sisk," says Lydia, hugging her stepmom.

"How's it going, Siska?" asks Johnny Hazzard, joining in the group hug.

"I have missed you, my dahlings."

"You should have come to Austin for Christmas," suggests Johnny Hazzard, out of politeness rather than practicality.

"Johnny, dahling, you are crazy. Your mother would burn my hair off."

Johnny Hazzard likes Siska. She makes him laugh. She is very good at diffusing tense situations and at turning potential tragedy into comedy. Mrs. Hazzard has never met her, and it's more than likely they'd get along in an uncomfortable sort of way. But still, all present know full well that Johnny's suggestion of a stepfamily yuletide is the stuff of fairy tale. So Siska's response about hair arson, though a little far-fetched, is just perfect.

She ushers the kids in and insists that Mr. Hazzard deal with the bags. Siska has, for the first time ever, painted a banner across the hallway of the apartment, which reads WELCOME BACK LYDIA AND JOHNNY. Lydia is a little taken aback; Johnny thinks it's very cool. A swirling mixture of dark reds, blues, and greens come together to form a vomitlike but heartfelt message.

The Hazzard apartment is as chaotic and disorganized as its two main inhabitants. There isn't a great deal of floor space in the lounge or dining room: Piles of books and papers litter the floor, unopened mail lines the fruit bowl, stacks of clothes wobble in corners and on chairs. There is a long corridor, decorated with Siska's brightly lit portraits of the Hazzards: Lydia, Johnny, and Mr. Hazzard. It's difficult to make out which painting represents which Hazzard. For a while last summer, Lydia was convinced she was the portrait that later turned out to be Mr. Hazzard. Siska was recently commissioned to paint the official portrait of the Belgian ambassador to Britain, so she is definitely doing something right.

Off to the left of the corridor are the two kids' rooms — Johnny's contains a lot of books, clothes, magazines, CDs, and games. To avoid bickering, Mr. Hazzard equipped both rooms with stereo systems, the same size beds, and TVs. But Johnny has a computer and Lydia does not — there is never true equality between siblings. At the end of the corridor gallery is the open-plan lounge and dining room. Beyond that are the adults' quarters — the master bedroom, a shambles at the best of times, and Siska's studio, a shambles at all times. Various types and colors of paint are strewn across the floor, and pretty much everything else for that matter. Siska's "work wardrobe" hangs on a clay coat hanger behind the studio door: more flowing gowns, blouses, and clothes that are trying hard to be capes. There are three unfinished paintings on the go at any one time. Siska has a tremendous work rate, but rather like a long-distance runner, she knows the end is somewhere, even if she can't quite work out exactly how far away it is.

Johnny Hazzard has been fond of Siska since he first met her. He and Lydia have accepted her just like they've accepted summers in London. Sure, there are minor flare-ups, but they remember that Mr. Hazzard was alone for three years before Siska came on the scene. He was an unhappy man, and, despite her unpredictability, she has filled a hole in the big man's life and never tried too hard to pass herself off as a second mom. More like a foreign, slightly batty aunt. Johnny respects this enormously. Up until recently, when Johnny considered himself a mere child (all of two years ago at the age of thirteen), Siska had him cackling with her fantastical, quirky stories. She would visit Johnny before bed and, sitting on the floor beside him, weave complex and fascinating tales of alleged Belgian and Dutch folklore. Johnny didn't care whether they were really real or not, because they were real enough. Siska's stories were, at times, as abstract as her paintings, yet somehow Johnny found a way to understand. He would fall asleep with the smell of Siska's sweet chewing tobacco in his nostrils, her soft and soothing voice in his ears.

Her fondness for Belgian comic books has rubbed off on Johnny, too. The country's long and fine tradition in comics has been brought to Johnny's attention; in his bedroom there sits a pile of books Siska has bought him over the years. *Boule et Bill*, *Tintin* (in English), and *Jojo*'s fantastic tales make up some essential jet-lag reading. There's something reliable about them. Sure, Johnny knows them all inside and out, but it feels very, very comforting to come back to his room every summer and have a journalist with a strawberry-blond quiff, a little boy and his naughty dog, and a mischievous, motherless youngster all patiently waiting for him.

Johnny and Lydia enter the dining room to find a veritable feast has been laid out for them. Finger nibbles, potato chips, the odd can of beer, and several pizzas sit begging to be gobbled on the overpriced glass dining table. Siska asks some polite questions about life in Texas. Lydia gives healthier answers than Johnny, who's content to fill his face with *choux* pastries, jam tarts, and bruschetta.

"Dahlings, I don't know how you can enjoy forty-degree weather," says Siska, referring to the Texan summer norm, in Celsius degrees.

"You say that every year," says Mr. Hazzard, but then again *he* says many things every year. There is something about this repetitive welcome home routine that appeals to Johnny Hazzard. He feels interesting, he feels loved, he feels the attention of two people he's rather fond of. The long, lonely flight is yesterday's news. Johnny Hazzard is content and his stomach is full.

FOUR

Rennes Bordeaux Toulouse Marseille Nice Paris Lille
Trondheim Oslo Stockholm Copenhagen Riga Helsinki
Krakow Minsk Kiev Odessa Moscow Rostov-on-Don
Sarajevo Chihuahua Guatemala Panama City Managua

Geography is not taught in the classroom. It is taught in the ad
breaks of American news channels. Unable to broadcast domes-
tic commercials, they resort to showing a map of the world littered
with city names and temperatures, accompanied by a soundtrack
of inoffensive elevator music. Just the tonic for a jet-lagged Johnny
Hazzard. He falls in and out of a slumber, waking to learn of the
unbearable heat in Beirut or the strange cold hitting Rome before
falling asleep again. The world is filtering in and out of the
Hazzard brain. Then he dreams of standing on a giant weather
map, leaping from Paris to Damascus to Okinawa to Auckland.

Thanks to the transmission of American news channels on
British cable TV, Johnny Hazzard's geography has improved.

The high school classes focus on eddies, erosion, and glaciers. Little wonder then that some of Johnny's classmates, when faced with the arrival of a math teacher from England last year, asked questions that included "Where did you learn English?" and "Where in England is Paris?" As outward-looking a city as Austin is, there will always be those who can only look inward.

By one thirty, Johnny Hazzard is curled up in the fetal position on his bed. The television is playing repeats of the '80s detective show *Magnum P.I.* Siska stands at the door and watches Johnny sleep. She smiles and walks to her studio, picking up a snack or two from the table on the way. Lydia is listening to an obscure British folk singer on her CD player. Mr. Hazzard sits in his office, tapping figures into his computer.

Once in the studio, Siska stands before a blank white canvas, brush in hand. She stands, and stands, and stands, and her mind is as empty as a Saharan lake. Siska is desperate for new ideas, but they seem to have gotten lost in the post somewhere. The Muse is blaming the postal service, and the postal service is claiming the Muse never sent them. Either way, Siska needs them badly, especially as she's just starting to make a name for herself on the London circuit and can ill afford a barren patch. She takes out a leather pouch of tobacco from her blouse pocket, molds a chunk no bigger than a piece of pineapple, places it in her mouth, and chews. The chewing normally helps.

Siska turns on her small stereo, listening, as she sporadically does, to teenage anthems of the '50s and '60s — today it's "Bobby's Girl" and "Poetry in Motion." Once these snappy numbers finish, she sighs, puts the brush down, and stares out of the window at the busy, car-clogged street below. The Muse has a lot to answer for.

The next day, Johnny Hazzard wakes up at two thirty. He pulls off the covers and feels immediately cold. He stands in his summer bedroom in white T-shirt and checkered boxer shorts and pulls back the curtains. He looks around the room, takes a deep breath, rubs his eyes, flattens his hair out, and, after initial confusion, realizes exactly where he is and where he will be for the next three months or so. The first morning is always the most disorienting. Johnny staggers to the bathroom, takes a pee, and heads for the kitchen. No noise from anywhere. After grabbing a bagel and slice of cheese, he goes to Lydia's room — the door is wide open, but she's not there. Her bed is made. In Austin, Mrs. Hazzard prefers beds to be made every morning. Johnny never makes his bed in London. This is one of the perks of having divorced parents. Johnny sits on Lydia's crisp, sheets-perfectly-folded mattress and looks at her bedside table. He recalls a similar moment last summer when he saw a scrap of paper with *JB* written next to a phone number. Lydia was eighteen and Johnny had been convinced she'd found love for the first time. She was her normal self until about halfway into their vacation, when she became uncharacteristically coy. She began singing in the shower. As happy a teenager as Lydia seemed to be, singing in the shower was not normal behavior. At first, Johnny was concerned, citing class-A drugs as a possible cause for Lydia's spontaneous outbursts of song. He confronted her one afternoon while they both watched a kung fu film on television. She denied having met someone. Johnny didn't believe her. The kung fu film reached its absurd climax and that was that. JB was never mentioned again, but Johnny was sure he was right and pleased with himself for observing behavior patterns and coming to clever conclusions. He felt as though he was beginning to understand people. He could tell something about them not because they said it but because they showed it. However much Lydia denied it, Johnny was certain.

Now, sitting here today, staring avidly at her bedside table, he remembers last summer, and he remembers all the subsequent events in the previous twelve months that have made him so confident in his ability to work people out. There was the time he just *knew* Kade had been given a massive verbal rollicking by his father, because he was talking in one-word sentences and avoiding eye contact. There was the time he was certain that his geography teacher, Mr. Legwinski, had received some very bad news. He was ever-so-slightly distracted in class, dropping books and leaving doors open. Subtle differences that most of the kids wouldn't have picked up on — or cared about. It later transpired that ice-cool Mr. Legwinski's daughter had been caught drinking on campus.

So yes, Johnny feels pretty boss about his psycho-detective abilities. And he can't help feeling that Lydia's quick exit, despite jet lag, means she's got something or someone very special to be doing.

Johnny eventually finds signs of life behind the closed wooden door of the study, where Mr. Hazzard taps furiously on his keyboard. Johnny can't be certain, but he suspects that his father goes through several keyboards a year. Most of the letters and numbers are faded, especially the *a*, *e*, and *h*.

"You'll give yourself arthritis, Dad."

"Aha!" exclaims Mr. H, like a magician would use "Abra-cadabra!"

"Slept well?" Johnny asks.

"Too well."

"How's it going?"

"Well, we're just trying to seal up this deal. Latest craze from Asia. Japanese teen horror movies. I gotta show you some, get your expert opinion."

Johnny gave up asking for details about his dad's business ventures some three years ago. Mr. Hazzard always talks about "we" and "us" when, more often than not, he means "me" and "I." His finger is firmly lodged in several business pies, most of which he doesn't bother to fully cook. But as lukewarm as those pies are, they're bringing in the cash. (Mr. Hazzard is no millionaire, but he can afford two trips abroad a year as well as paying the mortgage on the apartment and occasionally driving a car.) Johnny knows for certain that his father owns an English-language newspaper in Moscow and runs a successful dating website for professionals. Johnny is also old enough to realize those two facts alone explain why Mrs. Hazzard could no longer continue with her husband. Added to the newspaper and website are several import deals, the latest of which is this Japanese teen horror movie thing. Johnny tries to stay out of it.

"Where's Lydia?" he asks.

"Out with friends . . ." says Mr. Hazzard, returning his sights to the monitor.

"What friends?"

"The ones she made last year, I guess. That okay with you?" he asks, with more than a sprig of sarcasm.

"Sure it is," says Johnny Hazzard, with more than a sprig of annoyance. He returns to his bedroom and plays his NHL video game.

Having won every brawl in every game leading up to his Stanley Cup triumph with the Dallas Stars, Johnny decides to put some clothes on. It is now five forty-six and Johnny Hazzard lies on his bed, staring at his ceiling. He looks to his right, at the wall, and decides then and there to rip down his Texas Longhorns poster. He also tears down a couple of pictures of American models in bikinis. He places the posters in the trash can and checks the clock once more. Five forty-seven.

The sun is screaming outside and the thermometer by his window reads 26°. Johnny learned the metric and imperial conversions last summer. He sees flustered workers in suits and ties on the road below, feeling hot and looking bothered. *Love to see them working an August week in Austin*, he thinks to himself.

"I'm going out," he says aloud.

"Okay," replies Mr. Hazzard, before Johnny hears more violent taps as the Texan tycoon of Maida Vale seals a deal to buy Denmark or some other small nation.

Johnny Hazzard (splendid in baggy blue jeans, white socks, new skater shoes, and new yellow skater T-shirt) is taken aback. The last two summers, on the few occasions when he has been allowed to leave the apartment on his own, his father has insisted on asking where he's going and when he'll be back. Now it's just "okay." It is very hard to hate a father who is quite so liberal. Johnny Hazzard is torn between beginning to like the sound of this summer, and dreading the thought of his father getting all hyper-hippie and "son, wanna try a joint?" on him.

Still, he leaves without explanation, buoyed by his newfound freedom. After exiting the apartment block, he takes a left, walks twelve paces, and enters the DVD store. He picks up two new titles — one action, one animated feature — and walks back the twelve paces into the apartment block. He's back in the lounge less than five minutes after leaving it. But he's begun to wonder where the newfound freedom could lead.

After the movies have been watched, it's ten o'clock. Johnny feels bogged down with fatigue. Siska is still out and there's no sign of life from Lydia. Johnny and his father sit down to eat a late supper of chorizo and mashed potatoes. Conversation is limited, as Mr. Hazzard is constantly interrupted by phone calls from the States. Dialogue ranges from the ridiculous ("Well, can we hold the baby dolls?") to the alarming ("Can't you postpone paying for another twelve days?").

Johnny retires to his bedroom at eleven, finally falling asleep at about three. Still no sign of Lydia.

He wakes up almost twelve hours later, the television still on. Johnny can hear Siska and Mr. Hazzard talking in their bedroom. No sound from Lydia's room, though.

There is a CB radio in the lounge. On occasion, Siska has been known to use it as a source of inspiration. Johnny has never understood this; talking to overweight truckers and other lonely single men doesn't seem the most obvious place to find ideas for a painting. But then Siska isn't the most obvious of people.

Johnny turns on the CB and overhears a conversation between a wheelchair-bound Cypriot and a thirty-year-old computer programmer living with his parents. The wheelchair-bound Cypriot espouses clichéd philosophy; the computer programmer blathers on about a fantasy games website for single Europeans. He explains that in order to play, contestants must have webcams switched on to prove they are dressed in appropriate medieval garb. Johnny tries to engage in conversation on other channels, but no one seems to hear him. He tunes in to a husky-voiced man asking for "any ladies around Junction15 of the M25 for loud fun." He switches channels and appeals again:

"Hello . . . hello, y'all . . . anyone alive? Anyone a-fucking-live?"

"Hello," comes the reply. (Male, young-sounding, Cockney Londoner.)

"Hey, what's up?" asks Johnny.

"Oh, God. . . . where you from then?"

Johnny senses hostility.

"America. . . ."

"Oh, alright, mate? Overpaid, oversexed, over here," replies the voice. Johnny doesn't know what he means. But he doesn't like the sound of the guy, and switches the CB off.

He turns his attentions to the Internet. In Austin, Johnny uses the net for e-mailing, MP3 downloading, and instant messaging. But in London he logs on to the chat rooms. Specifically, Teenchat, London, Skating, and Texas. Conversations rarely last more than a minute.

<JH15> Hi
<KingRock> M or F? Asl?
<JH15> 15/m/London
<JH15> Hello?
Last message received 15.43

Boys don't want to talk to boys. Girls don't want to talk to boys. Johnny wants to talk to anybody. The girls are generally seeking young men over eighteen, who aren't supposed to be in Teenchat. The Texas channel is suspiciously quiet and mainly populated by parents. The London channel is fast becoming the battleground for cybergang warfare between single mothers and sexist eighteen- and nineteen-year-old boys. Johnny manages a twelve-minute conversation with Firebomb, a fourteen-year-old girl who lives in Portsmouth and loves London, cigars, and boys in makeup. They swap pictures — Johnny's is a year old, and he is shorter and considerably chubbier in the cheeks, but still significantly more attractive than Firebomb. Johnny Hazzard grimaces at the eyes pointing in different directions and the badly dyed hair, deciding enough is enough. He shuts down the computer and returns to the horizontal position.

He lies in bed and examines his fingernails. He picks at them, leaving them spotless. He cuts them. He takes a shower. Siska wishes him well. He lies on his bed again and scratches his bum. He begins to read a skate magazine from the previous summer. He goes through his *Jojo* comic book — *Jojo au Pensionnat* — all about the little boy being sent to boarding school. He's pleased he doesn't have to refer to his French dictionary too often to translate. The sun is excited again and the thermometer has reached twenty-eight degrees.

Siska passes Johnny's half-open bedroom door and pauses. She looks in, feeling only half-guilty and wholly interested. The unsuspecting Johnny takes out his skateboard from under the bed and tightens the trucks. He finds a sticker from last year's skate magazine and places it over a faded, tatty one on the board. Siska watches. He lies back on his bed, hugging his skateboard like he used to hug his teddy bear. Johnny Hazzard, who took up skateboarding in Austin some eight months previously, has decided he is going to take to the streets of London. Or more specifically, the South Bank, the London skateboarders' Mecca. He gets up, prompting Siska to dart off down the corridor, her flowy yellow dress trailing behind her like Count Dracula's cloak.

Johnny Hazzard tells his father he's "going out."

"Okay," comes the response.

Johnny pauses at the study door, watching his dad work.

"Don't you wanna know where I'm going?"

"Well, the video store, right?"

"Wrong."

Mr. Hazzard stops typing and looks up, removing his enormous reading glasses that looked out of style when Reagan was still in office.

"Oh."

There is a pause as neither of them says anything, and a smile spreads all over Johnny's face like an old egg cracking into a saucepan.

"Aren't you gonna tell me?" his father asks.

"I wanna go skating. On the South Bank."

"Okay, be back by eight. Siska's cooking a meal for all of us."

"Even Lydia?"

"Even Lydia."

"Surprised she's not busy sucking some guy's face somewhere . . ."

"Johnny. It's not like you to be jealous of your sister," says Mr. Hazzard, looking like the dog who found the bone.

"I might be bored but I can assure you I don't wanna be busy sucking some guy's face."

"What makes you so sure she's with a guy?"

Ha! How stupid he is, thinks Johnny Hazzard. *How clueless, how dumb, how totally unobservant*, he silently says to himself.

"I'm just sure. You gotta trust me, Dad," says Johnny, smirking at the remote possibility of such a thing.

"My son the telepathic guru," replies Mr. Hazzard.

Johnny is not entirely sure what he means.

"Well, I'll be seeing y'all later, then."

Mr. Hazzard checks that his son has enough money for the Underground ticket, a drink, and a snack, and lets him go. Johnny walks with a bounce in his heels, remembering a song he heard on the plane's in-flight radio station. "Mr. Blue Sky" by ELO bounces around his brain. Its speedy rhythm quickens Johnny's walk out of the apartment and into the elevator.

Unbeknownst to him, Siska has been watching the bouncy walk. She runs into her studio, grabs a packet of tobacco from her pocket, and begins chewing a meaty chunk. Brush poised, she starts to transform the clean canvas into a dirty swamp with some violent brush strokes.

> *Running down the avenue,*
> *See how the sun shines brightly in the city. . . .*

Johnny's humming along to ELO. His backpack on his back, his skateboard attached, his dad in the palm of his hand. He feels good. He feels the same way he did when he saw his mother's face after she checked his report card. The same way he did when his mom bought him the Pekinese (loving, intimate, enjoys having his ear scratched, named Pacino after Johnny's favorite actor) for his thirteenth birthday. There's a vigor, a verve going on today.

Johnny enters the Underground station. He's only traveled by himself on the Tube twice before, and both times went smoothly. He buys his return ticket from the machine, a little surprised at the hike in price, but then Johnny doesn't hold out much hope when it comes to London transport. He and his father were once stuck on the Underground when the train in front of theirs broke down. Irate passengers attempted to pry open the doors to make their own getaway. The driver began telling jokes on the PA system. A passenger tried to initiate an impromptu karaoke session. Somebody farted. Twice. The whole experience was comparable only to being thrown out of class by Mr. Legwinski for making lewd remarks in seventh grade.

Johnny comes out of Waterloo station and walks straight into humid heat. His T-shirt feels like an annoying layer of skin. Sweat droplets are dotted along his hairline and he admits to himself that he is feeling a little apprehensive. He's very much a novice when it comes to skating, and the idea of performing some tricks in front of the legendary crowd of South Bank skaters fills him with worry. He has seen these dudes on videos.

Johnny Hazzard walks around a little lost, aware of the spreading patch of sweat the weight of the backpack and skateboard have formed on his back. He ambles through a tunnel, past large patches of bird shit, too concerned about getting where he wants to be to acknowledge the young beggar who asks for spare change. Still not entirely aware of where he is going, he spots some skaters walking by in the opposite direction. Johnny sees a vast concrete space ahead, in front of an outdoor café. Spotting his first stretch of smooth slabs since arriving in London, the skateboard comes off the backpack and Johnny cruises, always aware of everything around him. He spots some BMXers to his right and some bespectacled, trench-coated thirtysomethings to his left.

Johnny read all about the South Bank in the magazines he had bought the previous summer. It was around then that Kade and

David had begun skateboarding, and Johnny thought it would be the logical thing for him to do. He had to admit Kade was often ahead of the pack when it came to good ideas — but then again Kade did have an older brother and two older sisters to emulate.

So, to impress the boys, he had brought home some more UK skating magazines, and Mrs. Hazzard had obliged his request for a skateboard — a mail-order board that had been put together by a young skateboarder in Boston. The whole package cost $80 and Johnny was very pleased with the result. His street, Olfman Drive, is suitably smooth, and he mastered the ollie within a month of starting. Kade and David often came around on Saturdays, and a routine quickly developed. From around eleven in the morning till two in the afternoon, skating. Trying ollies over everything from a banana to a crate of beer. The beer, or at least some of it, consumed afterward. Saturdays were perfect because Mrs. Hazzard has started working a full shift, now that she feels Johnny is old enough to be left home alone or with Lydia. The boys have only gotten drunk three times. All three occasions ended in carnage. The first time, Johnny and Kade spent an hour vomiting in the backyard, narrowly missing the hyperactive Pacino. David, as pickled as his friends, was deliberately throwing a ball toward his barfing buddies in the hope that Pacino would slide straight into the lake of sick. The other two drunken Saturday afternoons were led by a very enthusiastic Jack. Chain-smoking Jack, never without a pack of twenty, was a fourteen-year-old who felt he really ought to experience drunkenness before his fifteenth birthday. Hazzard Saturdays, as they became known, provided an excellent opportunity for a bingeing session. Jack arrived one particular Saturday, in January of this year, with a bottle of lukewarm vodka, insisting they all down shots. No one was man enough to challenge this suggestion. Johnny Hazzard learned he hated the taste of vodka. It was far worse than any medicine he'd ever taken, and twice as expensive.

Then, just a couple of months ago, when the days were beginning to really heat up again, Jack brought over some pot. Johnny felt a little bit excited and naughty. After four hours of kickflips, ollies, and grinds, the boys got royally stoned . . . and royally sick. Johnny Hazzard didn't feel peer pressure. He just thought it would be rude not to join in. And besides, he was the host. It was his duty to do as his guests wished. Kade said the joint made him horny, and disappeared into the bathroom. After five minutes, he opened the door and asked if Johnny had any pictures of Lydia.

"Shut up," Johnny Hazzard replied. Kade locked the door and got back to work.

Being doped was not a sensation Johnny Hazzard particularly enjoyed. "Beer beats bongs," he would try to tell the others. But Jack wasn't interested. Jack smoked anything — parsley, mint, thyme, banana skins. (He often claims to have "seen the stars" after smoking banana skins, having read about their hallucinogenic powers on the Internet. Johnny thinks it's bullshit.)

Johnny remembers the first high, the first binge-drinking session, the camaraderie he has developed over nearly a year of skating with Kade and David. Although Jack buys the clothes and lives the life, he refuses to participate in skateboarding itself (insistent on being different in any way possible), but regardless, the four of them are referred to as "skater dudes" by classmates. They worship Beastie Boys (Eminem is *way* too mainstream), dress in jeans large enough to fit two slim boys, and insist on belts that dangle down their legs in a second-penis kind of a way. But take away the clothes and the music, and there's something special between them. Skating is the antithesis to jock sports — to baseball, football, and soccer. It's an individual effort, but it's all about the team — about the friends really egging you on to do well. There's a mutual respect Johnny loves, a feeling of belonging that Johnny never experienced in his brief dalliances with the major sports at school. But most of all, the feeling of cruising and going airborne, the jittery sensation as the wheels roll over the concrete, a sensation that can be felt through the toes, ankles, and up the legs, and the exhilaration and pride of pulling off a new trick with aplomb — that's what makes skating so special.

Johnny looks down as he cruises past the Royal Festival Hall café and sees his belt is dangling. As he moves forward, he can hear the clattering of the wooden boards against the concrete ground somewhere nearby. This is the only sound Johnny Hazzard can hear, and it is electrifying and scary. He feels jingly-jangly with nerves, picks up his board, and sees for the first time what all the fuss has been about.

A dark and mythical ghetto. A car park. A concrete nightmare hijacked by kids and turned into something with character and energy. The skaters occupy territory immediately beneath the Queen Elizabeth Hall and Royal Festival Hall concert venues. There are different-sized chunks of concrete dotted about —

perfect. Pebbled surfaces provide evidence of failed attempts to ward off skaters in years gone by. Visitors to the theater, concert, and film venues nearby watch admiringly. Joggers scoff patronizingly. Bladers are reluctantly tolerated, in the same way you accept distant and usually annoying members of your nonimmediate family. Here beside the resplendent river Thames is a live street performance to rival the displays in the theater, cinema, and concert halls nearby. The South Bank is alive with a fusion of old and new culture. The atmosphere is creative and exciting, sinister and intriguing.

Johnny sees a bunch of kids, mostly male, mostly teenage, trying out tricks he wouldn't dare. Tricks he doesn't even know the names of. He sees some girls, which surprises him, but he's not complaining. Older skaters, clearly with years of practice behind them, shake their rumps as they try Caballerials on impromptu ramps. There are occasional cheers and ripples of applause as spectating skaters observe an impressive trick. Johnny Hazzard hasn't seen anything like this in Austin. There must be fifty or sixty people here. The jackpot has been hit. He finds a quieter spot by the entrance to the National Film Theatre and begins to practice. Nearby there's a small group of absolute beginners, maybe a couple of years younger. Johnny is aware of the sweat trickling down his back. But he picks up pace, the breeze feels as refreshing as ice, and he does a perfect kickflip. His self-consciousness slides away. Then he tries a second kickflip, only to mistime and send the board careening into the group of absolute beginners.

"Sorry," he says, approaching sheepishly, eyes stuck on the ground.

"It's all good," comes the barely-broken-voice reply.

Johnny looks up. "Thanks," he says.

"American?" asks one of the others, a skeletal fourteen-year-old.

"Yeah." The self-consciousness creeps back in.

"Where from?"

"Texas," Johnny Hazzard says, knowing full well there may be consequences.

"Cool," says the barely-broken-voice.

The kids look at Johnny, he looks at them, and he detects a little bit of hero worship. Being American is clearly scoring him cool-ness points.

"What brings you to this dump?" asks the previously silent, scrawny one with long blond hair.

"Actually, I think it's cool. We don't have anything like this where I'm from."

"I meant England," says the scrawny one with the long blond hair.

"Oh." Johnny forces a laugh. "My dad lives here," he says.

And there's a silence, and nobody can think of anything else to say. Johnny resumes his skating, and the boys resume theirs. Occasionally they stop to watch the American. Johnny feels embarrassed by the attention, wishes them well, and moves off. He walks through the dimmest and dingiest section. Guys video each other and take photos on digital cameras. A *thief's payday*, thinks Johnny Hazzard. He had been mugged in downtown Austin some months before, and, as much as he chastised himself for doing it, he couldn't help but think of the incident every time he left the house. Crime isn't a major feature of his hometown, which makes Johnny feel all the more stupid for being one of the few victims.

He approaches the balcony looking over the river Thames. He leans his back against the railings and watches the skaters. Several topless and hairless male bodies sparkle under the sun, which has formed a thick and uncomfortable layer in the air. Johnny thinks the guys have got guts — he would never take off his T-shirt. A cute girl skates past at speed in a tight green T-shirt and camouflage trousers. *Way out of my league*, guesses Johnny Hazzard, and he starts skating again, flipping some easy ollies.

Johnny continues for about a half hour. He's trying out a tailslide on a wooden crate, conveniently dumped there by somebody else. The attempts aren't going so well. He notices a largish presence looming peculiarly close behind him. A feeling of fear skids through his body. His brain tells him he's about to be mugged, grabbed by his backpack and tossed to the floor. Adrenaline racing, he skates away faster, stops by some concrete steps leading down to the river, picks up his board, and turns around to confront the demon.

41

A guy in his early twenties, with darkish skin and short, messy, dark brown hair, is pointing an expensive-looking digital camcorder at Johnny Hazzard. He is wearing a Beastie Boys T-shirt and baggy dark blue jeans, held up by an enormous silver-studded black belt. Sporadic facial hair decorates his face, looking a bit like someone's hurled a pot of black paint across it. Johnny Hazzard skates up, grinds to a stop a couple of inches away from the guy's feet, and picks up his board.

"Beastie Boys . . ." Johnny says, as though he's about to declare a long-winded theory.

"Yeah, Beastie Boys," comes the response, in American English although the speaker is definitely not American. "You like?" asks the mystery man, with a smile. Johnny Hazzard enjoys the guy's aura.

"Sure I like," says Johnny Hazzard.

"You can't front on that. . . ."

Johnny smiles and the gesture is returned. If the eyes are a window to the soul, the smile is the catflap, and a warm smile is an open catflap.

"Where you from, man?"

"Texas," says Johnny.

"Yeah? Where?"

"Austin."

"I been to Houston. Didn't like that place, man," says the mystery man. Johnny notices he does not have a skateboard with him.

"Nah, Houston sucks. I'm from Austin."

"Oh, okay. Never been."

"Where you from?"

"Brazil. South America."

"I know where Brazil is. You making a video?"

"Yeah. You heard of RedHead?" Johnny hasn't. "Skate store just behind the Oxford Street. The manager likes to have videos running."

"You're getting paid to video skaters?"

"Yep."

"Dream job, huh? You don't skate?"

"Sure I can skate."

There is a brief pause in conversation, during which Johnny and the mystery man size each other up.

"Mario."

"Johnny."

They shake hands.

"How old are you, Johnny?"

"Fifteen. How old are you?"

"Twenty-three."

"So you been skating ages."

"Eight years. You?"

"'Bout a year. I wish I'd started when I was really young, but . . ." Johnny shrugs. Mario smiles.

Mario asks what brings Johnny to London. He explains and asks Mario the same question.

"Spent two years in L.A. I wanted to come to Europe. I been here a year now."

"You like London?"

"Yeah. I miss my friends, you know. My family. But it's good here. I was seeing an English girl as well. You know."

Johnny doesn't know, but he makes sounds in agreement. And just at that moment, he's happy to be on the South Bank, happy to have made a friend, and happy to be in London. He can't be sure, but he doesn't remember feeling so *consciously* contented. The Brazilian invites the American to visit him in RedHead when he gets the chance. Johnny replies as though he's got a schedule and assures him he'll say hello before long. Mario continues videoing. Johnny decides it's time to head home.

"Mr. Blue Sky" is still banging about inside his skull. It should be irritating by now, but instead it just puts Johnny in an even better mood. Things are happening.

FIVE

"But he's not old enough. It's illegal."

"Since when do you give a shit about what's legal?"

Johnny and Lydia are engaged in combat, with Mr. Hazzard serving as UN peacekeeping troop extraordinaire. Siska's family meal is a tasty bit of cooking that is now just turning into indigestion fodder. The fight kicked off when Mr. Hazzard dared to suggest Lydia take Johnny out with her one evening. Even if it was just for an ice cream. Anything to give the poor guy something resembling a social life. Mr. Hazzard was feeling sorry for his son.

"No way." Lydia bangs the dining room table, narrowly missing the soup bowl.

"Dahlings, fighting will not find you solutions," says Siska. Her philosophy isn't the most useful in rows.

"I just thought it would be a nice gesture. Johnny's been twiddling his thumbs in the evenings. He's not twelve anymore, Lydia," says Mr. Hazzard, raising his volume.

"No, it's worse than that — he's fifteen. I'm meeting friends. It's all arranged. I can't bail on them."

"You've been out every night since you got here," Mr. Hazzard points out.

"So? There's nothing else to do!"

"So now you know how I feel," says Johnny Hazzard, meekly.

"I don't wanna take him out and that's the end of it," shouts Lydia.

"Fine. If I'm such a big fucking embarrassment . . ." Johnny's sentence trails off as he kicks his chair back and stomps off, heading for his bedroom. The line and the sentiment are more than a little bit calculated.

And sure enough, the calculation proves to be good math. Lydia is not an evil person. If anything, she lets herself be touched by open displays of hurt a little too often. Minutes after Johnny's departure, she appears at his door and leans in, finding Johnny in the customary horizontal position, staring at his ceiling, arms folded, mood apparent.

"So we'll go for a bit. But this isn't the start of some kind of joint social life, okay?"

"No, if you don't wanna take me, I don't wanna go."

Mr. Hazzard pokes his face round the door, looking to Johnny like a head without a body.

"Johnny, you're going," he says pointedly. And his head disappears.

"We'll go in a half hour," says Lydia.

She leaves, shutting the door behind her. Thrilled, Johnny Hazzard leaps out of bed, picks up the tub of expensive hair wax (rarely used, plenty left), and stands preening himself in front of the mirror. He takes off the sweaty T-shirt and replaces it with a short-sleeved black shirt his mother had bought him. And in five minutes, Johnny Hazzard has succeeded in making himself look a little less fifteen.

Lydia appears to have gone to less effort, but then again she doesn't really need to. She's never been one for forced appearances and, thanks to her simple good looks, she doesn't need to be. They leave the apartment and begin the five-minute walk to the Maida Vale Underground station. It's still uncomfortably humid, and Johnny is grateful the shirt is black.

"So who's gonna be out tonight?" he asks.

"Just a few friends."

"How did you meet them?"

"Jim. You remember Jim."

"No."

"We did photography in tenth grade. He moved here with his family two years ago."

Jim. J. JB.

"You dated last summer, right?"

Lydia turns and, although it's far from certain, she may well do a Wile E. Coyote–style double take with her head.

"What? No. Don't be stupid. Johnny you really talk some crap sometimes."

"I was only asking. . . ."

They traipse down into the Underground station, purchase their tickets, and head for Leicester Square, barely saying a word until they get there. Johnny begins to feel a tiny bit scared, but the fact he's out with big sis — for the first time ever — and in London, starts to soak in. What's worrying and stirring in equal measure is that he has no idea what to expect. He's never seen the inside of a pub. He's never drunk alcohol anywhere other than his house, or Kade's, or David's, or at one of the smattering of house parties that had begun popping up in the last six months or so. He has only been plastered three times.

Brother and confident sister walk through Soho, crammed full of Londoners enjoying pints on the pavement, celebrating as if the sun is going out of fashion. As Lydia leads her brother to what will be their venue for the evening, Johnny Hazzard feels his heart beat faster, his hands clam up, and he suddenly notices a small stain, possibly caused by the hair wax, on the bottom of his shirt. It's too late for that now. Lydia holds the door open behind her and Johnny follows inside this overdecorated and old-fashioned Soho pub.

"Okay, sit down and behave yourself," says Lydia, with a minuscule smile.

Johnny struggles to find somewhere to sit. Nobody looks at him very much. The pub is heaving, but he spots a stool and wooden chair that wouldn't have looked out of place on a pirate ship. He worms his way through a group of students, probably in their late teens or early twenties, and makes it to the stool. Lydia joins him some minutes later, with two pints of British beer.

"We could get so busted," she says.

Johnny shushes her and sips from his beer. He doesn't enjoy the taste a great deal, but that's not the point. Besides, he's confident it won't taste so bad after the first pint. He and the boys back home all agree that the first is the worst, the second slightly less awful, and the third just dreamy.

Johnny Hazzard does not feel at ease. He keeps his eyes peeled. He notices every detail: the number of bar-staff (three — two male, one female, the female being of grumpy and gallumping disposition, the males being of tanned and disturbingly worked-out appearance); the walls pasted with "English" artifacts, maps, tools, and weapons; the clientele (a true mixture, many student types, a couple of old men who ought to know better, one old woman in the corner talking to herself and smoking a roll-up cigarette). Johnny feels like a missing piece of a complicated jigsaw.

"You're making me nervous," says Lydia, unhelpfully.

"How d'you think I feel? How did you feel, for God's sake?"

"Will you relax? It's no big deal. Kids your age come to bars all the time. This isn't like home. If they card us, we'll say you left yours at home. If they ask us to leave, we'll leave. Simple. This was your idea, anyway."

"No, it was Dad's idea. Don't blame me."

"Oh, so you didn't want to go out?"

"I did but, I dunno, couldn't we get a pizza or something?"

"Listen to yourself. Look. This is London. You're out on a Saturday night. You're in a pub, drinking beer. This doesn't happen every day. Take your finger outta your ass and enjoy yourself."

Johnny Hazzard cannot think of anything to say. Lydia sips smugly from the beer.

An hour later, Johnny Hazzard has drunk two pints of beer and nobody has uttered the dreaded two letters — *I* and *D*. In fact, the barman came to the table, collected the empty glasses, and Johnny smiled, making eye contact for what felt like eternity but was probably more like half a second. Without ever delving into deep and emotional territory, he and Lydia talk about familial matters — Siska, their shared concern for Mom, their bemused confusion about Mr. Hazzard's latest ventures. As ever, the beer gives Johnny a woozy feeling in the head and a leaky feeling in the bladder. On his third visit to the toilet this evening, he is engaged in conversation by the man standing next to him at the urinal. Johnny Hazzard isn't so good at peeing when somebody is standing right next to him, not since seventh grade, in fact. But it's even harder when that somebody begins idle chitchat.

"Bloody jukebox ate my money!" exclaims the peeing man.

Johnny smiles, hands still on dick, pee still in bladder.

"What song did you want?" he asks politely.

"I have absolutely no idea."

Johnny now laughs politely. *Pee chat sucks*, he thinks.

The peeing man finishes his business and goes to wash his hands.

"Be warned. That jukebox sucks eggs."

And he's off. Johnny Hazzard closes his eyes briefly, thankful no one is around, ready to pee. Head woozy, shoulders relaxed, pee on way from bladder to urinal, so of course Sod's Law dictates that a burly man walks in and stands right next to him. Giving up hope, Johnny dives into the cubicle. The light does not work, and there is toilet paper all over the floor. Johnny cannot see where he is peeing, but the noise does not bode well. He flushes, washes his hands, checks his clothes and face (fine, just fine), and returns to the bar. Lydia is engaged in conversation.

"No way, that's not describing me at all," she is saying. A small crowd has gathered around the older sister. Two guys and two girls, obviously students, appear animated and happy-faced. Johnny is feeling gently merry. He doesn't want any more beer, which is just as well, as it would probably mean asking at the bar. That's a step into a great unknown, and Johnny isn't ready to make it a known unknown just yet.

"Ask my brother," she says.

"Ask me what?" he says, returning to the woeful stool.

"Gung-ho," says one of the student girls, lanky and with jet-black hair.

"She said gung-ho would be the best way of describing Texans," explains Lydia.

"That's kinda true."

The students cheer, smiling at Lydia, who can't believe her brother has been quite so disloyal.

"No, I mean listen," starts Johnny, getting into his stride. "Some Texans are assholes, but we don't all go around with guns, you know. Like, we're not Republicans. And we're not cowboys, before you ask."

Lydia feels slightly prouder.

"Most of them are, though, right?" says one of the student boys (awkward posture, green T-shirt, chewing gum).

"Yeah, but it's like he says. Not everyone's an asshole. Least not in Austin," says Lydia.

"Back home, some people call our family commies," says Johnny.

"How very tolerant," says the lanky one with jet-black hair.

Lanky jet-black's friend, equally lanky but with a short blond bob, joins in:

"Well, I'm not dissing you, but Texas has the highest death penalty rate in the States, right? That's a big deal. And racism . . ." She's slurring slightly.

"Yeah, but what's that got to do with us?"

"Well, you're Texans."

"Yeah, we're Texans. Y'all are English, should we blame you for the shitty weather?" asks Johnny, geared up for a fun-fight.

"That's totally different. How old are you, anyway?" asks lanky jet-black.

"I hate the death penalty, by the way. And what about the British in America? It was hardly a happy time," says Johnny.

The silent-one-until-now speaks up:

"The man is right."

Johnny Hazzard likes him. He is very, very rarely a "man" to anybody. The silent one continues:

"He's hardly responsible for all the problems in Texas."

"I wasn't blaming you guys. I was just saying, America needs to take a look at itself. D'you know what I mean?" says lanky with short blond bob.

"I think so, too. I'm telling y'all, we agree on this," says Lydia.

Johnny is relishing the interaction with people outside of his family.

Siska notwithstanding, he has never spoken to non-Americans about their views on America. Even if this is not precisely the sort of conversation he is used to having in Austin — where more often than not he is preaching to the converted about the USA's ills — he's enjoying being on the other side of the fence for once.

"So how long you guys known each other?" Johnny Hazzard asks his sister.

"I just met them," she replies.

"Oh. Well, I guess us Texans are kinda friendly, don't you think?"

Nobody has an answer to that.

"Can I get you guys a drink?" asks the ill-at-ease guy.

"No, I'm alright, thanks," says Johnny.

The students back off, slightly turning to talk amongst themselves. Lydia turns to her brother.

"This same shit happened last year. It gets so boring."

"They were okay," says Johnny, actually very excited at having met some new faces.

"Yeah, they were okay but . . . I dunno. People say things. Things they shouldn't say."

"Like what?"

"What do you think? They got a problem with us. Those guys were just trying to be clever. But some of the others . . . they can be ass-holes without knowing it. Or without really thinking it's bad at all."

Johnny suddenly remembers the crackly voice on the CB radio, talking about Americans — "Overpaid, oversexed, over here." He recalls Michael Moore. Here in Soho, London's liberal and cosmopolitan heart, it hits him for the first time quite how prone to attack *he* is because of his nationality. Bashing an American is not offensive; it's a global sport. And although he agrees with Lydia that sometimes it is wholly unfair and spawned out of ignorance, Johnny Hazzard decides that he cannot blame anyone for playing it.

Lydia decides it's time to go home. Johnny sounds achingly desperate.

"We've been out less than three hours. It's not even dark yet. What about Jim?"

"I guess he couldn't make it."

"Oh. Can't you phone him?"

"No. Let's go."

"Did you say you were meeting friends just so Dad wouldn't force you to take me?"

57

"Of course I did."

Uncertain if she is being sarcastic or truthful, Johnny is effectively ordered out of his seat and told to wait outside while Lydia goes to the ladies' room. Johnny wonders if she is actually telephoning the enigmatic Jim on her cellphone. He says his good-byes to the student posse. They half apologize if any offense was caused.

A big, bright door has been opened to a new, bright room for Johnny Hazzard. Things are making sense now. He's not a kid on a bike anymore, so why behave like one? What was he *thinking* playing video games and reading Tintin? He should have been out being social. Meeting new people. Now is the time, concludes Johnny Hazzard as he waits for Lydia by the pub door. The time to go outside, to meet as many people as possible. There is no time to waste — far too much has already slipped by. *I'm fifteen, for Christ's sake!* he thinks, a little merry-go-round still revolving in his brain. *I've spent fifteen whole years being boring. I can go to bars. I can really go to bars!*

"Let's go, Mr. Ambassador," says Lydia.

SIX

In what is a marked improvement on previous efforts, Johnny awakes at ten thirty (a mighty boner of Eiffel Tower proportions, slight dehydration).

After refreshing himself with a glass of iced water, he returns to his bedroom, noticing that Lydia's door is still shut, indicating she is inside and not out "doing her thing." Johnny sits cross-legged on his bed, hair a mess, iced water a delight.

"He's dumped her," he says.

He's sure that is what has happened. Lydia's fling has ended and she's locking herself in her room, feeling depressed and distraught. He begins to feel sorry for her. She was so good to him last night and yet in return she gets intellectual, snobbish Brits and a no-show from Jim. The more he thinks about the situation, the more concerned he becomes for her. She has never been one to talk very openly. The pain must be completely crippling, it must be leaving her in pieces. Now that they've crossed the great divide and mixed their social lives, even if it was just for one night, Lydia ought to feel able to get problems off her chest. Johnny decides today will be a pivotal day. He will lift her out of her grief, give her a cuddle, and tell her everything is going to be okay. He walks to her door and knocks.

"Lydia, it's me. Come on, let me in. Let's talk, okay?"

No answer. Johnny knocks again.

"Can I come in? We should talk about it."

Nothing.

"Come on, I just wanna help. I know you must feel pretty crap right now."

Mr. Hazzard approaches down the corridor.

"Lydia, let me in. Come on."

"Lydia left an hour ago," says Mr. Hazzard, then continues walking.

The jingly-jangly of unadulterated embarrassment travels through Johnny's body like mercury through a fevered thermometer. He opens Lydia's bedroom door. Empty. Bed made perfectly. Johnny decides he should go out, too.

It takes him about twenty-five minutes on the Tube to get to RedHead, Mario's skate store. Mr. Hazzard has given Johnny money to buy some new griptape. Johnny (baggy jeans, usual skate shoes, skateboard in hand) finds the store, sandwiched between two American chain stores. A glass door is covered from top to bottom with skate stickers. Johnny enters and is immediately faced with a staircase. East Coast hip-hop booms from below. He heads down, noticing more faded stickers lining the steps.

On the far wall of the basement, there is a large, appropriately garish red neon sign that says REDHEAD. The shop is small but crammed full — clothes, bags, wallets, jewelry, belts, skateboards, videos, magazines, books. There are two guys, about double Johnny's age, looking at the shoes. Three TV screens show footage of skateboarders from, it seems, hundreds of different locations. The music isn't too loud. Johnny can't see Mario, but he does see a young blond girl in the corner of the store, her back facing him, her face apparently glaring at the TV in front.

The only person who vaguely resembles a member of staff is a twentysomething guy folding hoodies and wearing a card that says REDHEAD on a chain around his neck.

Johnny approaches cautiously.

"Hey," he says, cheerfully. The guy responds just as happily.

"Is Mario here?"

"Nah, mate, he's not on today. His day off. Can I help?"

Johnny's disappointed. "Actually, yeah, I was looking for some griptape."

The shop assistant obliges, and Johnny pays at the register. A couple of older teens head down the stairs and enter this skateboarding dungeon. Johnny really likes the vibe. He spots a couple of very short and dark wooden stools, made into the shape of large hands complete with fingernails. Beside them, on the floor, are a bunch of magazines. The blond girl is still staring at the video. Johnny sits on the palm of one of the big hands and picks up a magazine. He doesn't realize he is holding it upside down because his gaze is fixed on the girl. She has on a skinny-fit red T-shirt with gold trim around the sleeves and neck. Tight dark-blue jeans are accentuating a cute butt. Her shoes are puffy and oversized and as blue as the jeans. The blond hair, bright and healthy-looking, comes down to the end of her neck. It's hard to tell in jeans, but the legs look valuable. Johnny wonders what the tits will look like. And he's curious as to whether the face will be grotesque, just to destroy the fun he's having. She'll have a boyfriend, anyway, fathoms Johnny Hazzard. *If it's not the gross face, it's the boyfriend,* he thinks. All the cute girls have boyfriends. All of them. Every single cute girl, especially the few who are into skateboarding. It is a law decreed by the gods. Johnny tries to read the magazine, the right way up now, but his eyes keep moving back to the girl. He checks out the TV she's watching and notices footage of the South Bank. He recognizes the young kids he met at the beginning of his session yesterday (the absolute beginners), puts down the magazine, and approaches the screen.

62

Standing a few paces behind the girl, he feels his heartbeat pick up pace, pumping blood faster. The butt really is fantastic. Fleshy but not fat. Slim but not skinny. Then suddenly it's Johnny Hazzard on TV. He's actually on TV. And he looks fine.

"That's me!" he proclaims, without really intending to say it out loud.

She turns around. The face is good news. It's not classic gorgeous, it's not even classic pretty, but it's hot.

The eyes are blue. The nose is small. There are no sideburns, and there is no mustache. The skin is tanned and, all in all, the face is easygoing. It's warm. Not a stain of tension on it.

"Oh, cool," she says.

And after just a few seconds, Johnny's moment of fame is over, but his inadvertent chat-up line seems to be doing the trick. She continues.

"You go down to the South Bank a lot?"

"Actually, no. It was my first time when Mario filmed me. Do you?"

"Yeah, well, I've only been skating a couple of years. I'm pretty bad."

"Ha, me, too. I been doing it about a year now, so I'm picking it up. . . ."

While rational thought is normally a calm and calculated process, when you're chatting up a girl you fancy the brain suddenly becomes sharper, faster, and a tad paranoid. Johnny had already slid his tongue across his front teeth twice in the conversation, anxious that some unsightly food debris might be wedged there.

"Where are you from?"

Memories of the Soho discussion make Johnny a little hesitant. He answers "Texas" rather than "America," and dreads her response.

The girl smiles broadly. It's a real smile.

"Austin is the capital," Johnny continues. "It's different from the rest of Texas. Like, really different. There's this campaign going on, it's called Keep Austin Weird. We like our weirdness." Johnny is aware he's talking too much. But she seems to actually be listening, to give a shit about what he's saying.

"I've only ever been to Los Angeles," she tells him. "Stopped off for a few days on my way to Fiji. I've been traveling on my gap year, you see."

Johnny isn't entirely familiar with the concept of a gap year, but it seems fairly straightforward: Take a year off between school and college in order to "find yourself" on far-flung shores. Or, alternatively, just smoke dope on a beach, eat fast food, and buy cheap, tacky nonsense made especially for Western tourists, whilst kidding yourself that you're learning.

"A gap year? Cool," he says, only half meaning it.

"What board do you have?" she asks. Johnny tells her. She looks impressed. They exchange names and handshakes.

"I never met a January before," says Johnny. And she laughs for the first time, a sweet and real laugh.

"What?" he asks, smiling. On the Richter scale of positive vibes, this encounter is a definite ten so far. A new experience for Johnny.

"Nothing, nothing. You've never met a January, I've never met a Texan."

"Well, we're not so bad," he says, meekly.

"No, I don't suppose you are."

"I was in this pub last night — me and my sister — and these guys started asking all these questions, thinking we're all cowboys in Texas," says Johnny. A cluttered sentence with the principal intention being to make clear he was in a bar last night.

There is a brief pause while they both think of something useful to say.

"So how old are you, Johnny the Texan?"

"Seventeen," he lies, with the skill of an Actors Studio graduate — no hint of hesitation, no clue that he's telling a fib. Pacino would be proud.

"You look a little older," she says, and that's enough. The jubilation is total — Johnny thinks she is the most fantastic female creature on Earth. He's on a roll — regularly called sir, allowed to drink beer in a pub, and now being told he looks even older than he is.

"Thanks," he says, a reply that completely fails to illustrate his unbridled excitement. "How old are *you*, then?"

"Eighteen," she says. Her smile reappears.

"Of course, gap year before y'all study, right?"

"Right. I love that y'all shit," she says, still smiling.

"Y'all shit?" asks Johnny, smiling in return.

"I've only heard that in the movies. I didn't think anyone actually talked like that."

Johnny cannot tell if she is being sarcastic, sweet, or cynical. He's still unsure of himself — or, more specifically, of his Americanness and how the gorgeous girl will react to it.

"It's funny to you?" he asks, gently.

"No, it's nice. I mean, it's different. The drawl."

There is another gap in conversation, when suddenly loud punk starts blasting from the speakers. Johnny shuffles, not entirely sure what will happen next. Seemingly out of nowhere, a tall, lanky Goth guy appears. He is baby-faced, with dyed jet-black hair and unfortunate bum fluff around the mustache and chin area. Like a pair of Mr. Hazzard's dungarees, this facial hair really shouldn't be seen outside of the home.

"January, I'm done," says the lanky Goth's deep voice.

Johnny feels the instant crush of disappointment that normally follows statements like "I've got a boyfriend," "I'm straight edge," and "You carry on skatin' around here, boy, and I'll call the cops." It's the kind of crushed sensation that Johnny's been experiencing all too often lately. January has a boyfriend, and a pretty ugly one at that, and once again Johnny Hazzard is staring disappointment in the face and struggling to think of something to say. In fact, disappointment isn't just staring at him — it's picking a fight. Johnny feels listless, drained of energy.

"Well, let's go, then," she says to the lank. Johnny Hazzard has one of those split-second thought processes that only ever materialize in times of crisis, panic, and/or flirtation.

If she was truly interested in me, she wouldn't suggest leaving like this. It doesn't make any sense, he thinks.

"It's been nice chatting," she says.

"Yeah, you, too. Maybe I'll see you at the South Bank or something?" he says, hopefully.

The lank scowls at the American.

"January, come on, I'm starving," he says.

"Yeah, I'd better go. Well, I'll be skating tomorrow probably —"

"Afternoon?" Johnny asks.

"Yeah, probably. See you around."

January turns and leaves with her head-to-toe-in-black boyfriend. Johnny watches her go. The noncommittal vagueness of her answers annoys him. He fully intends to head down to the South Bank tomorrow afternoon, but there's no guarantee she'll be there. However slim the chance of seeing her, it's a chance worth taking.

The sales assistant smiles to himself. On the TV screens, thirteen- and fourteen-year-old guys fall off their skateboards and boastfully show cuts and bruises to the camera.

SEVEN

Johnny Hazzard is at the South Bank by one o'clock. It is not a bright day. It is, instead, the sort of day when the sun occasionally and politely asks the clouds if it can interrupt. When the clouds are feeling especially generous, which is about twice every hour, they allow the sun a few moments to shine. The ever-polite sun then returns to its resting position behind the clouds. This farce continues for days on end. *The sun really ought to improve its self-esteem and assertiveness*, Johnny Hazzard thinks. *In short, it needs to become more of a bastard and stop pandering to the miserable clouds.*

With the weather so average and unsatisfactory, Johnny is not so inspired and the South Bank is not so busy. He begins to recognize some faces from before as he busily looks out for January. He doesn't want to miss her, so he keeps circling around the area. He rests, sits on his skateboard, and drinks a can of soda. He skates a bit more. He gazes over the river Thames. He looks and looks but cannot find the girl. After two hours of this, he counts his losses and heads back to the Waterloo Underground station.

As he skates across the large square of smooth concrete in front of the Royal Festival Hall café, he begins to feel like an idiot. *We never fixed a time to meet, she is way older and better-looking, and I'm a dickhead for even imagining this would be a date,* he tells himself. Then, making a mockery out of his predicament, his wheels jam on a piece of raised concrete. He trips, falling off the board and grazing his right elbow.

"Fucking A," he says.

"Hate it when that happens," she says.

Johnny, lying on the ground like a shot pigeon, looks behind him. There she stands — January, tall and fine, skateboard under her arm.

"Oh, hey," he says. "Sucks, doesn't it?"

"Howdy, pardner. You heading home?"

Johnny stands up.

"Yeah, I was down here for a couple of hours. It's pretty dead, anyway."

"I just got here with a friend."

"Cool, cool," Johnny says, painfully aware of his inability to come up with the right words.

"You should put something on that cut," says January, referring to the grazed elbow, which now has a brook of blood flowing out of it and down his forearm.

"No, it's nothing. I've had worse. Bet you have, too."

"Yeah. Worst was when I cut my cheek open. Put me off for weeks," she says with a smile. "I'd still clean it up if I were you."

"Yeah, you're probably right." Courage. Clarity. Johnny Hazzard goes for it: "So, erm, maybe do you wanna skate some other time?" Right now, he would take January as a friend. The sort of friend you secretly fancy and pine for desperately, but a friend nonetheless.

"Sure, we're always looking for new skate friends. It's only really me and my friend," she says. Johnny wonders what gender this friend is, if it's the lank, and if *friend* actually means *boyfriend*. All in a split second.

"Why don't you give me your number or e-mail or whatever," she says, casual enough to make it sound as though she wouldn't be hugely put out if he didn't.

"Yeah, definitely," he says, overflowing with eagerness.

They swap details on scraps of paper. Johnny knows he has to ask another question before they part.

"Does your boyfriend skate, too?"

"My boyfriend? No."

"Oh, right," he says, calmly.

"He doesn't skate, but he doesn't not skate. Because I haven't got a boyfriend."

She smiles. Johnny does, too. They look at each other while the smiling continues.

"If you're talking about the guy at RedHead, that's my brother."

"Oh, *cool*," he says, giving away his relief.

"Anyway, I'd better get back to my friend. She's by herself over there. See you around, okay?" Her expression is indifferent, passive, impossible to read. It could be that she is being dismissive, but it could just as easily be that she is being shy.

Johnny waves her off and skates back to the Underground station. He doesn't trip once.

He makes sure the scrap of paper with the contact details is safely in his pocket some twelve times between Waterloo and Maida Vale.

* * *

Lydia is IM-ing friends in Austin. Johnny is anxious to get online and e-mail January to suggest hanging out at the South Bank sometime soon. He does not want Lydia to sense his urgency, so he plays it cool and casually asks her if she's finishing any time soon. Lydia, however, is engrossed in fast-typing conversations with the gang back home, and she's in no rush to wrap things up.

An hour or two after arriving home, he finally manages to access his e-mail.

hey January,

how's it goin? it's Johnny here, the Texan guy from RedHead. it was good to see you today. you will be pleased to know I have put some antiseptic on my elbow and its all good now. ☺ thanks for the medic advice. . . .

anyway if u wanna meet up that's cool. i'm really having a good skate every time I head down to the south bank. would be fun to go again with someone I actually know! e-mail me back if u wanna go. i'm not so busy now, so just tell me what works for you.

later

Johnny H

The reply comes within ten minutes.

Hello Johnny H the Texan guy from RedHead,

I'm kinda busy this week. But maybe start of next we could meet for a skate and chat. How about Monday at like 2 pm? Hope that is cool.

Bye,

J x

Johnny hasn't been so excited by a computer monitor since the first time he and the boys downloaded a live recording of a Beastie Boys concert from Japan in seventh grade. He doesn't think January has made an official date, but it's close enough. And the x at the end is always a good start. He replies with a quick confirmation, goes to his room, and listens to some music to mark the occasion.

The days between the e-mail and the skate date are as empty as usual, but Johnny's mood is lifted by the thought that he's going to see January again. It pops into his head first thing in the morning and last thing at night. In between times, he is thinking about it: What he'll wear; what moves he'll try that will make him look skilled, but not stupid if he spectacularly fails; what kind of things he should talk about; how he'll get over the age lie; what will happen if her friends come; what will happen if they don't. These concerns are neither frivolous nor troublesome. They are exciting concerns. They are new concerns.

Lydia, on the other hand, is on cloud one. She still goes out to see the friends Johnny knows nothing about, but she is particularly introverted and moody. She reminds Johnny of the Lydia of a few years ago — the midteen sister who would fly off the handle if you asked her how she was. Although she's not quite as aggressive, she is just as silent and angst-ridden. Johnny the psycho-sleuth wants to know more, but he figures it's best to let Lydia have her own space. He's convinced she's hurting badly, that she needs her family's support.

But the self always eclipses the other, and Johnny's too wrapped up in his own glee to do more than support. He ponders e-mailing January again, then decides he doesn't want to seem too eager. He begins to worry that she'll forget or not turn up at all.

EIGHT

On the morning of the not-date, Johnny Hazzard has slept a good seven hours, from three A.M. to ten o'clock. He wakes up and immediately feels excited.

He takes a long shower, has a leisurely shave, and annoys Lydia by being in the bathroom for so long. He puts on some of the birthday aftershave and styles his hair briefly.

"This is not a date, stop acting like it is one," he tells himself, staring at his face in the mirror. He stays in that position for a couple of minutes. He is reminded of the Thanksgiving shaving incident. A few evenings after last year's Thanksgiving weekend, Johnny went to David's place to hang out. Bored and in possession of clippers and a razor, David offered to shave the Hazzard head. Johnny thought it was the best idea David had ever had and duly allowed his hair to be shorn down to just a few centimeters in length. Looking at himself in the mirror, Johnny was pleased with the end result. It made his eyes stand out and he looked a little tougher than before.

"How about your eyebrows, dude?" asked David.

"You're not shaving those off," Johnny replied.

"No — better than that. I'm gonna *style* them," said David, a little mysteriously.

Johnny had no idea what eyebrow-styling involved. In the kind of what-the-hell mood he found himself inhabiting with more and more frequency of late, Johnny allowed his friend to shave three narrow lines into his right eyebrow. It actually didn't look so bad, but Johnny felt embarrassed by it. The attention at school mainly consisted of strangers laughing at him in the corridors. It was a teenage experiment Johnny Hazzard would not be repeating. But it is a small leap from experiment to experience. And without experiment, experience is just a dream.

Johnny smiles when he thinks of the eyebrow incident, his reverie interrupted by a loud "Johnnyyyyyyyyyy" coming from outside the bathroom door, courtesy of a fuming Lydia. Eyeing himself one last time, he sees there are a couple of zits that need popping and eyebrows that need plucking.

Once the popping and plucking is complete, Johnny heads to the lounge, eats a bowl of sugary cereal, drinks a glass of fresh orange juice (Siska insists on the expensive stuff), and watches a movie for courage. Today it's Woody Allen's musical comedy *Everyone Says I Love You*. It's happy, but cynical enough not to leave Johnny with a gooey heart and gooier mind. Tim Roth's singing is enough to undermine any sentimentality. Johnny Hazzard is ready for his not-date.

He puts his almost-empty pack on his back, picks up his board, leaves his bedroom, and heads for the front door.

"Where you going, looking so smart?" asks Mr. Hazzard. Johnny feels like the boy thief who's been caught with his hand in the piggy bank.

"Er . . . where does it look like?" he replies, pointing to the board.

"Oh," says Mr. Hazzard, scratching his neck and returning to the study.

Johnny doesn't even think he looks that smart. He hopes it doesn't look like he's made too much of an effort. The buttoned short-sleeve shirt is perhaps more formal than a T-shirt, but it's clearly a skate label and nothing too sober. "I look fine," he says to himself before stepping foot out of the house, hand in pocket to confirm once more that the e-mail and phone number scrap of paper is still in there.

He assures himself yet again that it is not a date as he skates from the Tube station to the skate ghetto. And there she is, by herself, sitting on her board and watching some of the others. He has seen her and she has not seen him. Johnny stands perfectly still

78

watching her for a short while. Her face looks happy, but is without a smile. She is peaceful. She scratches the bridge of her nose, then pulls her hair back behind her ear. She takes her cellphone out of her pocket and checks it — Johnny knows she's seeing if he's called her or sent a message. Her attention is distracted from the phone by a skater in front of her, and she smiles as someone pulls off a frontside 180. This is January. Watching her just being herself feels like an honor. Johnny is transfixed. Then she spots him, waves, and he walks over.

Once the pleasantries are over, it's down to the serious business of skating. January is pretty good on the board — certainly Johnny's equal. But now that he's here with her, Johnny is far more interested in talking to her and finding out more. He wants to know what made her choose skating, especially when there are so many more boys doing it than girls.

"Maybe that's exactly why I took it up," she jokes. At least, Johnny thinks it is a joke. "I've always wanted to get into it. And a few of my girlfriends from school wanted to as well. So we just did, a couple of years ago. I never really thought of it as a boy thing. It's not like football. Sorry, *soccer* . . ." she says, playing with him.

"I knew that," Johnny says, equally playfully. "We're not all dumbasses, you know. . . ."

"I should hope not," she replies. "But then again, I'm not sure the evidence is in your favor."

Johnny frowns.

"Some of the peeps your country has elected. Shit actors and brain-dead muppets. Doesn't make the great U S of A look so good, I'm afraid. Relax, I'm not blaming you for the world's problems."

"Thanks," says Johnny, smiling.

"Just most of your compatriots," she says, cheekily, before skating off and landing a successful kickflip.

Johnny is taken aback. Although he doesn't disagree with her, it's still odd hearing it so vociferous from someone who isn't an American (or who isn't Siska).

"I can't say you're wrong," he says.

After just half an hour of skating, January suggests going "somewhere quieter." Suddenly Johnny's heart starts beating faster, louder somehow. The not-date is metamorphosing into a date. Johnny hasn't prepared for this consequence. But there isn't time to dillydally. It's a simple choice: Go with the girl or go home.

"How about a coffee?" she asks cheerfully.

Johnny Hazzard does not drink coffee, but he's not about to disagree with the cute girl's suggestion. Besides, she's eighteen and, aside from scoring with a celebrity, this has to be the best thing that can happen. An older girl. A girl who has experience at being experienced.

"I spent six months traveling," begins January, as they perch on uncomfortable chairs in a chain coffee store. Johnny sips from a dangerously hot hot chocolate. January is on the equally dangerous watery lattes. "Vietnam, Cambodia, India. Then Australia. Then L.A. and Fiji. It was amazing. Have you ever been to those places?"

"Never," says Johnny, almost hypnotized by January's coolness.

"Oh, you should go. I've made so many friends. It's funny because before I left I was really kinda scared about going abroad on my own. I met up with some friends from here, but for the most part I was by myself. I thought I'd be very lonely, but you know what? I met so many new people. In Australia especially. So many people who were like me."

"Well, I've been across Europe and seen some of the US. That's more than most Americans," says Johnny, desperate to appear at least a quarter as worldly-wise as January.

"Yeah, isn't it like seventy percent of Americans who don't even have a passport?"

"Something like that. Not my family. We've all got passports." Johnny smiles, happy to dispel this myth that every single American is a dumbass who hasn't traveled farther than the local mall.

"Where have you been to in Europe, then?" she asks.

"France, Ireland, Germany, Spain. Oh, and Portugal."

"So it must be kind of weird, your dad being so far away?"

"I can't complain. I was a bit unsure about this year, but I think it's all working out well. I'm glad I came."

There's a moment that January could fill with a flirtatious comment, but she opts to smile instead. There's a whole lot of smiling going on this afternoon.

The conversation continues in this happily light vein for a while. Johnny isn't entirely focused on what January is telling him. It's almost as though he's stepped out of his body and is watching this absurdly fantastic situation unfold. It wasn't meant to be like this. It was meant to be a summer of overcastness. This happiness just won't do. He needs something to complain about.

"How do you *afford* this gap-year shit?" he asks.

"I worked for six months. And got a loan from my parents."

Johnny thinks that's wonderful. He thinks the traveling is wonderful. He immediately develops a desire to visit Australia and Fiji and India.

"The people are so poor, but so happy," January explains. Johnny's not concentrating and unsure precisely which people she's talking about, but he nods in agreement, so *grateful* to be in this conversation. He keeps reminding himself that this shouldn't be happening. She shouldn't be talking to Johnny Hazzard. She's far too pretty, far too clever, far too *experienced*. But, above all, far too mature. An eighteen-year-old giving Johnny the time of day? Absurdity. Nonsense. The stuff of sticky dreams. Johnny is paranoid he's going to give away his real age. He isn't helped by making remarks like,

"Graduation's in four years — I mean *two* years. . . ."

But January is as dreamed-up as Johnny is. Doe-eyed and straight-backed, she's flowing through Johnny's every word. They exchange skateboarding stories, Johnny careful not to sound too much like a fifteen-year-old stoner. He needn't be.

"Hash cakes! I can make a mean hash chocolate chip cookie," January says enthusiastically.

"Yeah, I figure I should try one out. I don't like to smoke."

"Me neither. I'll make some for you."

There. She has spoken magic. That commitment to the future fills Johnny with a very hot sensation. He's warm and anxious to know more.

"So where do you live?"

"Finsbury Park. North London. Yourself?"

"Maida Vale. Not far from here really."

"Closer than Austin, anyway," she says, as you do when trying to avoid pauses.

"About five thousand miles," says Johnny. "But it's not far anymore."

"How do you mean?"

"Nowhere's too far anymore. You can chat on the Internet, make a phone call for cheap dollars, send an e-mail. Instant world. That's the name of a song by a band I know back home in Austin. And I bet you could download 'Instant World' in five minutes sitting in your bedroom in London."

January concurs. Unlike its population — or perhaps because of it — the damn world keeps on shrinking.

"And your world and my world have a special relationship, apparently," says January.

"What?"

"America and Britain. The 'special relationship.' You must have heard of that?"

"Yeah, I have. Don't get what's so special about it, though."

"The fact we're so close. UK and USA, that is. You scratch our back, we scratch yours . . ."

"Is that so?"

"Yep. Apart from the Second World War, when we had to wait for you guys to get bombed before you did any back-scratching."

"Well, sometimes we can be kinda slow on the uptake. You know, it takes us a while to realize exactly what's going on. . . ."

"Hmmm . . . I can believe that," she responds. "Relationships only work if . . . if there's give and take." She pauses, allowing the ambiguity of the conversation to sink in. "The special relationship seems to be us doing what you tell us to do."

"Really? Is that so?" asks Johnny, picking up the charge of the moment.

"Yes, it's plain to see. We sit on your lap. We seem to find it more comfy that way."

"You find it more comfy that way . . ." he repeats. "So you think that we're close enough as it is. In our *relationship*."

"You know, that depends."

"And what does it depend on exactly?" he asks.

Johnny looks dead ahead at January, face blank, pupils dilated. She continues, "Blind loyalty isn't good. You have to tell each other when something's not right. When you're doing something wrong."

"But also enjoy it when we're doing something good."

January nods this time.

"Two nations separated by a common language," says Johnny, remembering something he had heard on TV a while ago.

"Well, we don't *have* to be separate."

"That we don't," says Johnny.

They look each other in the eye, and there's a sense of mutual understanding. It doesn't take as much courage as Johnny would once have thought it would to say, "So, do you wanna meet up, maybe tomorrow night?"

"Hmm . . ." January starts, ominously. "No, tomorrow's no good." And Johnny feels stupid and dumb for ever imagining there was chemistry between them. What was he thinking, anyway? She's eighteen. "But tonight's good, if that suits you?"

Bingo.

"Yes, tonight. Great. Okay."

"Where?"

Johnny is stumped. "I don't know the nightlife so well," he confesses.

"So let's meet at the South Bank. We can go to the Film Theatre or something." *She's so damn easygoing,* Johnny thinks. *Isn't this kind of thing supposed to be a nerve-racking nightmare?*

Like a lemon lozenge, January soothes.

"Cool, okay," Johnny says, summing up his state of mind.

They arrange a time and say awkward good-byes. Johnny isn't sure if he should kiss her on the cheek. He decides that might be a little too forward at this stage and opts against. They leave the coffee shop and stand in the doorway outside.

"See you tonight, Johnny the Texan," she says. Then she walks away into the crowds. Johnny stays rooted to the spot, watching her disappear. He knows that somewhere in that crowd is this gorgeous, wonderful girl with a vat of charisma and the greatest butt in London, and what feels the best, what makes Johnny feel so amped, is that she likes him. Excluding Jessica Travis, this is the first time this has happened. He'll always be grateful for that.

Johnny Hazzard's journey back home is hazy. He's on the run with the sun, completely dazed. Upon arriving at the apartment, he says hello to Siska and jumps into the shower. He gives his armpits an extra-hard scrub. Standing in front of the mirror, a white towel tied around his waist, he pops a zit or two on the sides of his nose.

Johnny returns to his bedroom and shuts the door, locking it with the key. He removes his towel and stands in front of the long wall mirror, gazing at his naked body. He feels confident about his balls today. Some days, Johnny worries they are deformed, others he is sure they're just fine. Since the day they dropped, he's been worried, and not a single biology textbook or website has given him complete peace of mind. But today, they look normal, and their best friend the dick looks respectable. He turns around, twisting his neck so that he can see his own back and butt in the reflection. He turns again, and looks some more. He practices a smile or two (minimalist cool, enthusiastically broad). He takes some steps up to the mirror and checks his stubble growth (hardly any at all — kissing should be fine). It's only four forty-five. The date is not till eight. So he looks at himself some more. Minimalist cool smile. Enthusiastically broad smile. Tilt to the right and pout. Tilt forward and pout, looking up as though through the eyebrows. Loud and irritating knock on the door.

Johnny immediately grabs his towel from the floor and covers his dick and balls. He remembers the door is locked and drops the towel again.

"Johnny, dahling, you are eating dinner tonight?" It's Siska.

"I'm heading out at seven fifteen."

"Your father and sister aren't eating in tonight. Shall we dine at six?"

"Cool."

Johnny dries his hair and begins getting dressed. His "going out" wardrobe is not substantial. In fact, it's virtually nonexistent. There are some overly formal shirts, a couple of preppy polo shirts, some uncomfortable, ill-fitting Docker trousers, and the black shirt he wore last night. But that shirt is smelly, and it just won't do. No chance of asking Siska to clean, dry, and iron it. That would involve explaining why he's so eager to wear it. It's going to be hard enough making up an excuse to leave for this evening's date. Johnny opts for tradition over smartness — a clean white T-shirt, the baggy jeans, the obligatory skater shoes. He tucks his belt into the loop, avoiding the second-penis hang. It's now only four fifty, but Johnny thinks it's never too early to look good, so out comes the wax. He experiments with some new tufts and quiffs here and there, all of which make him look like a recently hatched chick. He reverts to the "I-haven't-spent-much-time-on-this" scruffy look, which of course takes a good five minutes of styling. Johnny's reveling in the self-indulgence. He's not used to bothering to make himself look good.

Johnny tries to show enthusiasm for Siska's scrumptious, hot *curry de poulet vindaloo* but he's so nervous it feels as though a feather is stroking the inside of his stomach. He asks Siska for permission to go out, explaining he will "probably catch a movie." Siska lends him her cellphone. As the time to leave approaches, he tries to relax in his bedroom but the feathery feeling won't let up. Johnny distracts himself with a Tintin book — *The Castiafiore Emerald*. There is a time and a place for the Michael Moore, and in his room an hour before this first date is neither. The opening line of Tintin dialogue, as spoken by the thunder-tempered Captain Haddock, strikes Johnny as being appropriate:

"Ah, the merry month of May! Spring, the sweet Spring . . ."

It is the last day of May. Johnny takes this rare moment of happiness from Captain Haddock as a good omen.

Meanwhile, back in the studio, there are more half-empty packets of tobacco than paintbrushes. This is a clear sign that Siska has the inspiration, that the Muse's ideas have finally arrived in the late post. Two canvases are on the go: the one she started after watching Johnny be bored and a new one. It's by no means a certainty, but it appears she is sketching — in blue chalk — an outline that looks remarkably like Johnny himself.

* * *

The South Bank was created for balmy summer evenings. In the dark, you can't quite make out how hideously ugly the concrete truly is.

With its string of bright bulbs shining like a row of stars against the dark blue, thick evening sky, there's a hint of Paris about it.

Johnny Hazzard strolls through the skate mecca, past kids and after-office grown-ups with their kicks and spits. The slightly older crowd is actually more impressive than the juniors; these guys, in their late twenties and midthirties, have the wizened "been there, done that" vibe going on, and they're not so interested in the image, or in impressing one another. To Johnny, the thirties seem like a pretty cool time of life for a guy. He figures that if these dudes aren't growing up, he won't have to, either. So many thirty-something Austinites are carrying on as though they were still twenty-one — not in a childish, jerk kind of a way, but in a "fuck what's expected of us" kind of a way. Johnny looks at the skater "boys" in their midthirties and thinks they're cool. There is nothing wrong with it. Far from it, it's good. These guys aren't trying. And Johnny knows that's the main aim — to be cool without really trying.

He walks up to the arch that sits below the frenetic Waterloo Bridge. Under here, opposite the National Film Theatre cinema, there are five rows of creaky wooden tables covered in books — the bizarre, the esoteric, the crudely populist — and the stalls are beginning to wind down for the evening. A violinist busker and his Yorkshire terrier entertain passersby and drinkers sitting on the outdoor tables of the Film Café. This painfully thin musician has a long Santa Claus beard and wears a bright-purple scarf around his waist. His dog sings along to the violin, with an impossibly tuneful whine.

As Johnny Hazzard loses himself in the strains of the fiddle, a panic begins to rise through his slim fifteen-year-old body. The seriousness of the situation hits Johnny Hazzard like a shot of serotonin in the vein.

"Just what the hell am I doing?" he asks himself. "She thinks I'm seventeen and she's the most beautiful girl I've ever met."

91

That pretty much sums it up. Johnny Hazzard is staring at the starting line of the annual Shit Creek Regatta, and he's misplaced the paddle.

"Hello, you," says January.

"Hello, you, too."

She wears the puffy blue oversized shoes, the blond hair is shining, the gray trousers flare at the bottom and are tight in all the right places, and the white shirt is terribly sophisticated, with an eagle embroidered across the buttons in the middle. She looks the bomb. Johnny feels woefully inferior.

"Well, shall we catch a movie?" she asks. As before, Johnny's not in the mood for disagreeing, although he'd rather be somewhere he could watch her instead of a screen. He still can't believe this is real. That it's actually happening. That *she* is interested in *him*. Johnny half expects David to jump out from behind a bush and announce he's been set up for some sort of MTV prank.

Until that moment, Johnny's determined to do his best impersonation of an experienced seventeen-year-old, keep the y'alls coming fast, and remember every tiny detail so the Austin boys can hear all about it. *Every tiny detail*.

They head through the busy Film Café and into the main lobby of the National Film Theatre. Johnny quickly realizes the patrons here aren't average cinemagoers. There are several thick black Buddy

Holly glasses, numerous black and brown leather blazers, and not a piece of popcorn or foul frankfurter in sight. Tonight's movies reflect the clientele. There are two options — a Swedish movie called *My Life As a Dog* and an American one called *The Apartment*, which Johnny has already seen. So they choose the Swedish story — "a poignant and bittersweet tale of a boy coping with his mother's terminal illness, set in the beautiful Swedish countryside of the 1950s." It doesn't exactly scream "date movie," but Johnny Hazzard thinks "poignant" and "bittersweet" are good signs.

January insists on buying the tickets, which suits Johnny just fine, and also impresses him properly. This girl has the right idea.

There are fifteen minutes before the film starts, so it's straight to the Film Café for a couple of fruit smoothies. It is a curious place. There is no music, but there's buzz and bonhomie nonetheless. The mix of people is eclectic and vaguely reminiscent of Austin. The food is prepared in full public view, behind a glass screen with CHEF'S THEATRE written across it. The chefs are certainly giving it a performance worthy of the National Theatre, which is just next door. They shout at and berate their kitchen assistants. The clientele seems terribly sophisticated and intelligent, and while Johnny realizes it's a cool place, he feels self-conscious and stupid. Whenever anyone nearby laughs, he is sure they are sniggering at him. He is not normally a paranoid person, but the nerves are getting to him. January perceives he is uncomfortable, and cuts straight to the chase.

"Are you seeing anybody right now?"

What a nice, grown-up question, thinks Johnny Hazzard. *You just don't get asked that in high school.*

"No, I'm not," he answers. "You, too, right?" he asks, sounding desperately hopeful.

"Yeah. I was kind of seeing someone —" (Johnny Hazzard has no idea what this means, but it sounds quite neat) "— before I left for traveling, but it fizzled out. We weren't really suited."

"Oh. You weren't in love . . ." says Johnny, aware that he's sounding ridiculously naïve.

"Love? No no no. It was just fun. He was older, actually. I'd never gone out with an older guy before."

"How much older?"

"Just a couple of years. Anyway he's yesterday's news," she says decisively, and takes a big gulp of the banana-and-orange smoothie.

Johnny feels a little slapped by that last comment. He wonders, ever so briefly, if one day he'll be "yesterday's news." A split second later he wonders if he'll ever be "today's news." Then January starts talking favorite movies and everything's back to fluffy again. Johnny can talk about movies until the cows come home. Or indeed, the horses. Movies gave Johnny his first taste of independence at age ten, when Mrs. Hazzard gave him permission to go to the Dobie Mall on Guadelupe Street by himself and watch the Marx Brothers classic *At the Circus*. He loved the film, fell in love with Groucho, Chico, and Harpo, and came home singing "Lydia the Tattooed Lady" at his poor sister. The conversation gives Johnny confidence — he knows his stuff, he's in his element, and he's explaining who Austin's very own Richard Linklater is when a voice comes over the PA system declaring the imminent start of *My Life As a Dog*.

They take their seats. There are no trailers, no ads for deodorant — just the movie. Johnny is hooked within the first five minutes. The story centers on a fatherless boy whose mother is terminally ill. Johnny has no personal experience of such grief, but he can relate to little Ingemar, the film's twelve-year-old hero. Maybe it's because he has spent so much time away from his own mom, and he knows what it's like to worry, and to cry yourself to sleep missing her touch and her sensible words. Maybe it's because he's known the loneliness the boy has felt; the solitude of grief cannot be all that different from the solitude of being in London.

Johnny Hazzard does not touch January throughout the screening. It's not that kind of film. Besides which, he is utterly gripped. A cinema is not a date venue for Johnny; it's a place to enjoy movies. The final credits roll and the place quickly empties.

Once outside, January checks her cellphone and turns to her date.

"Well?"

"I loved it. Didn't you?"

"Yeah. He's adorable. I want to take him home and make him my little brother," she says keenly. Johnny is unsure what to make of that critique.

They return to the smoky Film Café for a drink. Johnny is feeling cocksure. He swaggers to the bar and begins his conversation with the barman with a "Hey, what's up?" before ordering two pints of lager.

Back with January, Johnny drinks quickly. He likes the mellow, dreamy half-high a pint of lager gives him. January seems to be less affected. Conversation, both before and after the alcohol, is easy. Despite the age lie, Johnny feels real. He also feels uncertain. He so desperately wants to be accepted and liked. But right now he cannot figure out whether this is just friendship, whether January is just treating him as the younger brother, or whether it's something more. Nevertheless, Johnny enjoys the moment. And he makes a confession.

"I cried before the end of the movie," he says, filling a gap in conversation. It seems like a mature and modern admission to make.

"So did I. You'd have to have a heart of stone not to," she says, slightly stealing the Hazzard thunder.

"You know, I think I could really identify with the little guy. Being sent away from home, spending time in a new place, having to make new buddies. I haven't really made any buddies until this year. The summers have been long."

"I hear you. It's hard to arrive somewhere knowing nobody. You just get so desperate for company. That's what makes you feel so down — not having any friends you can talk to. But you say you've made friends this time around?" she asks, eyes on beer.

Johnny feels January *does* hear him, and knows. "Well, only Mario," he says. "The RedHead dude. And y'all, of course."

"All of me?"

"Yep, all of you." January smiles. Johnny is unsure. Unable to think of anything witty or flirty to say, the best he can come up with is —

"Is that okay?"

January giggles. Johnny feels small, as embarrassment spills over his face like a bottle of milk that's been dropped on tarmac.

"Yes, it's okay. Y'all can be my buddy, too," she says, with a smile as bright as her blond hair.

"That's good, because tonight's been fun," says Johnny. How can he put into words what he's thinking without sounding like a complete chump? *Why can't I find the Tarantino or the Allen or the Scorsese words? I sound so fucking young,* he thinks, staring aimlessly at January, who's still smiling. *When am I going to be able to say good stuff?* And January quickly leans forward, places her lips on Johnny's and gently slides her tongue through them into his mouth. *Why don't I have the good words? Where are they?*

Holy shit, she's kissing me. His cheeks feel as though someone has just injected them with hot, hot lava. His hands moisten so quickly it feels as though he's dipped them inside a bowl of honey. His head is spinning like a magic merry-go-round filled with the happiest kids — it's not dissimilar to the feeling induced by the alcohol that balmy Soho evening with Lydia, only this time it's one hundred percent natural. Johnny Hazzard realizes he's delirious. His tongue and January's are dueling like two angry octopuses. After a healthy twenty seconds of tongue tennis, he pulls back.

"You've had practice," she says, still smiling.

"Well, you know, once or twice," says Johnny. And those words will do just fine. The detail is in the cockiness. Johnny Hazzard has told the truth and got away with it. Because at this moment in time, the truth sounds unbelievable enough to be perfectly believable. January is none the wiser, the evening is just about perfect, and the painfully thin violinist is finally playing something upbeat.

NINE

The next time Johnny Hazzard sees January, it is at her house in Finsbury Park, North London. Two days after the first date, Johnny rings the doorbell. About a second later, the door is answered by a boy of about the same age as Johnny, dressed entirely in black, with black nail polish on one hand only. It's January's brother, with the kind of expression on his sour face that screams *Fuck off, I'm busy*.

"Yes?" he says, in an accent as polished as January's.

"Hey, what's up? Is January home?"

"Who are you?"

"Johnny. We met before," he says, putting a hand out to shake. The boy in black does not oblige.

"I'm Doll."

"Good to meet you, Doll. So is January in? She's expecting me."

"Wait there."

And the door slams in Johnny's face. Moments later, January leans out of an upstairs window and shouts down that she'll be with him in a minute. Johnny feels very nervous again. Doll has derailed him.

January, minus shoes, comes to the door and lets Johnny in.

"Sorry about my brother — he's fifteen," she explains, and Johnny feels a pang through his torso. He talks quickly to disguise his guilt.

"No worries. I mean, he was cool, probably just not too sure about opening a door to a stranger and all. So how's it going? Everything okay?"

"Yeah, everything's just great."

She puts her arms around Johnny's waist, and he doesn't know where to put his. She kisses him quickly on the lips, and is about to go in for a second, slower, more longing kiss when Doll appears at the foot of the stairs.

"Put it away," he says. The grumpy frown has grown — it now looks as though his whole face is a big unibrow pointing southward from forehead to chin.

"Fuck off, George," says January, arms no longer around the Hazzard waistline.

"George?" asks Johnny.

"He didn't introduce himself as Doll, did he?"

"Yeah, he did."

"Oh, grow up, *Doll*!" says January, competing for the Miss Sarcasm title. "Your name is George — get over it."

"My name is whatever I want it to be. Are you two going to be in all day or do I get some peace?"

"No school today, Doll?" asks Johnny, not wishing to get into the name game.

"Study leave, Dollar Boy," explains Doll.

"That's enough, George," says January, ratcheting up the tension levels. "Piss off."

"Why should I have to leave?"

"Your mascara is all over your eyelids," January replies.

"Bull," says Doll, his face going from frown to concern in a split second.

"She's not kidding," says Johnny, trying to help Doll out of a makeup-hell scenario.

"I didn't ask you, Dollar Boy," says Doll. A good foot shorter than Johnny Hazzard, and considerably scrawnier, this kid is really overinflating the balloon. Fortunately, Johnny is in no mood for confrontation.

"Whatever, dude. Believe me or don't, but we're going out, so you have a good day," says Johnny, taking January's hand. Once January puts on some shoes, picks up her purse, the couple exit, and the boy in black, the frown having returned, scoots up the stairs and into the bathroom to adjust the errant mascara.

January is taking Johnny on a window-shopping tour of London. Carnaby Street (a far cry from its heyday, too many chain stores, no tangible style), Oxford Street (hideous all around), Regent Street (legendary, still a cut above the rest), and Covent Garden (not as quirky as it once was, fantastic skate store). At precisely half past twelve, having strolled down Oxford Street and approaching the mayhem of the crowded pavements at Oxford Circus, Johnny Hazzard takes the plunge and puts his arm around January's shoulder. If she had seen his panic-stricken face before he did the deed, his cover may well have been blown. The heartbeat speeds up, the hand stays dry, and it now sits comfortably and nonchalantly over January's left shoulder. She links her left hand fingers with his, and Johnny feels as though little can go wrong.

The romantic moment, however, doesn't survive the zealous Krishna crew. Within seconds of joining, they are forced to break to allow a gang of Hare Krishna singers to dance on by; behind the devotees, a couple of drunk homeless men have joined in the revelry.

On the slow stroll down Regent Street, January retakes Johnny's hand. They enter Hamley's, the gigantic toy store, which, it seems, contains at least five hundred thousand children at any given time.

"Let's be kids," says January. And kids they become, for the best part of an hour, playing with the fluffy tigers, giraffes, pigs, and ducks, trying out computer dance mats, chucking boomerang planes into the air, squirting each other with bubble pistols. There's a lot of laughter. *This is what dating's all about*, thinks Johnny Hazzard.

After picking up a couple of sandwiches, which Johnny remarks are "weedy and outrageously expensive" compared to their Texan counterparts, the couple continue to check out clothes and CDs. Inevitably, the all-important issue of music tastes comes up during a visit to Soho's small and perfectly formed record stores. Johnny talks about his long list of favorite bands — the classics (Beasties, Rolling Stones, Beach Boys, Nirvana, Foo Fighters) and the new alternatives (Cold Calling, The Tins, Stevie Wolland, The Halloween Masks).

After doing the only thing one can do in a record store — split up and reconvene twenty minutes later — they go for a soft drink and talk music. They find a shared taste for '70s punk bands like The Undertones, Buzzcocks, Sex Pistols, and the ever-cool

Blondie. Johnny explains about the legendary South by Southwest Festival. He says he has seen a number of bands, and even befriended a few, on the Austin scene. Johnny isn't trying to sound older than he is, but he's succeeding. The truth is, thanks to a mother who knows how to bring up a boy, he's been exposed to the kinds of experiences some of his classmates have to wait until they're eighteen to taste — he has been on the right track to acquiring the much-coveted savoir faire. He attended his first Austin concert at a small, greasy bar at age fourteen. While the under–twenty-one venues are few and far between, there are some cool ones, and Johnny tries to go to them twice a month. Kade is his main music companion.

"The trick is to stay behind afterward," says Johnny, sounding like a wise, old professor. "This one time, me and Kade stayed after the concert and got chatting with this dude. Turns out he's the singer's brother. We both got invited to the after-party at the singer's house in Westlake — that's like this rich part of town. We're two kids at this party with this bunch of guys and girls, and people are so friendly and talking to us. It was an awesome day."

"That happens a lot?"

"No, that was a one-off. But, you know, we make friends at these concerts. Music is where it's at in Austin. If you don't like music, you're not gonna like it. That's what my sister tells people."

Johnny is then drawn into a conversation about Lydia. He finds himself getting tangled in a particularly tricky labyrinth of lies, as he says Lydia is nineteen, which, according to the previous big lie, only gives them two years of difference. This makes the tense relationship he describes slightly harder to believe. Still, January seems to fall for it. So far, so good.

* * *

Johnny Hazzard returns to Maida Vale at three thirty in the afternoon, tired and happy. Mr. Hazzard is working hard. Siska and Lydia are not in. Johnny takes off his T-shirt and lies on his bed, looking at the ceiling.

So this is love, he thinks. *It's not overrated after all.* And he begins to worry about precisely how one puts on a condom.

TEN

The joie de vivre, the *joy of life*, is captured in a kind of feeling Johnny doesn't remember having since he was eleven. It's a return of that childhood mood. The sensation of riding your bike really fast around a tight corner on a sunny day in May and knowing that your day couldn't get much better. He's not the kid on the bike anymore, but that incredible feeling isn't hard to remember.

Mealtimes with the Hazzard clan are filled with subtle and not-so-subtle questions regarding the increasing number of hours Johnny spends out of the apartment. Johnny explains he's skating, or hanging with skating buddies. He's fairly certain Mr. Hazzard and Siska have bought it. But Lydia knows. As if her wry smiles weren't evidence enough, on one particular evening she pays Johnny a visit as he's reading Tintin before bed.

"So what's her name?"

"I don't know what you're talking about," says Johnny, deadpan.

"Sure you don't. Just don't get too excited, bro. Remember you don't live here."

Lydia leaves, and Johnny is left with some rather cynical advice he really doesn't want to take to heart. But Lydia knows what she's talking about. She still hurts.

Johnny and January's romance is what many might describe as "whirlwind" (*an event that happens much more quickly than normal*), but love is never anything other than whirlwind. If, indeed, it is love. But Johnny can't believe it's anything else. Because everything feels possible — *everything*. Johnny keeps reminding himself that he's only seen her a few times, but he just knows this is it. All he has to do is be truthful with her about the whole age thing and he's cruising for a first proper relationship. So it's happened quickly and, yes, it could even be described as "whirlwind," but how many loves don't come about in a strange, mixed-up whirl of ideas, emotions, instincts? And this has to be love because suddenly little else is as important to Johnny Hazzard as his beautiful girl. She is the proverbial first, the last, the everything. Suddenly, returning to London during the year is all that's on Johnny's mind — and he's still more than two months away from leaving. He jumps off his bed and switches on the computer, checking out online prices for flights between London and Austin. To date, Johnny has never bothered to research these things; tickets have, naturally, always been paid for by the parents. But he decides it might be time for him to find some work, save up, and pay for a flight back to see his girlfriend. Johnny remembers hearing there may be some part-time work going at Tekgnar, the popular Austin skate store. He types out an e-mail to formally apply for the post, before thinking it might be better to wait. The e-mail is saved in the drafts folder.

The next morning, Johnny is up at nine thirty and goes straight to the floor. Twenty push-ups, followed by twenty sit-ups, then a shower. Johnny feels good in that shower. The pecs are gaining definition. He turns to the mirror opposite the shower and swings his chin up and his head to the left, striking a moody pose worthy of an underwear model. Johnny Hazzard, Mr. H-O-T.

Today is extra special because with Mr. Hazzard, Siska, and Lydia out for the day, Johnny has invited January over for some hash cookie action. He makes sure his room looks clean but not anal, sprays on some deodorant, adds a splash of the birthday aftershave, and looks at his naked self in the mirror again. He studies himself. He looks at his bits, knowing it's only a matter of time before they're called into frontline action for the first time in their lives. Knowing that the pleasure won't just come from his own hand. Knowing positively that, very soon, he'll look at those bits and they'll have changed. They won't be just his anymore. They'll be a little part hers. They'll have been shared. He's certain. No more fantasizing and kissing the right arm in a ridiculous childish way. The fun might begin today. Although scared, the kind of scared he has never felt before, he's excited that it might be about to happen. And, despite the fear, he has never been more ready.

* * *

January brings over come chocolate chip cookie mix and a tiny polythene bag filled with skunk. As they mix the concoction, she and Johnny watch daytime talk shows, sitting on the couch in each other's arms. They put the cookies in the oven and Johnny takes January on a tour of the apartment. January is curious about Lydia but Johnny doesn't say too much. There is a hairy moment in Johnny's bedroom when January reaches for his passport. Fearful of a cover-blow, he grabs it away from her and jokes that he's not ready for her to look at his awful picture just yet. She laughs it off, completely unaware that she was seconds away from realizing she's dating an underage boy. A *boy*.

The oven bell rings. They stand in front of the oven door, peering through the glass at their cookery experiment as though studying a specimen of rare bird in an aviary.

"They sure look like cooked cookies," says Johnny Hazzard.

"We'll let them cool a bit," says January, seeing that Johnny is ready to stuff three in his mouth. "And only eat one, they're fucking strong," she advises.

After waiting ten minutes, January and Johnny feed each other a cookie, interlocking their arms. This is January's idea. Most of what goes on is, as Johnny doesn't quite have the guts to suggest things himself yet. Besides, it's easier this way.

They steal a few pecks on the lips as they munch down the cookies, then move to the world's most comfortable couch. Within an hour, the full impact of the magic hits Johnny and January. The visuals are provided (courtesy of a cartoon channel) by *Garfield and Friends*, *Top Cat*, and *Hong Kong Phooey*. Things hit cruising altitude with *Snagglepuss*. Suddenly, "Heavens to Murgatroid" and "Exit stage left" are examples of the driest wit, the sharpest humor.

The inevitable giggling is interrupted only by long kisses. Johnny feels his style is improving with every tonguing. The high makes him feel dislocated from his body, almost as if he's watching himself kissing January from somewhere above. It makes the kiss feel even better. He's in less of a rush than before. Now it's a few lips-to-lips kisses, then the slight protrusion of tongue, then the tongue tennis, then a pullback and some dry kisses on the neck. It's a style. Johnny has his own kissing style. The boys back home most certainly do not.

January is visibly impressed with her boy's technique, but she needs a glass of water. Between them, they consume two liters of mineral water during that afternoon. With the effects wearing off around the time *The Smurfs* hits the screen ("Why is there only one girl?" January asks), they decide to call it a day. January takes the remaining cookies with her. As she places them in a Tupperware box in the kitchen, Johnny Hazzard grabs her by the waist. Their hips touch and their faces smile naughtily. Johnny's still flying, even if he's close to a landing.

"Don't go," Johnny says, finding the words now coming very easily. The cookies have, if anything, eased articulation.

"I don't want to," she says.

"Let's hide in the bathroom," he suggests, breaking into a fit of silly giggles. January joins in. "No, you're right, you'd better go," he concludes. "So when do we get to hang out again?"

"Hang out? I was kind of hoping we were more than hanger-outers now," says January, smile broadening.

"Oh, really? Does that mean you're my girl?" asks Johnny, bold and bright.

"No. It means I'm your *girlfriend*. I'm nobody's *girl*," replies January, pointedly but still with a pleasant smile.

"That suits me," says Johnny, going in for a couple of quick kisses. "I'm happy," he says, simply and plainly, yet full of meaning.

And Johnny Hazzard *is* happy. He doesn't need to wave his arms in the air, run through the sea, sing along to "Something Tells Me I'm Into Something Good," or walk around whistling. But he is reminded of reaching top speed on his bike and making tree houses and inventing new games. It's that kind of happy. A real kind of happy, that even the finest hash chocolate chip cookies would struggle to equal. But, unlike those childhood experiences of just a few years ago, today's happiness is directionless, without warning and all-consuming. Put simply, he is lost in the most wonderful maze. He is lost in January and in all the possibilities she represents. He looks at things differently — he appreciates things he didn't even notice before. So, amid all the wonderful chaos is a startling clarity. The clarity that tells Johnny Hazzard he *is* into something good. He's the angler who's taken home the prize catch, the gambler who's cleaned up the casino, the president who's won in a landslide.

This kind of lost suits Johnny Hazzard just fine.

ELEVEN

"The Japanese teen horror movies have arrived," announces Mr. Hazzard, patting the table with his silver fork, with all the grandness of a CEO at an AGM.

Johnny Hazzard sits at dinner that evening with Siska, Mr. Hazzard, and a frumpy Lydia.

Siska has made some enormous omelettes and served them with new potatoes.

"Great," says Johnny.

Mr. Hazzard and Lydia look up, surprised at the apparent enthusiasm. The family has heard these announcements countless times before. Johnny hasn't expressed any interest since he was ten.

Lydia returns her concentration to the new potatoes.

"You want me to watch them, get my expert opinion?" asks Johnny.

"If you don't mind, that'd be great," says Mr. Hazzard.

"Sure, no problem."

Siska and Mr. Hazzard exchange a look of concern.

"Lydia, dahling, what's new?" asks Siska.

"Nothing's new. I'm pretty bored, really. . . ."

"You want to help me with the *vacances*?" Siska had previously mentioned her plans to arrange a family trip to Belgium, taking in the capital, Brussels, Bruges, and Ieper. Johnny had grunted in approval, a commitment that feels like it was made an age ago and that he is beginning to regret with the advent of recent developments.

"On the net?" asks Lydia, who couldn't sound less interested if she tried.

"*Oui*, we're running out of time, dahling. You like to help?"

"I guess," is Lydia's noncommittal reply.

Maybe because he is on a natural high, maybe because he is on the tail end of a cookie high, maybe because he wants to counter the forces of Lydia's negativity with something pure and true, or maybe because he has lost his sanity, Johnny Hazzard (eyes fixed on the omelette) comes out with a —

"I've got a girlfriend."

Lydia looks up at her brother, incredulity across her face. Mr. Hazzard smiles embarrassedly. Siska smiles enthusiastically. Naturally, she is the first to speak.

"Dahling, who is the lucky lady?"

"Her name's January. I met her at the skate store."

"Dahling, you sly fox! Didn't I say it was love?" she asks Mr. Hazzard.

"Whoa — I didn't say love," Johnny points out.

"That's just as well," Lydia interjects.

"Don't get snippy," Johnny says.

"I'm not, it's like I said before. Watch your back, Jack."

"I don't need the advice, sis."

"So tell me more about January" is Mr. Hazzard's first, suspicious contribution.

"Interesting name . . ." says Lydia, slicing a potato in half, her knife banging the plate loudly.

"She's just a student. She's cool, she likes to skate. It's just started, really," says Johnny, and it feels light and easy to speak.

"Well, if you need any kind of help . . . you know, with sensitive issues," starts Mr. Hazzard.

Siska is not impressed. "Pfft! Don't be stupid, dahling, he knows what he does. Shit, Johnny knows more about sex than you do." Down her mouth goes half a glass of red wine.

"Siska!" says Lydia.

"Your father sounds like a boring old guff," says Siska, sitting very straight-backed in her chair and smiling at Johnny, her glasses defying gravity on the end of her nose.

Mr. Hazzard is resigned to being second in command to Siska. He looks at her with mock anger and returns to his dinner, before asking Johnny if he will introduce January to the family.

"Er, I don't know. We only just met, you know."

"You take your time, dahling. But if you do bring her for dinner, I'll make something nice."

"Where does she live?" asks Mr. Hazzard, the suspicious streak in his voice continuing.

"Place called Finsbury Park. North London."

"And she lives with her parents?" Mr. H continues.

"Of course. Who d'you think she's gonna live with?"

"I don't know."

"She's okay, Dad. Trust me," he says, knowing full well he's asking a lot of his father.

But Mr. Hazzard, like his ex-wife back in Austin, is a keen advocate of the "hands-off" approach to parenting. This comes somewhere between the "hands-on" and "fuck-off" approaches; that is to say, he is neither too involved nor too disinterested in his kids' affairs. The balance is just right, allowing Johnny a certain freedom to make his own decisions as to what is right, what is wrong, and what he should never do again. Of course, there are occasions when Mr. H has had to implement some strict codes of discipline. But groundings are not part of the Hazzard armory. He prefers to negotiate, calmly and patiently. No shooting from the hip.

The result could have been messy. Johnny might have become a vicious rebel. Instead, he's become a sweet rebel, a bit like his sister, although in very different ways. Notwithstanding the offer to discuss "sensitive issues" — clearly one he had been thinking about since Siska first whispered her suspicions about Johnny's love life — Mr. H demonstrates an admirable cool at the dinner table and, although he doesn't express it, Johnny is pleased.

And an hour later, the tobacco is being chewed and the paint is flying over the canvas. Johnny has given Siska the greatest gift. That evening she compiles a small sketch of squares and circles, which she names "Undiscovered."

TWELVE

"Ladies and gentlemen, I know you've been waiting for this moment for a very long time. Yes, folks, it's your prom night band — Austin's very own purveyors of fine rock 'n' roll. Please put your hands together and give a warm high school welcome to the sensational, the incredible, the *phenomenal* Johnny Hazzard and the Hurricanes. . . ."

The room goes into delirium. High heels stamp the floor. Guys put their fingers into their mouths and whistle loudly. Girls scream. Teachers applaud. Ears prick up. Everyone gets ready for a sight of the local legends.

And then there's a disturbing quiet. The band has not appeared. The announcer, Mr. Hardcourt (one of the school's deputy principals), looks slightly embarrassed. He takes a handkerchief out of his dinner jacket pocket. The dinner jacket is two sizes too small now and his wife has told him he must replace it. The handkerchief mops his bald head.

"There he is!" screams a girl.

And, indeed, there he is — in a sparkling sky-blue suit, velvet collars, black ankle boots, and a taut haircut. Guitar in hand, over shoulder, Johnny Hazzard appears at the door to the hall, his three-piece standing behind him. David is the drummer with sticks in hand. Kade is the bass player with bass poised. Jack is the keyboard player, hands in pocket, bemused look on face. The crowd is going wild. The screaming continues, the whistling is so loud some teachers are putting their fingers into their earholes to avoid perforated eardrums.

The band walks through the hall, parting the crowd like Moses parted the Red Sea. The promgoers are only too happy to make way for this local hero. The screaming seems to intensify as Johnny Hazzard and the Hurricanes take to the stage.

Mr. Hardcourt hands Johnny the microphone stand.

"Thank you, Austin," says Johnny, greeted with more teenage bedlam. "I am Johnny Hazzard. These are my Hurricanes."

Before the screaming has a chance to fill the room again, David begins the beat. A rhythm suspiciously similar to "Wipeout" is soon accompanied by a loud and pulsing riff, played by Johnny Hazzard. In turn, the riff and beat are soon joined by some funky '60s organ sounds courtesy of Jack the bemused keyboard player. To great cheer, Kade the bassist completes the sound with some fast plucking.

These are the Hurricanes. This is the prom. Johnny Hazzard is the star.

At one point, during the third song of the show, a pair of girl's underwear lands at Johnny's feet. Three women faint throughout the course of the evening. Miss Simbio, the biology teacher, comes right to the front and dances with the kind of enthusiasm normally aided and abetted by class-A drugs. But nobody at this prom needs class-A drugs. They're off their heads on Hazzard. Miss Simbio gives Johnny the most obvious puppy dog eyes.

Before Johnny knows it, Miss Simbio's on stage with him, giving it the sexiest dance he's ever seen. The normally ice-cool Hazzard is taken aback. The prom king and queen stop dancing and begin staring. So does everybody else. Mr. Hardcourt's bald head is wetter than a henpecked insurance salesman. With one foot on the stage and one foot off, he's considering pulling the plug.

"Go, Miss Simbio!" shouts Tim Kipton, the prom king.

The crowd begins cheering Miss Simbio. Using the microphone stand as her pole, she's giving a performance worthy of the sort of club your mother warned could only get you into trouble.

Johnny's singing continues . . .

"Everytime I see you, girl,
I know you'll drive me crazy, girl,
Won't you let me go, girl,

Let me be and let me grow, girl,
I can't keep seeing you, can't you see?"

Miss Simbio's dancing like a deranged four-year-old. The crowd's loving it. She's dirty dancing all over Johnny Hazzard. The Hurricanes look on, accepting their fate as B-list players in the Hazzard phenomenon. They'll get some girls alright, but not till the show's over and the Catholics who have slipped out of their bedroom windows are anxious for a slice of the rock 'n' roll star cake.

The song finishes. Miss Simbio jumps onto the wild crowd, surfing it. Johnny Hazzard, always one for the great improvisation, turns to his band and says, "Boys, 'Surfin' USA!' Two three four . . ."

With just those seconds of warning, the band is away. Johnny kicks off with the famous riff and Miss Simbio is carried across the hundreds of excited teenagers' heads, as the Hurricanes (with backing vocals provided by Kade and Jack) whoop everybody into a frenzy with the Beach Boys' eternal summer anthem.

Things couldn't get much better.

Why the hell do I always wake up when the dream couldn't get much better? is Johnny Hazzard's first thought of the morning. The sun is shining through a gap in the curtains. It's a beautiful city morning. Johnny Hazzard loved the dream, and determines to write it down later in the day.

THIRTEEN

It is three days after the cookie fun, and with three hours' warning, Mr. Hazzard announces he and Siska are attending a dinner party with a few other American ex-pats. Almost instantly, Johnny is on the phone to January inviting her over for cocktails. The couple has been talking of making cocktails for a while. Johnny has no idea where to start, so it's just as well Mr. Hazzard has a *101 Great Cocktails* book ready for reference.

January comes over at around eight. She brings a bottle of vodka, a carton of lime juice, and some whipped cream. They enjoy a customary "hello, how are you?" snog and get straight to work in the kitchen. The White Russian (vodka, Kahlua, whipped cream) is heavy-going. The refreshing Woo Woo (vodka, cranberry juice, peach schnapps) goes down like a storm. Johnny places two pizzas in the oven. While they bake, January makes a Sea Breeze (yet more vodka, grapefruit juice, and cranberry). They are both quite sizzled as they gorge on the mozzarella and tomato. Johnny is just in the middle of eating a slice, when he realizes he must level with his girlfriend. The charade has gone on long enough. Inspired by the Woo Woo, encouraged by the White Russian, and toughened up by the Sea Breeze, he decides it's time to tell the truth. To blow his cover. January catches his stare and laughs at him.

"What?"

Seated at the same dinner table where he admitted his relationship to his father and Siska, he decides he's going to be just as frank. Only this time he has a whole lot more to lose. Johnny Hazzard opens his mouth, but no words come out. *Dammit, Scorsese. Damn you, Tarantino. And fuck you, Woody. Where are the words?*

"January, I'm fifteen years old."

There follows a lengthy pause. January shows no real expression. Johnny panics because he can't read her face.

"I'm sorry," he says, fearing the worst. "I didn't want to lie, but I thought you'd hate me if you knew I wasn't really seventeen."

January stares a bit longer, still saying nothing, either in face or in voice. Johnny Hazzard is as uncertain as he ever wants to be.

"Well. Fifteen," she begins. "Fifteen . . . that's the same age as George."

"I'm not like George," mumbles Johnny.

"What's that?"

"I said I'm not like George. I'm not a kid."

"I know. And I know why you lied. And you're probably right. If I'd known you were fifteen, maybe I wouldn't have taken things any further. But . . ."

The "but" hangs in the air for what feels like an hour.

"But you know what? I'm glad I know. I don't care that you're fifteen. I like you, Johnny Hazzard."

Moments earlier, he'd have bet his life on a negative. He's just heard a positive. He leans over and kisses January on the lips.

"Thank you," he says.

Johnny Hazzard is now indebted to January.

The lips are numb with cocktail. The minds are twisting and turning with cocktail. The weather is fine, the temperature high, the atmosphere as humid as it is tense. Johnny starts to kiss January with a new urgency. A new and exciting urgency, which feels almost primitive. As he does, he can't help but think of documentaries about wild animals. He can taste the pizza on her tongue. Now she's ruffling his hair with her hands, infected by the same mood of quickness. He kisses her neck, she moans quietly and appropriately in pleasure. And without forethought, it just feels like the right thing to take her T-shirt off. She begins gasping ever so slightly. Johnny takes his own T-shirt off hurriedly. The T-shirts are on the floor. Quite suddenly, Johnny feels exposed and convinced that January will think he is too skinny, too pale, too boyish. He is very aware that she is looking at his body, and paranoia pours into his head. He tries to make the concern vanish by increasing the speed of his foreplay. Hands are exploring backs. Johnny is aware of his hard-on, but doesn't want her to notice just yet. He leans forward closer to January and kisses her neck faster. January's moans get louder, an expression of pure pleasure. Her neck has a faint trail of Johnny's saliva adorning it. She takes his right hand and places it on her right breast. While Johnny feels it, he remembers Jessica Travis. Then, desperate to get Jessica out of his head, he realizes his eyes have been closed for almost the entire duration of the kiss. The eyes open, and it really hits him now — it's eight thirty, he's sitting half-naked in his dining room, he's feeling up the most beautiful girl he's ever met. And she's taking her bra off. The bra is on the table. And in front of him is a pair of wonderful, wonderful breasts. They are the most wonderful things that Johnny Hazzard has ever seen. Johnny takes her hand and leads her over to the world's most comfortable couch. He lies across it and January lies on top of him. He holds her tight in his arms. He doesn't care that she must now know he's hard. He doesn't care about anything other than her. He strokes her hair and kisses her neck. She groans. He's thinking about the next step, but really doesn't want to be the one to initiate it. The couch suddenly feels claustrophobic — too short and narrow. The hard-on softens a degree. The panic seeps in. Johnny Hazzard knows sex is just around the corner, but like the kid on the first day of school who doesn't want to say good-bye to mom and walk through the school gates, he really doesn't feel sure about going around this particular corner.

"Do you want to?" asks January.

"I . . . I." Johnny's mouth goes so dry. "I need some water. Let me get some water. Then yes, yes please," he says, aware that he is sounding like a complete fool.

Johnny leaps up, goes to the kitchen, and, with shaky hands, pours himself a glass of ice-cold mineral water. The mouth as dry as the Gobi suddenly feels a whole lot better. But the lack of knowledge is frightening. The kind of frightening that makes him think up stupid ideas. *I could just tell her I'm really tired and I've got a bad infection and maybe we should try another time*, Johnny thinks. He immediately decides this is the worst idea he's ever had. This kind of frightening leaves Johnny aware of his every physical flaw, from mole to zit to scar. Johnny is a cowboy, not a professional. If sex was his business, he'd be laughed out of town having racked up huge debts and a reputation as lousy as Nixon's. Johnny Hazzard is frightened, alright. But he has to do what he has to do.

While the anxiety keeps rushing in, so too does the water. Half a liter later, the spot has been hit and Johnny feels refreshed. He's still nervous and suddenly cold and even a bit shivery. Yet the air is still sticky and sweaty and uncomfortable. It's a classic muggy June city night. But Johnny Hazzard is cold.

He returns to the couch.

She's not there.

He begins to worry that she's made an exit as hasty as one of Snagglepuss's. An instant regret creeps in. "Why didn't I just go for it?" he asks himself. *Fuck, shit, Jesus, shit*, he thinks. The fear gives way to embarrassment and anger.

"I'm a dick," he says out loud, frozen to the spot, his face staring into midair.

"Keep me waiting any longer and I'll get cold feet," comes from the bedroom corridor.

Johnny smiles. He heads to his room, his baggy jeans drooping below his navel, the belt hanging loose. He pushes open his door and January is lying on the bed, looking at a USA passport.

"Jonathan Evan Solomon Hazzard, your picture really sucks," she declares, cracking into laughter. It's humiliating, punishing laughter.

"Bitch!" shouts Johnny, diving onto the bed and tearing the passport away. He's still unaware of what will happen next and very aware of how unprofessional he appears to be, but at least the ice has been smashed.

A clap of thunder, and torrential rain starts. The kind of summer rain that is accompanied by that strange but attractive smell of water hitting the pavement and road for the first time in ages. Winter rain has no such fragrance. This is warm and inoffensive rain. It's not a problem. They begin kissing again, mouth to mouth. Johnny is a pantheon of concerns. Is he kissing too fast? Should he, the male, make the first move? Can January sniff the inexperience on his breath, or — worse still — last night's onions?

Seconds later, January is undoing Johnny's belt. And Johnny is undoing January's. The skate pants are around the ankles. His black cotton boxer shorts are stroking her white undies. They are cut high on the hip and appear to be expensive, designer, shape-accentuating underwear. She slowly slips off her pants entirely. The way she removes them is the sexiest thing Johnny has ever seen.

January whispers into Johnny's ear, "Are you sure?"

He answers by pulling down his boxers. Again, Johnny begins to worry about what she'll think. Is he too small? Is he too average? Are his balls normal? Has she seen a far more impressive set? He doesn't have too much time to worry; January takes his hands and puts them on the elastic of her underwear. She gives his hands an instructive tug downward, and Johnny knows that she wants him to remove her underwear for her. Slowly, his fingers slide underneath the cotton and pull. The tight white slides away and is replaced by supple flesh. This is the first time Johnny has seen a girl in all her glory. He is transfixed for a few moments; as he pulls the underwear off her ankles, his eyes stay on January's groin. He is fascinated and excited and completely, woefully unsure.

Johnny sits up next to January, whose eyes have narrowed. He opens the top drawer of his bedside cabinet. He takes out a

Transworld Skateboarding magazine and finds a condom underneath. The magazine has been strategically placed to hide the condom so as not to give the impression that Johnny ever thought sex was a certainty. He struggles for a short while with the wrapper, then puts on the protection. He has practiced this. January puts her arms up over her head. She spreads her legs open. Johnny knows she isn't dry. She seems happy to take the backseat here, and allow Johnny to take the lead. The trouble is, Johnny isn't entirely sure what he wants to do, what he can do, what is acceptable and what is not. It is most unfortunate, really. He's waited for this day forever, fantasized about it a thousand times and visualized all the wild stuff he'd do, and when it comes to it, he feels rather stuck and silly.

Slowly and carefully, Johnny Hazzard begins to have sex for the first time. He prefers to call it *making love*. January's noises and movements suggest she is enjoying herself. Johnny joins in with the odd groan himself, to make her feel good about things. It takes a few moments for him to locate, and then a little longer to build up to a decent rhythm. But he begins to move magnificently. Right now, Johnny feels at one with everybody and everything. His rhythm is harmony itself. She places her warm hands on his bum, which makes him move quicker. She holds his buttocks, then strokes his smooth back. He tries to hold out as long as possible. His face remains fixed to hers for most of the duration, but he keeps his eyes closed, out of fear more than anything. The slightest suggestion in January's face that he is doing something wrong, the slightest hint of a laugh, would be crushing, so the eyes are best kept shut. His caressing hands speedily switch from her hair to her breasts to her stomach. January's moans become louder and more regular. The two bodies are beautifully sweaty now, slipping and sliding against each other. It doesn't matter that it's a bit messy; it feels, for want of a better word, natural. Johnny feels great. He reckons five minutes is long enough. A small but pronounced scream of satisfaction brings the lovemaking to an end. The unprofessionalism rears its head as he moves off January and sits beside her on the bed. She pulls him back down to her face and kisses him some more. He reciprocates. She slides her hand up and down his leg and back. She loves the feel of Johnny's skin. She steers his head toward her ear, and Johnny guesses at what he ought to do. The ear-licking is clearly doing the trick; January moans, and exhales, and smiles. Johnny isn't hard anymore but it doesn't matter; his girlfriend is loving what he's doing. She's actually loving what he's doing. His tongue wanders around the ear, and he moves down, kissing her neck. January's exhaling reaches a climax. She grips Johnny's hand tight and bends her legs so her knees point up to the ceiling. She moans one last time, quietly, contentedly.

Then a muffled noise begins. It's coming from one of the neighbors — up above, it seems. It can't be — it really cannot be *"Je T'aime Moi Non Plus."* The sensual sounds of Jane Birkin gasping and Serge Gainsbourg seducing fill the Maida Vale air. Johnny has never heard it before — he keeps on kissing. January laughs.

"What the hell is this song?" she asks.

Relieved that the tension has been busted, Johnny smiles. "I don't know. But you're perfect. You're so perfect. Thank you."

"You don't have to thank me," she says.

Johnny almost says "thank you" again before stopping himself. Instead, he holds her tightly. He doesn't want or need anything else in the whole world. He leans in, placing his left leg over her right leg. His right arm rests on the pillow; his left hand strokes January's hair. Nothing is said. He feels her breath over his left arm. It is warm. It makes him feel relaxed, tranquil, and so far away from difficulty. Neither of them speak for three minutes.

Then Johnny Hazzard sensitively detaches himself from January and goes to the bathroom to clean himself up. January peeks out the window, looking at the pouring rain. Johnny comes back into the room and peeks out as well. Rain has never looked better. It's semi-light outside; the sky sags with rain clouds.

January puts her underwear back on. Johnny Hazzard turns and looks at his girlfriend lying on his bed. The same bed he cried himself to sleep in on so many occasions in the past. The same bed he slept in at age ten, eleven, twelve. It is a different bed now.

The girl sits up, her head resting against the wall. The Birkin/Gainsbourg song comes to an end.

"I'm glad that's over," she says. "The song, I mean."

"Oh, yeah. Kinda corny."

Johnny sits down on the bed in his boxers. He feels more awkward now than when he was doing it.

She leans over, embraces him, and blows gently into his ear. He enjoys it and smiles. She tickles his chest. He returns the gesture. They fall back onto the bed and lie there, the increasingly aggressive rain dampening Maida Vale but not their moods. And, aside from the traffic, the rain is the only sound. They lie in each other's arms for five minutes, January stroking Johnny's chest, Johnny holding her hand tight. Nothing has to be said. They are together. Johnny Hazzard has never known anything like this. He has been accepted. Nothing else matters.

It's nine o'clock. January decides not to risk a parental bust and says she will go. The couple plan a few dates before January heads off to visit family in Yorkshire for two days. After that, Johnny is going to Belgium. They are both dreading the ten days they will be apart.

January leaves Johnny Hazzard's apartment, her cheeks red, his redder. Once she has left his apartment, Johnny clears the remnants of the cocktail party and heads straight to bed. He can't sleep for a while, though. With the soundtrack of the rain accompanying his thoughts, he begins writing down what has happened to him so far this vacation. And he concludes that it isn't a vacation at all. It's an experience. A vacation is an escape, a lame bit of fun away from the rigmarole. This whole trip to London is far more than that. It's an experience and, by putting pen to paper, it's an experience Johnny is determined to remember every tiny detail of. He lists what January was wearing, the ingredients of the drinks they made, the weather conditions, the thoughts that ran through his head before, during, and after the sex. He ends up writing for over an hour. Mr. H and Siska return. Johnny slips on a T-shirt and turns off his light. No more talking tonight. Just hopes for happy dreams.

FOURTEEN

The dreams aren't exactly what Johnny Hazzard thought they would be. To a dream analyst, flying on the back of a gigantic eagle through Congress Avenue in Austin's center, up toward the state capital building and onto the UT campus, before coming to a rest on the clock tower probably means a lot. But to Johnny Hazzard, it's just unacceptable. He wanted to dream about what had gone before, about January's soft, ringless fingers and flawless body.

The following morning, Johnny calls January on her cellphone.

She says, "Nothing you can say will change what I think about you. You do know that, don't you?"

Johnny is possessed by a new and swirling kind of a sensation in the stomach.

It feels incredibly good to know that someone worries about him, cares about him, wonders about him. To know that someone somewhere is thinking about him, about what he's thinking, curious for his opinion on something she hears or reads about. To know that someone will do things for him without expecting anything in return. That he can call her and she'll listen, that he can tell her about it all — every last fear and hope, every secret and desire. To know that someone likes him for all his good and bad — for what and who he is. High school is about the precise opposite: about altering what and who you are to seem more likable, more part of the gang. The fake dimension to some high school friendships becomes more obvious to Johnny today. This, on the other hand, is so much easier and truer. Yes, it feels incredibly good, and Johnny Hazzard has never felt it before. To know that he's no longer alone is to know everything that is important.

In other words, the lost is becoming slightly more found. Johnny remains happy, floating around in this bright blue chlorine-free swimming pool of weird new feelings, as long as the pool is never emptied. Because that's how it feels — like constantly swimming, but without too much effort. It's all just happening, without trying hard. It's not like sitting up till midnight on a Sunday finishing up a history paper for first thing on Monday morning. Nor is it like trying to complete a switch backside flip. And it's nothing like trying to persuade David that Marilyn Manson isn't that kid from *The Wonder Years*. Because it all feels so simple, it's all just happened, like the jigsaw pieces have been chucked into the air and they happen to have landed in exactly the right places to make the puzzle complete. It shouldn't be this easy. It shouldn't happen so quickly when you're not even looking for it. Yet it feels so entirely right and so obvious and, above all else, exciting. Everything is January: the hot chocolate Siska makes (and my

God, she makes it so brilliantly) becomes a question — *What would January think? I'll have to get her to try it.* The cute T-shirt in the window becomes a daydream — *January would look great in that.* And it's the way she manages to sneak her way into everything that makes it so exciting.

Sitting on the comfortable couch, looking at the switched-off TV, his hands behind his head, Johnny Hazzard is certain. He's found love.

And, like the ruthless alarm clock that crushes the heavy sleeper's fantastic dream, an idea bangs at Johnny's happiness, trying its best to disturb it. It comes to Johnny seconds after the certainty of love has come to him. The idea that he'll lose her. As ridiculous and childish as it feels to him, he's scared.

FIFTEEN

Johnny Hazzard, Mr. H-O-T, awakes with a hard-on and, in a break with routine, whips the bed sheets off and lies there, staring at his boxers.

After he tires of this, he stands and looks in the mirror. Hair still a mess, he tenses up his chest and arm muscles and looks at himself a little longer.

I'm hot, he thinks. *I'm actually hot.*

There is no such thing as leagues anymore. Once upon a time — like, last week — Johnny Hazzard fell into the minors. In his mind, anyway. He was destined to date minor league girls, marry a minor league girl, and, if they were lucky, spawn a major league child who might hope for better days ahead.

Suddenly — unexpectedly and beautifully, and through no real hard work — Johnny has been propelled into the majors. And a mighty fine league it is, too. The fields are better-kept, the stadiums are fuller, the players are of an altogether higher quality. It's a pleasure and privilege to be in this league, and Johnny knows it might slip past him at any moment. He could be sent down at the drop of a cap. So he must work hard at staying there.

January's acceptance of the fifteen-year-old Austin kid has far-reaching implications. It means that Johnny can expect to get it on with the beautiful ones now, not just the mediocres, or the leftovers. There is no reason why he shouldn't go for the top girls. Not that Johnny is after the rest of the league, given that he has the champion.

Johnny Hazzard has often thought of his sister as being a major league girl. Last Mardi Gras, Johnny and company hit East Sixth Street to see what all the fuss was about. The boys were either fifteen or just sixteen. They hadn't seen so many real, live breasts before. There were tits all over the place — big, small, vinegar, melon. Johnny's better side was trying to tell him this whole "festivity" was degrading and, at best, ridiculous. Guys — many of them equipped with video cameras — would surround girls and offer them cheap, tacky beads in exchange for a flash of breast. It was hardly up there with New Orleans. And, as Austin celebrations go, the February Mardi Gras was lame-orama. Lots of jocks and preps walking around, smoking cigars in their latest pair of dull khakis and characterless polo shirts.

But with all that womanhood on show, it would have been rude not to look. After the fourth pair of breasts, Jack had wisened up and was using his lack of height to craftily worm his way through a throng of salivating, grunting men to get a front-row view.

It was during this festival of carnal desire that Jack told Johnny how much he liked Lydia.

"Johnny, your sister has the best pair of tits I ever seen."

"You've never seen them, Jack."

"I saw them underneath that white linen shirt the other day. That's good enough for me."

"Shut up. That's my sister you're talking about."

"I know. Isn't it great? Your sister. And she's the hottest."

"Would you shut up? You're pissing me off," exclaimed Johnny, before slapping his friend around the shoulder.

"Hey, amigo . . . chill out. I'm paying your family a compliment. Your sister is on it — "

This compliment, which the boys often used, always prompted the same reaction from Jack, David, and Kade — a rendition of the Beastie Boys' "She's On It." Johnny was not amused.

Kade had joked about his crush when the weed made him horny and he asked for a picture of Lydia, more out of cheeky humor and desperate randiness than anything else. But Jack was serious.

Since then, Johnny has often thought about Jack's words. He knows his sister's good-looking. But he never considered himself to have the same share of the family's beauty DNA.

Until now. Until this very day.

A couple of days go by, during which Johnny finds he does not need to "relieve" himself of any sexual tension. Instead, he watches movies, calls January, and talks with her about nothing in particular (for a particularly long time), and plays the odd game of chess with Mr. Hazzard. Johnny loses every time, and Mr. Hazzard apologizes. Anxious to win, Johnny asks Lydia for a game.

"Chess is for losers," she announces. "You seen the chess club at school? Those guys — and they are *all* guys — haven't been near a shower since the last millennium."

With that, she returns to her room. Johnny worries about her reclusiveness, but won't let Lydia hijack his happiness.

SIXTEEN

It is a gray day, and Regent's Park is not busy. January takes Johnny for a stroll and a picnic.

She says it's one of her favorite London spots in the summer. "On sunny days, it's full of people sunbathing, reading a good book, drinking wine, playing frisbee. It's so chilled out."

On this particular Monday, though, there are only a handful of tourists and joggers. The couple find a relatively secluded spot by the desolate football pitches, where the grass is lush and smells of summer. It is a little after one o'clock. January takes out her shopping bag of food and shares sandwiches, crisps, and juice with her boyfriend. They eat and talk, and January begins to tell Johnny about her course at university.

"I'm dreading it, really," she says. "I've been dreading it since I got the results last year. In fact, I've been dreading it since I took my exams. I think I've always been a bit scared of success. The pressure is higher when you succeed, isn't it?"

Johnny does not know.

"I do well at school, too," he volunteers, "but I'm not scared of success. I just go with the flow."

"Maybe that's it. Maybe I need to let go," says January, finishing a strawberry yogurt. Johnny eats a slice of chocolate cake. "I think uni will be cool, though. I'm looking forward to it, definitely. All my friends who have already gone are having a blast."

"I'm sure you will, too. You'll make lots of friends." This feels like a very abstract conversation to Johnny. To him, college is centuries away.

"Yeah, I know," she says.

"So long as you don't make lots of boyfriends, I won't mind," says Johnny, jokingly . . . but in the way that you say stuff jokingly when you are actually deadly serious.

"As if," she responds, before kissing him.

"Mmmm . . . strawberry," says Johnny.

January laughs. Her lunch completed, she lies back on the grass and looks up at the sky. There are smatterings of blue across the gray. Nothing is said as Johnny finishes his cake and reclines, his hands behind his head. He and January look at the sky for a few minutes, without a word being uttered. But it feels comfortable. The silence is easy, the pause is not pregnant. Here are two people who are finally comfortable in each other's company.

January twists around so her head rests on Johnny's tummy. Doctors might have a thing or two to say about the weight she is applying to his stomach so soon after a hearty meal, but then doctors usually drink and smoke more than the patients they advise to cut down.

"What do you think you'll be doing in ten years?" asks January.

"Ow," Johnny responds, as his girlfriend's head hits a painful bit of small intestine.

"Sorry," she says, lifting her head.

"A bit lower," he requests. She rests a little lower down the torso. They keep their gazes on the sky as they talk.

"Ten years. Hmm. I really don't know, but I hope I'm a journalist by then. And I guess writing for a skate magazine would be the best way to start. But, you know, if the *Washington Post* comes calling, I won't say no."

"You know what you want to do. That's lucky. Not many people do."

"Blame my mom. She always has the news on, always has newspapers in the house. And she's always asking questions. . . ."

"I can't wait to hear what she asks you about me," says January, smiling.

"I can," says Johnny, not smiling. He is well aware that his mother will be happy for her son, but very protective. "What about you? Where do you see yourself?"

"I have no idea. That's the scary thing. I suppose I want to live abroad, but that's about all I know."

"Where?"

"I wouldn't mind trying America. There's this great city called Austin, apparently."

"Now that would be cool," says Johnny, playing along.

"Doesn't it ever scare you?" she asks.

"What?"

"Whatever's going to happen tomorrow and the day after. Aren't you scared about what you'll do after school and college?"

"No. Not yet. Maybe that'll come. But I know where I want to go."

"That's very good. I wish I did."

"It'll come," he says, sounding like an understanding grandfather. "My dad changed his career when he was like forty. People take time to get their shit together and work out what the hell they want to do."

"What does your sister want to do?"

"I don't think she knows. She loves her music, though. She writes lyrics and poems a lot and she's got a good voice. I think she might wanna chase the music thing. And Austin's the place to do that."

"But she doesn't know for sure, right?"

"Right."

January seems reassured slightly by that news.

"So is there any music in your veins?" she asks.

"No. None. I can't sing for shit."

"That makes two of us."

"I took piano lessons for a year when I was ten. The teacher refused to continue. She told my mom I had to stop. I was that bad."

January giggles.

"I learned recorder at school," she confides, "with all the other kids. I was useless. Then again, who wants to play recorder?"

"So tell me more of the bands you're into," says Johnny.

"Hmm. There are so many. Let's see now . . . Bowie, Beatles, Kinks, Beach Boys. I prefer the old school. Rage Against the Machine, the Chili Peppers. Is that acceptable, Mr. Cool?"

"It sure is."

There is another lengthy and relaxed lull in conversation. Cars and birds can be heard, but no conversation. Johnny consciously feels more comfortable with a girl than he ever has before. He is truly relaxed. Nothing could perturb him. This is bliss. Around three minutes later, January starts talking again.

"Sun or snow?"

Johnny thinks for a short while.

"Snow, because I've only seen it like three times."

"Favorite color?"

"Orange."

"Blue."

"Hope that's not anything to do with your mood," he says.

147

"No way. Not now, anyway. Now I couldn't be happier."

"Me neither."

"Country or death metal?"

"Death metal, but that's a killer question. They both suck. Especially Texan country."

"Lasagne or pizza?"

"Lasagne. My mom's homemade. Simple."

"Me, too," she says, chuckling. "Well, not my mom's, or your mom's, but lasagne all the same. Okay . . . beer or wine?"

"Beer."

"Good book or good movie?"

"Impossible. I'm gonna use the Fifth Amendment on that one."

"Not allowed."

"I'm a Texan, I can do whatever the fuck I want. We're better than you. You've seen the bumper sticker, right? There are two kinds of people in the world: Texans, and those who want to be."

January laughs, and Johnny is off the hook.

"Okay, I got some for you," he says. "James Dean or Tom Cruise?"

"James Dean. Hands down. That one was easy."

"James Dean or Johnny Hazzard?"

"I'm gonna use the Fifth Amendment."

"That's not allowed. You're not an American citizen."

"In which case, I will choose Johnny Hazzard on the grounds that he is alive."

Johnny laughs.

"You're a cheeky monkey," she tells him. He likes that.

"Okay, here's one I gotta know, 'coz girls are supposed to be weird like this. Sex or great chocolate?"

"Your questions are too damn hard."

"There you go — I'll make a good journalist, then."

"Yeah, you'll be good at interviewing presidents, not girlfriends."

"Thanks, but you haven't answered the question."

"I'm thinking," she says, still staring up at the clouds.

Johnny gives her ten seconds.

"I have to press you. Answer the question. The public has a right to know."

"Well, let me explain. Great chocolate and sex are supposed to kick off the same hormones and chemicals and stuff. So it's a close call, but I'm gonna go with sex. Especially if it was like the other night."

Johnny grins naughtily and memory meteors whiz through his head. He thinks of her breasts, the touch of her hands on his buttocks, her smooth and shiny hair, the moment he climaxed.

"I'm pleased to hear that," he says proudly. "You weren't so bad yourself."

January reaches out her right hand and slaps Johnny on the chest.

"Cheeky monkey!" she says, before resting her hand in his.

"It was great," he says. "You were great. It was awesome."

"I think so, too," she says.

There is a gap in the conversation, during which both Johnny Hazzard and January contemplate the evening in question. Johnny's thoughts begin to travel from his brain to his groin, and the effects are evident to January, whose head is nearby.

"You cheeky, cheeky monkey!"

"I can't help it. It's your fault anyway for being so damn fucking hot," he jokes. This is not the kind of joke he would have been able to make just a few weeks ago. And it is not the kind of thing he would have ever imagined saying to a beautiful London girl in a beautiful London park. And that sums up Johnny's current mood of excitement — the unpredictability of this summer. A feeling of imminence hit him at Bergstrom International, and that was the clue that something significant lay ahead. But he had no way of knowing it would be this. And the routine of high school, of the same classes and same hot and doped Saturday afternoons, suddenly seems far away, alien and wholly unattractive. What is attractive is the element of surprise that has characterized this summer, the fact that Johnny could not have imagined these things in his wildest dreams. What is attractive is the girl resting on his tummy.

"You're a horny, cheeky monkey, aren't you?" she says, hornily.

Johnny doesn't say anything. January twists herself upright and looks down at her boyfriend, smiling. Her smile is electric, and Johnny feels the voltage. He sits upright, and they kiss hard. Johnny's boner does not relent. He passes his hand over January's hair and down her back. The thin white sleeveless T-shirt she wears provides easy access to what lies beneath. He puts a hand under her T-shirt and feels her breasts, slowly, delicately. Johnny knows what he's doing. He has acquired the savoir faire. He is, after all, a horny, cheeky monkey.

The kiss calms down, and Johnny slips his hand out from under her top.

151

"Let's go somewhere quiet," she says. The words are music to the Hazzard ears.

Without saying a word, they put their trash in the shopping bag and walk, hand in hand. Johnny is uncertain — he is even a tad nervous — but at the same time he is confident that whatever January has in mind, it will be memorable. They walk for about a minute and find some bushes. January takes a quick peek over her shoulder, sees that no one is in the immediate vicinity, and walks behind the bush, taking Johnny along with her.

"This is crazy," he says, and starts kissing her again. She removes her sleeveless white T-shirt, and throws it to one side. She is sitting on the grass with just a white bra and jeans on. Johnny leans straight down and kisses her breasts through the bra, before taking it off and kissing the naked skin. January groans. Johnny is bursting with excitement — there is so much he wants to do. He takes off his T-shirt, and January is straight on to his chest, kissing it all over. He feels good about everything. Absolutely everything.

January begins fumbling with Johnny's button fly. She undoes the buttons, and begins to spank the cheeky monkey. Johnny closes his eyes and his face contorts. He is wearing the kind of expression that, if you were unable to see what was going on below waist level, could easily be an expression of pain and misery.

After a short while, January begins using her mouth. Johnny feels instantly great about himself, and then a twinge of guilt because he thinks he is in control, and that excites him. Johnny feels he is just lying back and being pleasured. She's doing all the work. Does it get much better than this? As January continues doing all the hard work, he cannot stop thinking about how cool it is to finally experience this, and how amazing it will be to tell the boys.

January believes *she* is in control. She continues to please him, getting faster and faster. Johnny runs his hands through her hair. He wants to say something like "You're so fucking sexy, you're a horn machine." This is what he is thinking. He cannot say it.

Johnny is close, but does his darndest to hold out. January keeps on going. Johnny catches a glimpse of her naked breasts moving about and this turns him on even more. The full, pervy absurdity of this outdoor sex hits him and that makes him excited, too. Johnny's groans get a little louder, January quickly returns to the spanking of the cheeky monkey, and the sex is complete. Both are out of breath, and both are elated.

January smiles at her lover. Johnny just looks at her with intense eyes, eyes that are so full of love for what they're looking at they're almost insane. January cleans up using some tissues.

January passes Johnny his T-shirt.

"We'd better be careful," she says. They both laugh and put the T-shirts back on. Johnny buttons up and hugs his girl. They hold each other and kiss on the lips.

"Are you okay?" he asks, feeling that he has just obtained the better side of the deal.

"Very okay," she replies, feeling that she has just obtained the best side of the deal. As the giver of pleasure, she has control. Johnny's happiness is, quite literally, in her hands. And she is satisfied by the knowledge that she is Johnny's first. January will never look at Regent's Park in quite the same way again. Johnny, on the other hand, cannot believe this is happening to him. It is not too good to be true. It is beyond that. It simply *cannot* be true. Johnny Hazzard has found experience; he has finally arrived at the destination of savoir faire.

* * *

Three days pass by, during which Johnny and January go skating and take a long walk along the river. During the stroll, January invites her boyfriend to a special evening. Johnny has another rite of passage to go through: meeting January's friends. They're gathering in a Maida Vale pub, just a few minutes' walk from the Hazzard apartment. The evening has been planned for some time now, as January hasn't seen some of them for a long while. Now she's keen to show off her fella, although they've agreed not to bring up the age thing.

"It'll just make our lives easier," says January.

Johnny does not want to rock the boat. He's happy to keep quiet, and to lie if he has to.

As the evening approaches, he is feeling a little nervous, but itching to get *out*. To see and to meet. To do exactly what he realized he ought to be doing after that night in the Soho pub with Lydia. That night — that first step — now feels like a million months ago.

Johnny arrives early and, with a half-second's hesitation, goes up to the bar and asks for a beer. The barman, himself very young, does not ask for ID. Johnny Hazzard is on top of the world, looking down on creation, and the only explanation he can find is that he's been a very good boy in a previous life.

January arrives soon after, with two of her friends: James (preppy, John Lennon glasses, unfortunate goatee, likes you to know everything he knows) and Susan (eats up classic literature as fast as she eats up doughnuts, short, beautiful blue eyes). Johnny shakes hands. He finds it easy to talk. They ask about Austin; he tells them about Austin. James looks down his considerable nose throughout most of the conversation, busily smoking long cigarettes. Johnny gets a bad vibe from this particular motherfucker.

Susan, on the other hand, is terribly enthusiastic. She tells Johnny how much she loves Ernest Hemingway, "despite him being an unadulterated bastard." Johnny knows little about Ernest, so nods and smiles. She says, "Gore Vidal is just my cup of tea," and asks Johnny who his favorite American authors are. "Elmore Leonard," he says, because he recently read *Tishomingo Blues* by accident. "But I'm reading Michael Moore right now," he adds. James sneers as he takes a long drag on his long fag. Susan looks like she's about to climax.

"Oh my God, he's wonderful. He's the best. You're so lucky to have him!"

"Yeah, I guess. But he only exists because we're unlucky enough to have so many jerks around."

"Oh, absolutely. I mean, yes, you're so right. But let's be grateful for small mercies. Or Michaels!" she says, looking at January, who fakes a laugh.

Susan is a decidedly minor league girl, despite her stunning eyes. Johnny feels superiority over decidedly minor league girls. And boys, for that matter. He is in charge of the conversation and of the mood and he feels absolutely comfortable with that. James, although hard to categorize, is definitely a dick. Dicks are less predictable.

"What about you, James? You like to read?" Johnny asks. He tries to sound neutral, but it's impossible; the disdain is there to be picked up on.

"You could say that," James says, with the sort of smug smile that you only normally find on a politician's self-satisfied face after he's duped the nation.

"James is going to study English literature at uni," explains January. "He went traveling on his gap year, too."

"Oh, where did you go?" asks Johnny.

"South America," comes the reply. "Brazil, Argentina, Uruguay, and Chile. Ever been?"

"No."

"Great time. Really great. Changed my perspective."

Johnny finds this last sentiment hard to believe.

Over the next half hour, the group is joined by a steady trickle of January's pals. With the exception of Tom (rugby player, deep voice, stout legs, cozy personality), they are all girls. And they are all major league. Johnny Hazzard thinks he could have them all if he was a single man. Despite not being a single man, he is getting a very positive vibe indeed from Rosie (tall, long brown hair, sympathetic smile). She is one of January's oldest friends. She sits opposite Johnny, and he notices her black bra straps peeping out of a very skimpy and low-cut number. When a woman is wearing a particularly low-cut number, it is asking far too much of a guy to stop his gaze from drifting toward the breasts, however engrossing the conversation. There may yet be a scientist who proves there is a magnetic connection between the male eyeball and the female tit. Regardless, Johnny's eyes wander in midconversation, and the more he notices himself doing it, the more he seems to be unable to stop himself from doing it.

January is otherwise engaged in catching up with school friends. She doesn't notice the overt flirting going on. Rosie asks Johnny every question she can think of about life back in Texas.

"So you don't ride horses, then. . . ." she says sarcastically.

"I've never been near a horse. And I hate rodeos," he says, which she finds sidesplittingly hilarious.

Rosie asks what brings Johnny to London. He explains briefly. She wants to know how different the two countries are.

"Every year I think we're more alike," he theorizes. "Austin's way smaller, of course. But I've been around the States. We're louder, that's for sure. But we think the same things. I've been around Europe, too. Nowhere is more like the States than London," he says.

"Louder. Hmm. . . ." says Rosie, before a small cackle.

"What?" asks Johnny with a flirty smile.

"Well, I'm glad you said that, not me," she says, getting properly serious for a moment or two. "But you know here in London . . . one advantage we have is that we're just a couple of hours away from a completely different culture. Jump on the train and you're in France or Belgium or Holland. Then you're a stone's throw from Germany or Denmark or Spain."

"Yeah, you know back home you can drive for a whole day and still be in Texas. It's bigger than France. And I can see why most of us don't leave the States. We have every type of weather and vacation and a bunch of time zones. But it's a shame people don't want to explore more."

And with the cross-cultural bit over, Rosie tells Johnny she likes his hair.

"Thanks. Nobody in Austin ever tells me they like it."

She tells him she likes his accent. He says he likes hers. And when Rosie gets up to go to the toilet, Johnny Hazzard knows he could have her. He imagines her slowly taking off her black bra and exposing her breasts, and before he knows it he's thinking of his head resting in them. He's imagining her standing naked, then and there in the pub, her index finger calling him over to play. He goes hard under the table.

"Bloody ridiculous about that Schwarzenegger," says James.

Johnny goes instantly soft under the table. He nods and smiles. He doesn't want to give James the satisfaction of an easy poke at Americana.

"Well, what do you think?" says James, cheekiness fueled by a couple of glasses of French red wine.

"I think he sucks," says Johnny. His attention is firmly on the girl behind James, standing at the bar. She looks about twenty, with short, spiky, naturally blond hair. She's wearing tight blue jeans and a minuscule white T-shirt. She's screaming sex and Johnny is screaming it back. If only she could hear him.

"I mean, as a Texan you must acknowledge the ongoing trend of

Americanization," says James, with all the pomposity his nineteen-year-old face can muster.

"Americanization?" asks Johnny.

"Yup, I mean your culture is basically becoming our culture. You see kids on the street trying to be Yankee fans, or Raiders fans, or imitating rap stars. Have you noticed that since living here?"

"Not really. I guess I'm not as observant as you, James."

"Nothing against American culture, but it's sad we're losing our own."

"Are those Levi's?" asks Johnny.

James's face crumbles.

"Yes, actually."

"And CK glasses?"

"Yes."

"You know, I hadn't thought about it before. But I think you may be onto something," says Johnny Hazzard. "Another wine?"

"Not for me," comes the snippy reply.

Johnny checks with his girlfriend and goes to the bar to buy two pints. He stands beside the spiky-haired blonde and sneaks a look. Once upon a time, he would have looked at a girl of her age and appearance quickly and awkwardly. Not anymore. Johnny turns, checks her out for a good few seconds, makes eye contact, half smiles, and looks away, confident he's made his point. It is the knowledge that he's been speedily promoted to the majors in this sudden pubescent acceleration, the conversion from Mr. Wanna-be to Mr. H-O-T, that makes Johnny Hazzard truly feel like he can achieve anything he wants to achieve. He's not about to be unfaithful to January, but the option is thrilling.

Johnny finds the beer comforting and relaxing. He ends up rather woozy, as does January. They leave the pub, along with the others, at around ten o'clock. Johnny is to be home by ten thirty. An inebriated James heads home to Kensington by taxi. Everybody else is taking the Tube. Rosie gives Johnny a kiss on the cheek. "Glad I got to know you," she says, with a squeeze of his arm.

"The feeling's mutual," he replies. As she walks off, Johnny is careful not to let January see the horniness her good friend has inspired in him.

January walks her boyfriend home to the apartment block. In the hallway downstairs they steal a kiss. A slow-eyed Johnny invites her to come upstairs and meet the family.

"Not now. When we're sober," she says.

"Awww, you're no fun," he whines.

They kiss. He puts his right hand on her right breast, his left hand on her left butt cheek. For a second or two she lets him, then she stops the kiss and takes a step back.

"Calm yourself down, Romeo," she says.

He takes a step forward.

"Does that mean no fun tonight?" he asks.

"Yeah. You're drunk. Go and sleep," she says, good-humoredly.

They have one last good-night kiss and Johnny goes upstairs. He sits in the lounge, in front of the television, alone, watching a late-night Sinatra movie, *The Naked Runner*, his legs wide open. Thinking of January's breasts and butt, he falls asleep in this position, waking up two hours later to find the Sinatra film has been replaced by an ancient and turgid American sitcom.

Johnny Hazzard walks to his bedroom, deliberately ignoring his dental hygiene, and strips off, falling asleep naked on top of the bed sheets.

SEVENTEEN

According to Shakespeare, the course of true love never runs smoothly, a sentiment reinforced by every two-bit philosopher who is probably a greedy womanizer and, through his own self-ishness, has lost a couple of good women before singing Charlie Rich's "The Most Beautiful Girl in the World" into a whiskey tumbler in a blues bar at two in the morning. So it comes as little surprise that neither Johnny nor January is particularly keen on their imminent family holidays. They arrange to meet for a fare-well rendezvous before her trip to Yorkshire and his to Belgium. It just so happens to be the longest day of the year, the summer solstice. January suggests watching the sun go down from Waterloo Bridge. Mr. Hazzard does not grant permission for Johnny to be out so late. Especially not on a bridge. So instead, they elect to meet earlier in the evening and enjoy the extended daylight. During the organizational phone call, January says she will bring a joint. "We're to share the joint equally," she declares. "And we're to share everything from now on, okay?" Johnny is

163

not in the mood to be disagreeable. "Including baby photos," says January.

"Baby photos?" replies an incredulous and more-than-confused Johnny Hazzard.

"Baby photos."

"Shit. You know it's serious when she asks to look at the baby photos," he says.

January laughs, makes the final arrangements, and leaves Johnny to ask Siska to root out some baby photos of Hazzard Junior. He approaches her in the studio. Empty bags of tobacco lie across the floor. A large chunk of the green stuff is lodged in her left cheek, a brush lodged in her right hand. Her wedding cake hair looks more upside-down cake.

"What for, dahling?"

"I just wanted to see some. Where does Dad keep them?"

"Can it wait? I am in the middle of the journey," she says elusively.

"Well, I'm going out soon. Can't you just tell me where they are?"

"Dahling, I don't know where my passport is, nevermind your baby photos. I need time to find them."

"Well, can't you go now?"

"Johnny, my sweet, I'm working. Later!"

She returns to the canvas and Johnny returns to the bedroom.

A couple of hours later, Siska emerges from her studio, looking as though she has spent the last few days in solitary confinement. The rings around the eyes, the disheveled hair, the pasty face — Siska is in need of a holiday. She goes to The Cabinet in the dining room. Every house has The Cabinet, the piece of old furniture inside which lurks the useless, the mundane, the ancient. Candles, unwanted gifts, shit cutlery, birth certificates, out-of-date contact numbers for the gas and electricity companies. And, in this case, a photo history of the Hazzard family. After initially hearing exasperated cries of "Shit!" and "Bugger!" with the distinctive Belgian twang (usually accompanied by the clattering sound of assorted items falling to the floor), Johnny is aware of the silence. She's either fainted from artistic exhaustion or given up the baby-photo mission. Johnny leaves the comfort of his mattress and goes to the dining room. He sees Siska, her back toward him, her head pointing downward at something Johnny Hazzard can't quite make out.

He catches a glimpse of her face. She looks lost in whatever it is she's holding in her hands. Johnny shuffles and Siska is woken out of her reverie. Johnny approaches, asking Siska if she's found the baby photos yet. Siska says nothing, but offers Johnny the bundle she has been looking at so peculiarly. Johnny stands by

165

his stepmother, who kneels on the wooden floor, still looking sweetly unkempt.

The bundle contains more than just baby photos. There are pictures of hippie-ish Mr. and Mrs. Hazzard in Zilker Park, Austin. Of toddler Lydia holding baby Johnny. Of Mrs. Hazzard proudly showing off her new baby boy to the camera. Of Johnny's first day at school. Of Lydia and Mr. Hazzard rowing in Austin's town lake on a bright summer's day. Of five-year-old Johnny blowing out the candles on his birthday cake, his mother proudly standing on one side, his sister lurking sinisterly on the other. Unwittingly, Johnny Hazzard slips into the same lost kind of a look that Siska held just moments earlier. He sifts through the pictures, careful not to show too much emotion or display any kind of a thought pattern in front of Siska. But he lingers longer on the pictures containing his mother. And he misses his mother. On this year's trip, he hasn't thought of her as much as he once did. It takes a photo to remind him that he misses her. Events of the present have eclipsed longing for the past. Yet the past is still there, biting at his ankles.

"Thanks for finding these," he says to Siska.

"No problem," says Siska, exiting on cue, aware as usual of when and where to do what and how.

Johnny takes her place on the floor and continues looking through the hundred or so photos. He finds one in particular that he looks at for a good sixty seconds. It is him, Kade, David, Jack, and a kid they used to hang with named Michael. The five of them, age ten, sit on their bikes, waving at the camera. And although they're only ten, and it's only five years ago, Johnny is hit by a kind of instant and brief sadness. He knows he'll never be like he was ever again. An obvious realization, but a realization nonetheless. The sadness quickly and seamlessly turns into a kind of relief. Because to Johnny Hazzard, this is the summer he has finally left those years behind. He takes four baby photos and a couple of kiddie ones, and leaves the rest in the open drawer of The Cabinet.

The picture of his gang is on top of the pile Johnny leaves behind. In each ten-year-old face there is a sight of each future, a crystal ball in each pose and expression. There's Kade, half smiling and looking pissed off at the photographer. Perhaps because he looks younger than the others, he appears just to want to get on with it, ride his bike faster than anyone, start skateboarding before anyone, start sexing before anyone. Beside him is Jack, the only one wearing a bicycle helmet, mommy's boy, already plump and wearing a look of concern that will later be countered by an absurd chain-smoking habit. David, a little more baby-faced than he is today, looks cynically at the camera as if it's the dumbest photograph in the world. Michael, the kid who moved to Delaware, is practically not there. And Johnny Hazzard. Some people say that when there's a death in the family, the relatives have death in their eyes. In this picture Johnny has divorce in his eyes. He looks hurt, alone, distant. And yet his pose is determined, confident, and full of Texan swagger and the machismo of the ranch. He's a young boy who wants to be noticed.

* * *

Johnny meets January at the South Bank, board at the ready. Despite the concrete car park ambience, this is the new romantic hotspot in London. It is six o'clock. They have a few hours to enjoy the longest day before Johnny has to head home. Johnny suggests a spot of skateboarding. He is proud of himself for having come up with the ideas for a change. The couple agree to share their baby photos on Waterloo Bridge at the end of the evening, after a solstice smoke.

The South Bank contains a smattering of dedicated skaters, most of them not teenagers. Johnny is impressed by January's ability. They skate for about forty-five minutes before Johnny notices a familiar face approaching in the distance. It's Mario, clutching his skateboard with his left hand and an English girl with his right.

"Hey, that's Mario!" says Johnny. "Come on." They go over to interrupt the Brazilian's bankside stroll.

"'Sup Mario?"

"Hey . . . how are you?"

A smiling Mario shakes the Hazzard hand.

"I went looking for you at RedHead. I found her instead," says Johnny, proudly holding January's hand and showing her off like she's just won Best in Show.

There are some introductions and more smiles. Mario's girlfriend (tall, dark brown hair, cannot take compliments) is called, most unfortunately, Henrietta.

"You guys going for a skate?" asks Johnny, full of enthusiasm.

"No, we're just taking a walk. We're going to the Solstice Festival in Clapham," says Mario. "You wanna come?"

Johnny could explode with enthusiasm by now, but he knows there's no way he can evade Mr. Hazzard's curfew. It's a polite declination, then.

"Come by the store whenever you like," offers Mario.

"Yeah, it'd be cool to hang out," says Johnny.

While the boys talk, the girls briefly and discreetly examine each other and their boyfriends. They smile fondly as they part. Mario gives Johnny a hug and pat on the back. Johnny Hazzard loves London.

* * *

"You know, although there's cars and buses and shit, it's blissful up here," says January nearly two hours later, lighting up a joint and passing it to her boyfriend.

Standing on Waterloo Bridge, looking down at the river Thames and over at the Houses of Parliament and Charing Cross, and the London lights twinkling in the longest day, Johnny feels no fear.

He has never felt so at ease. He has never felt so attached to a place or a person. He belongs and they are together. There is, however, one small thing —

"What are the laws here? For dope?" Johnny asks.

"Er . . . why?"

"Well, I just thought. We're out here in the middle of the city smoking dope. It's kinda risky, don't you think?"

January giggles. It can't be the gear already.

"You've got to loosen up, Johnny Hazzard. This isn't America. You don't get killed for breaking the law here."

Johnny Hazzard wants to explain the complexities of federal laws versus state, but decides instead to say, "No, but I'm a foreigner. They could stop me coming back and shit. And I wanna come back," he says, unable to complete the sentence with a "to see you" but confident that January has gotten the idea.

"We won't get arrested, silly. Besides, they don't arrest you for smoking dope anymore. Unless you have intent to supply. And the only person I intend to supply is you, so stop worrying."

She leans over and kisses Johnny on the lips before returning to her spliff.

"You need to see the world," says January, suddenly.

"What?"

"It didn't even cross my mind that we'd get into trouble, smoking a joint here. When I was traveling, it was just the done thing. In Goa, Cambodia, Vietnam. Wasn't a big deal. I think everyone should go to Vietnam and Cambodia. See a different way of life. I'd never seen the developing world before. It totally changed me. I don't get so pissed off about small things now."

Johnny Hazzard is enjoying the moment too much. He's loving the romanticism of Waterloo Bridge, of the snail-slow setting sun, of the lights along the river Thames, of the warm summer night. He doesn't want to spoil it. But he knows that January has just said the dumbest thing he's heard in a long time.

The joint is completed. They kiss, with tongues, and it's so slow, and so full of meaning. Johnny Hazzard has never experienced a kiss full of meaning before January. He has never kissed someone he really, really likes before January. It feels different; it feels sharper, and livelier, and so much more fun.

January asks Johnny to be totally honest about her friends.

"I liked them, totally honestly," he says, with a small giggle.

"You didn't like Becca, did you? I could tell. You thought she was stuck-up. We all think she's stuck-up."

"I wouldn't say that," says Johnny. "She was a bit stuck-up, but I don't think she had it in for anyone else. . . ."

Johnny cannot say that he found three of them very attractive, one moderately attractive, and one half-attractive. Love might mean honesty, but there's a limit to everything. He can, however, say that he thought James was a dick.

"James was a dick."

"Hey, he's one of my oldest friends. We used to bathe together, when we were three."

"Do I get that honor, too?"

"Maybe. . . ." January grins and kisses him on the neck before moving up to the mouth for a full-scale snog.

"But he's kinda snobby," insists Johnny.

"Well, he's had a certain type of childhood. The very, very rich type. It's not really his fault."

Johnny frowns.

"How about your friends? Would I like them?"

Johnny thinks of his high school class first, then Kade, Jack, and David second. *No, I honestly don't think you would*, he thinks.

"Yeah, they're cool," he says. "Kade especially. He's like my best friend — well, I have three good friends, but Kade's the best. We all skate, hang out together, the usual."

"What would they think about me?"

Johnny thinks. The strong skunk hits him hard. He looks inside his hazy head for a decent answer.

"They'd want a piece of your ass."

January laughs and slaps his bum.

"Well, they'd think you were hot," he says. "You ever gonna meet them, then?" he asks, full of hope, and a bravery only the skunk could provide.

"I'd like to," she answers.

"I'd like you to, too," he says, softly and embarrassedly. "I grew up with those guys. We've done everything together. Well, almost everything."

Johnny tells January about a few of those experiences, but he's terribly aware of how insignificant they seem beside stories of mountain climbing and helping Cambodians fish for their dinner. Eventually, January steers conversation to Johnny's family. Standing in each other's arms, overlooking the Thames, Johnny feels invincible. There's nothing he wouldn't say to his girlfriend. He talks, perhaps for the first time, of exactly how he felt when his parents announced their divorce. He tells January about the initial shock, then the lonely nights in London, the anger, the crying — especially the crying.

"It felt like nothing could go right. And it was scary. I thought it would never end. But it did, and I got on with things."

"Would it have been easier if your dad still lived in the States?"

"Probably. But I don't blame him. I mean, he's opened me up to new stuff, being over in Europe. I've seen things most guys my age from Austin would never have seen. I've done stuff most of my friends have never heard of. I'll always be grateful for that."

January slides to the pavement, her back resting against the bridge wall. Johnny sits beside her. They hold hands. January listens with a serious expression that almost looks like she's putting on the kind of face she thinks she ought to put on when someone says something difficult and emotionally charged.

"I used to miss my mom so much," he says and, quite abruptly, his face begins to crease and dip downward, and drops of tear appear. He tries his best to control his face and turns his head away from January. She grips his hand tighter and strokes the back of his head.

"It's okay," she says, gently. "It's okay, don't be afraid to cry in front of me. Don't ever be afraid to cry."

And he turns his face back, looking straight ahead. The crying has stopped, but the tears are still there.

"I couldn't sleep. It was really hard. I think the few years after the breakup were the hardest thing I'll ever have to go through, you know."

"I understand," she says, although she doesn't really believe she can understand that which she has not experienced. "Wasn't your sister any help?"

"I like Lydia and all, but we're not really close. I don't know. I thought things would change when I got a bit older."

There's a lengthy pause when neither of them says anything. Johnny feels vulnerable but in the most positive way imaginable. It's not as if he's opened up to one of the boys, or to a teacher, or even to Lydia. All those might use the knowledge to their own gain. But the point is, they wouldn't truly understand. Not in the way January does. Right now, Johnny Hazzard feels he can tell her anything. And, moreover, he wants to.

"I don't blame my dad and I don't blame my mom. 'Sometimes these things just happen,' she said. And she was right. It wasn't a big blowout with arguing, or affairs, or anything like that. They just drifted. And although it messed me up, I can understand it now. It's just what happens."

"You're so calm about it," January says. "I don't know how I'd have reacted. I'd probably have flown off the handle. Or just got totally fucked up."

Johnny can well believe her. At the time of the breakup his school therapist warned him of "temptations to numb your pain." He likes to think he's avoided most of them so far.

"A lot of me is a front. Well, not anymore. But most of the time it is," he says.

"I thought a lot of you before. But I think more of you now," says January, resting her head on Johnny's shoulder. He holds her close. He recalls the loneliness of before, and sitting here, above London and its folkloric waterway, the most beautiful girl in his arms, he doesn't remember a time he's felt less alone.

* * *

Johnny could stay cuddling January for the rest of his life. But that would be inappropriate as well as irksome for the back.

So, after an hour of almost wordless bliss, just sitting there as the night sky slowly takes over from the day sky's longest shift, Johnny Hazzard bids January farewell for now.

"Call me if you can, okay?" she asks. "Take care and be good," she says.

"You take care, too," he says, letting go of her fingers.

Johnny agrees. He doesn't want to see her walking off. He knows it'll be over a week before he sees her again. A thousand thoughts race around inside his head — *Why did Siska have to arrange this stupid holiday? Nobody wants to go. It's going to be shit. I can't go ten days without January. Damn you, Belgium!* As January walks away, Johnny is about to turn in the opposite direction and begin his journey home. But he stays absolutely still, watching her. She walks slowly, elegantly. This is her just being herself, without front or pretense. She keeps on walking, until she becomes a distant dot, swallowed up by a dozen distant dots.

EIGHTEEN

Johnny does not even attempt to disguise his resentment. He quickly regresses into a heightened version of pre-sex Johnny. That is to say, prone to mood swings, a conviction that everybody is out to get him at every available opportunity, and a suspicion that his parents are still treating him like he was a young boy. Even Siska comes in for the Hazzard attack.

Watching a popular soap opera, Siska does what she always does when the art is flowing: She knits furiously. Johnny sits to one side of her, Mr. Hazzard to the other, reading *The New York Times*.

"This show is so stupid, Siska," says Johnny.

No response.

"Siska! This program sucks."

Still nothing. Mr. Hazzard is in his own world, too. Lydia is reading in her bedroom. Johnny Hazzard is invisible.

* * *

It is six A.M.

The ferry leaves at seven thirty A.M.

The Hazzard clan has, between them, overslept, spent too long in the bathroom, left packing to the last minute, and misplaced a passport — Siska's passport, of course, which turns up in one of the many cavernous drawers of The Cabinet.

A bleary-eyed and less-than-thrilled Johnny Hazzard emerges into the lounge first, his small carry-on containing limited clothing. Ready for the holiday he doesn't want to go on, he waits for the others, looking about as grumpy as somebody who has just woken up at shit o'clock ought to look.

The wait proves lengthy. Lydia is having a minor tantrum over the dryer, which she claims didn't work as it should have done the night before, leaving her with a severely diminished wardrobe. Mr. Hazzard is tapping away at his laptop, desperate to complete some e-mails before leaving work behind for the weeklong sojourn. And finally there's Siska, who has decided at the last minute to pack her sketchbook and artistic accoutrements, after having made the proclamation the night before that "an oliday is an oliday. I will not work."

179

But Johnny Hazzard is inspiring her in lots of different directions and she cannot possibly pass up such an artistic roll. The paint is coming.

* * *

The clan packs into the car and Mr. Hazzard races through the London traffic at a perilous pace. Remarkably, defying all known laws of time, gravity, and common sense, the Hazzards make it to Dover in time for their ferry to Calais, from where Mr. Hazzard will drive to Belgium. The plan is to arrive in Bruges, the city of canals and chocolate, by late afternoon.

On the ferry, Johnny Hazzard decides he needs some time to himself. The weather is gray and overcast, naturally. The sun is lurking somewhere behind the thick clouds, itching to break through and shine on the miserable sods down below. But the clouds are being their usual, stubborn, pigheaded selves and not giving way. Johnny stands on the deck. He looks up above.

Mr. Blue Sky, please tell us why
you had to hide away for so long?

Whoever heard of a song dedicated to the sky? he thinks.

In front of him is an English Channel of negativity. The river Thames of cheer and optimism feels like it's a thousand miles away. Johnny Hazzard thinks of January and little else. He remembers their night together. Every little detail. He must not forget any detail. Not one. Otherwise, the moment will be lost

180

forever. The memory of that night must always remain as vivid and as true as the experience itself, otherwise what is it? It's meaningless. With obsessive compulsion, Johnny runs over every moment of the great night, making himself so hard in the process. Johnny Hazzard has no idea how he will cope without his girlfriend this week. It scares him. He goes to the ferry canteen, where the cheese and crackers take a long time to go down the throat, making him feel sick.

Mr. Hazzard's insecurity driving on the European mainland plays havoc with even the calmest of nerves. At almost every roundabout, Lydia cannot help but let out a "Jesus Christ!" as Hazzard Senior narrowly misses a lorry, bus, tractor, or, on one occasion, all three. Johnny tries to ignore the occasional yelps of panic from Siska and the frantic cursing of Lydia and, most of all, the appalling highway skills of Mr. Hazzard. He buries himself in an easy read. Well, easy providing he can ask Siska for definitions. *Jojo au Pensionnat* is the twelfth installment in the saga of the little boy from a single-parent family. As the car plows its way through France and into Belgium, leaving a trail of irate French drivers in its wake, Johnny tries to lose himself in the elegant comic strip with its fine attention to human detail (absurd noses, eccentric hair, cocky grins). He's no linguist, but the Siska Factor plays its part and he understands *most* of the language.

However, Lydia soon tires of the sporadic vocabulary queries, opens her rucksack, and hurls a pocket French dictionary in Johnny's direction.

On page seventeen of *Jojo au Pensionnat*, the little boy's

grandmother, the rock of his young life, has to have an operation and cannot look after him. So he has to stay at a boarding school while she recuperates. Jojo can think of nothing worse than sleeping in his school. His cheery father tries to keep up the boy's spirits — *if you experience a moment of cafard*, he says, *never forget to whistle. Always whistle.*

cafard — **coup de** ~ fit of the blues; **avoir le** ~ to be feeling down, have the blues, be feeling gloomy; **avoir un coup de** ~ to be feeling (a bit) down in the dumps

Johnny feels he's just beginning to *avoir un coup de cafard*. But, unlike little Jojo, whistling won't provide a remedy.

Siska gives her copassengers a potted history of Belgium as the Hazzard wagon crosses the border into Belgium's north coast, which is in the region of West Flanders. Half reading from the guidebook and half improvising as any good history teacher should know how, she informs her dozy audience they are entering the Flemish half of Belgium. As Johnny will discover, when referring to the locals, the term *Belgian* is as ambiguous and unhelpful as *American*, in the sense that a Texan is considered worlds apart from a New Yorker or a Hawaiian. Just like America, or Iraq, Belgium contains several different groups of people living under the same hefty and occasionally leaky umbrella. Siska continues with the facts: Belgium used to be part of a cluster of territories known as the Netherlands. Throughout history, war and treaties resulted in these Netherlands being owned by the Spanish, the French, the Austrians, and the Dutch. It wasn't until 1830 that Belgium found independence, on an August night at the opera. The Theatre de la Monnaie in Brussels was playing the new opera *La Muette de Portici* (*The Dumb Girl of Portici*). The story centered on the uprising of the Neapolitans against the Spanish. (Siska says she saw a production of it in the late 1970s, and it sucked.) Nevertheless, on that fateful evening in 1830, the crowd, inspired by the epic scenes of suffering and triumph on the plush Brussels stage, kicked off their own revolution. The streets of the capital were soon full of bourgeois and proletariat alike, fighting for their independence from the Dutch. The Palais de Justice was taken under siege and the flag of Brabant was raised over the town hall. Days later, the Dutch gave up, and in January of 1831, Belgium's independence was formally recognized. Siska lets off a "Hooray" at this point. "*Vive l'opéra!*" she exclaims, clapping.

You know a country has a colorful and rich history when its leading figures have names like Philip the Handsome, Philip the Good, Charles the Bold, and William the Silent.

But despite the spirit of unity that the opera inspired, Belgium was — and still is — effectively two nations living uncomfortably side by side, with a capital city that straddles both cultures. Brussels is home to the European Union and NATO. French and Flemish (and English) are spoken. The rest of the country is not quite so bilingual; French was once the language of the elite — the very same people who, in 1831, wrote the country's first constitution. It took more than sixty years for Flemish — which is an inch away from Dutch — to be recognized as an official language. This is an awfully long time to wait, when you consider the North has always been the Flemish region, making up a majority of the nation's population. Whereas the southern Wallonia region is home to a minority of French speakers. There is also a German region, alongside the border with Germany. This tiny community of seventy thousand is a throwback to the Treaty of Versailles, put into effect after The Great War (First World War) in 1919. The region was given over to Belgium as part of the treaty, then later claimed as part of Germany by the Nazis, then liberated once more by American forces in 1945.

An official language divide was made in 1962, and a bitterness remains between the Flemish and the Wallonians. But the truth is, neither region could survive independently, so the marriage of convenience serves its purpose.

And then there are the colonies. In 1885, King Leopold managed to somehow get his claws over vast sections of central Africa. In 1908 he gave his control of these countries over to the Belgian nation. The Congo remained Belgian until 1960. Inhabitants of the former colonies now make up a chunky part of the Brussels population.

In other words, here is a nation of different languages and cultures, with a long and bloody history of conflict and clash, glued together by some rather unsticky glue. So it's just as well that since 1945, Belgium has enjoyed a relatively tranquil and peaceful time, making the headlines for its food and drink rather than its war and bloodshed.

* * *

The family spends the first two days in Bruges. The weather is a dismal mix of torrential rain, drizzle, and occasional sunshine. This rather destroys the romance and beauty of Bruges, the closest northern Europe gets to Venice: Its canals are legendary, but not as famous as its chocolate.

Given the romantic nature of the city, many couples choose to take their holidays there. This does not make easy viewing for Johnny; whenever he sees a couple enjoying each other, he can't help but think of January. He is in no mood for happy holidays, so he maintains a low profile. The baseball cap is on, the peak's shadow casting a protective pall over his eyes, which are a giveaway to his feelings. Lydia, by contrast, seems chirpier than she has been in London. The family's first port of call is a Siska-recommended chocolate shop where Johnny buys himself a box of twelve (pralines, truffles, white chocolate). They are so gorgeously rich, he can only manage two. Sitting in the spectacular Grote Markt (or Grande Place, or Great Square — all Belgian cities and larger towns have one), Johnny wants to be sharing this moment. Seeing the spectacular, experiencing the exhilarating, tasting the scrumptious — these are all things Johnny feels he ought to be doing with January. He is angry with himself for feeling like every corny boy-band song lyric ever written, but he really understands how it is to feel like a half not a whole.

After browsing some of the shops, where Siska nearly blinds an American tourist with her extravagant red umbrella, they head for the canal tour at noon. The drizzle is now light, and the dark clouds appear to be drifting. The queues are hefty, but the Hazzard family manages to squeeze into the last four seats on a boat. The other tourists are colorful and enthusiastic. There are the usual disinterested teens, noisy kids, middle-aged couples, and twentysomething relationships. And then there is the tour guide.

This man in his early fifties wears a filthy cap and aviator shades, holding the microphone in one hand and the barge's steering wheel in the other. In truth, he spends most of the time with his wrist resting on the steering wheel, halfheartedly guiding the boat through the water. This is not the kind of man you'd leave your dog with.

Johnny and Lydia sit right behind him, and Siska and Mr. Hazzard sit to his left and right, respectively. The fun and games begin when the guide starts his narration. The microphone is positioned so close to his lips that he is, effectively, chewing the thing. This makes it hard enough to make out what he is saying. But the real killer is the fact that neither Johnny nor Lydia can work out whether he is speaking French, Flemish, or English. The "Fremlish" combination is nothing short of extraordinary. This stream of incomprehensible dialect starts out as a challenge; Johnny tries his damnedest to make out the English language section, but it ain't happening. The man is clearly trilingual, but he is so used to the routine that he no longer bothers with the minor things — such as articulation, diction, and clarity.

Johnny begins laughing and, in that horrible way that takes hold of you when you desperately don't want it to, he finds it impossible to stop. He listens to the guide, starts laughing, bites his lip, tries to stop laughing, succeeds in reducing it to just a smile, then remembers why he was laughing and begins laughing again. Lydia notices, and she, too, can't help herself. Brother and sister put their shades on. But tears drip down underneath the black lenses, as their bodies, seized by the laughter syndrome, contort and contract. This is hysteria.

Mr. Hazzard is not amused. Siska is somewhere on her planet, listening and apparently understanding. The guide's blasé approach to barge-steering leaves a few tourists gasping and a few ducks gawping.

Then, like an annoying cold, the laughter begins to spread. A fortysomething couple from New Zealand behind Johnny and Lydia are also laughing. Johnny and Lydia's tears still stream. Finally, the barge docks, the tour is over, and the siblings can let it all out on dry land. Siska is clueless. Mr. Hazzard thinks it was a "worthwhile and fascinating experience." Johnny and Lydia haven't laughed so much, together, since they were young kids.

* * *

From Bruges, it's on to Brussels. Siska has many friends here, as well as family members — some she enjoys seeing, others she calls "Christmas card relatives," for that is their only medium of communication. It is decided that the best way will be if she goes off and does her thing while the other Hazzards see the sights. The first stop is the twin-towered Cathédrale St. Michel, a huge building that was started in the thirteenth century and took another three hundred years to build. Johnny is not one for religious buildings, but even he is impressed by the pulpit of awesome intricacy and darkness; it's the kind of pulpit you'd be shit-scared of delivering a sermon from. You could recite the whole Old Testament from memory, but it still wouldn't be as impressive as the object you're standing in. This is a pulpit and a half.

From the religious to the absurd — the *Manneken Pis*. Unfortunately, the national symbol of Belgium is a little boy holding his dick and taking a piss. There are little pissing boy chocolates, lollipops, mini statues made of copper and stone, T-shirts, pens, pencils, rulers, erasers, mouse pads, bottle openers, corkscrews — you name it, the little boy is pissing on it.

So what a disappointment that the Hazzards, nobly but rather hopelessly led by a map-wielding Mr. Hazzard, can't find the damn thing. In fact, they walk straight past it three times. So small is the monument, hundreds of tourists seem to walk straight on by, bewildered. The truth is the little boy is tiny, and wholly underwhelming. The spectacle is an antispectacle. Far more exciting for Johnny is the waffle shop next door. He decides to attempt his first French of the trip, and asks for a *gaufre avec sucre et chocolat* (a waffle with sugar and chocolate). Then it hits him. There is a *girl* behind the counter (no older than January, startling blue eyes, chestnut-brown long hair, red g-string visible above trousers, long eyelashes). She shoots a smile as Johnny speaks. It's not a mocking smile. It's the flight attendant's kind of smile. The kind of smile that sex is made of. Mr. H-O-T is back in business and Johnny hits a brief, but very welcome, high.

Johnny, Lydia, and Mr. H take a short walk up to the Grande Place (aka the Grote Markt and the Great Square). This place certainly is Grande (or Grote). Johnny has not seen anything like it before. The tall, stunning buildings almost don't feel real. The gothic Town Hall is an awesome, intimidating sight. This building is actually the only one in the square that was not battered to pieces by the French in 1695, which is all the more noteworthy when one remembers that it was the primary target. Johnny reads about this in the guidebook and instantly thinks of his own country's armed forces, and the notorious "miss the target" debacles of recent conflicts. It's an age-old tradition, it seems.

The bars and restaurants, housed in colorful seventeenth-century buildings of extraordinary detail, aren't the bars and restaurants of East Sixth Street. Johnny can see history all around him, ancient history by American standards, but recent by European ones. The square drips class, style, and architectural vision.

"This is pretty good," says Lydia.

"I've never seen anything like it before," says Johnny, finally as enthusiastic as he was during the canal tour.

They vow to return for lunch at one of the eateries, after taking a tour of a couple of museums on the Grande Place — the Museum of Cocoa and Chocolate, followed by the Brussels City Museum. Not much is said on museum tours. It gives the tourist family a chance to think for themselves by pretending to be, or by genuinely being, engrossed in the displays and the history. Johnny would rather sit in the Grande Place admiring the buildings than be wandering around mediocre museums thinking of January. He is desperate to ask her how she is, to hear her voice, and to feel her breath and touch her. What makes it all the more difficult is the complete lack of communication — no chance of e-mailing or phoning or anything. That's just cruelty. These are difficult moments for Johnny. Now, a few days into the holiday, he is no longer content in the self-indulgence of thinking about his girlfriend twenty-four/seven. He has had enough of the misery that comes with the thinking. Unable to transfer the thoughts into actions, he now wants something almighty to distract him.

Lunch on the Grande Place is impressive, but not almighty enough to kick January thoughts out of the mind. The Hazzards decide to split for an hour and meet up again at the Town Hall. Johnny grabs his hour of freedom with both hands and feet. Things have been relatively cool with both Lydia and Mr. H, but breathing space is helpful. So naturally Johnny does the most obvious thing when given sixty minutes of free time — he wanders into a porn shop.

This is not strictly possible. Nobody *wanders* into a porn shop. It is, more often than not, a calculated and planned decision that usually requires a degree of courage and embarrassment. At least, that's what Johnny feels as he walks past the store, takes a peek inside, walks back, pretends to tie his shoelaces, feels nervous, thinks he's being a dick, then thinks *what the hell?* and walks through the creaky, embarrassingly loud wooden door.

Inevitably, the door-that-needs-oiling causes the other customers to look up at Johnny. He smiles faintly, then sets his sights on the floor, closing the door behind him. He is convinced he'll be busted and asked to leave. The shopkeeper (male, young, diligent-looking, a Georges Simenon novel in hand) is not what Johnny expects. There are two other browsers in the store: a middle-aged dude (no hair, thick-rimmed glasses) and a guy in his late teens wearing trendy jeans and a hooded top. Neither looks particularly pervy or weird. This is disappointing to Johnny Hazzard, who was hoping to find a gallery of weirdos in such a place.

This store that he *calculatedly walked into with purpose* is particularly eccentric. There is no order to the magazines — they are piled up in dusty heaps all over the large room. The windows are clear glass — no blacking out to spare the patrons' blushes in this establishment.

Johnny Hazzard has never been inside a porn shop before. He has heard about the famous Amsterdam red light district, and he understands that Europe is generally more chilled out about the whole matter, but he never really considered exploring until about half an hour ago. A mixture of boredom, desire for adventure, and post-first-sex horniness has led him in. Plus, of course, the fact he is Mr. H-O-T. And, thankfully, it doesn't feel sleazy, or dirty, or especially naughty. It feels more like one of the old bookshops on London's Charing Cross Road, in which rare and ancient titles can be found or traced (although you won't find many Dickens first editions in here). There's an air of weird sophistication amid the *Asian Boobs*, *Sexy Sluts*, and *Double Action*. Johnny isn't entirely sure where to begin, but he is aware that there is something for everybody — the *specialist* sections confirm Johnny's suspicion that there is nothing in the world that doesn't turn *somebody* on.

Johnny meets Dolly (blond, fluffy) on page ten of *Brust*, a German magazine. He grows fond of Dolly as he sees her in various states of undress. She has alluring green eyes and firm thighs, but conversation isn't her greatest facet.

The noise of the creaks in the door disturbs Johnny's getting-to-know-you period with Dolly. He looks up as a couple walks in. They seem so disappointingly normal. Thirty-five years old perhaps, wearing sensible trousers. They begin to browse the collections. Johnny finishes with Dolly and puts her back on top of one of the piles. He finds an ancient batch of black-and-white porn, which seems to be rather expensive. In one box, between modern, bright, glossy porno magazines there is a hardback book with a creased dust jacket: *Second World War Uniforms — Women*. Johnny has absolutely no idea what it's doing in there.

The couple continue their analysis of the literature. The guy calls over his partner and shows her one magazine. Johnny tries to get a look at what it is, but he can't see. The couple share a joke in French, giggle naughtily, and head to the counter to pay up. Johnny is intrigued. The two other customers continue their studies silently and meticulously.

Suddenly aware that if he were to buy something, Lydia and Mr. H's first question would be *what's that you bought, Johnny?* he decides to leave the shop. But it is his first porn shop, and he shall not forget it. And, with a few alterations and exaggerations here or there, it'll make a great story to tell the boys back in Austin.

NINETEEN

The next two days pass slowly. Then it is time to move again. Next stop: a living history lesson of misery and carnage. Not exactly what Johnny's mood needs right now.

The small West Flanders town of Ieper was the location of three enormous and gruesome battles between 1914 and 1917, involving troops of the British Empire and Germany. The events of almost a century ago have not been forgotten — nor are they likely to be. (Not least because the town's thriving tourism is primarily thanks to that brutal conflict.) The reminders of the Great War are everywhere in and around Ieper. But this is not a town trapped in its past. In aesthetic terms, the area was flattened after the war and has been entirely rebuilt since. To be precise, nine centuries were wiped out in just four years. Yet, despite the death and mass destruction, the town's character is not stuck in 1918. Although Belgians suffered, the soldiers who died were primarily those of the British Empire and Germany. The town has moved on, but hasn't forgotten its past. Perhaps this sentiment is best expressed by the motto of the In Flanders Fields Museum in Ieper: *remembering the future*.

Upon arrival, Johnny Hazzard is thoroughly depressed. He fell asleep on the car journey from Brussels, and wakes to the sound of heavy rain clattering on the car roof. Mr. Hazzard parks down a side street and the family unloads its stuff, the umbrellas proving a hassle rather than a help. Led by Siska, who has been here only once before, "centuries ago," they troop along the empty square looking for their hotel. The rain worsens, and the thunderclaps begin. There is no time or inclination to notice the splendid Cloth Hall, Town Hall, or St. Martin's Cathedral.

"We've been all around the square once already," says Johnny, impatiently.

"Here it is!" exclaims a sodden Siska.

The hotel is located above a bar/restaurant. The outdoor chairs and tables look pathetically lonely with the rain pounding down on them. The lights of the ground floor are very welcoming. Ten or so guests eating and drinking look up in shock when the Hazzards pile through the door, carrying six bags between them and drenched in enough water to fill a small bath.

Johnny goes to his room and, before unpacking, heads straight for his bed. He kicks off his shoes and turns on the TV. It's CNN International. He flicks over to a local channel, covering the news in Flemish, and despite the language barrier, decides to leave it on as background company while he begins his comics reading.

After five minutes, the rain intensifies, and the thunder begins. The first few claps are quiet and distant. In his mind, Johnny compares them to the sound of shells exploding during the constant barrage of attack of the Great War. He is largely ignorant about the conflict, but Siska has given him a basic history.

Johnny returns his attention to the book, when a sudden and much louder, closer bang of thunder follows a flash of lightning. January is far, far away, and he wants to be with her so much, he feels sick. It is a different kind of longing; this is not the way he misses his mother. That was more of a dull ache. This is a sharp pain. Johnny cannot and will not admit it to anybody else, but he feels as though he just cannot wait, as though the few days until he returns to London are a few days too many, and he will be unable to cope. That is it: Johnny is scared he cannot cope with the time.

A half hour later, at about seven o'clock, Siska knocks on Johnny's door. He lets her in.

"Dahling, you have not unpacked?"

"I'm too tired," mumbles Johnny, plonking himself stubbornly back on the bed.

"We are going for dinner. *Allez!*" she demands, before leaving.

Johnny buries his head in the pillow. The rain reminds him of that magical night with January. He goes through that evening in his head, every last detail. The same kind of detail the Belgian architects of years gone by applied to their constructions. It's all about the details; they must never dim, and they must never leave. It's an important ritual every few days to remember every single thing there possibly is to remember, from the smells and sounds to the words, the order of the touches and the act itself. Nothing must ever be forgotten. Even though thoughts are increasingly frustrating, he must cling to the one thing he has of January — the memories. He is petrified of forgetting the memories.

Then he has an idea. It's an obvious one, but it will require a little detective work. Johnny decides he has to call her. It's the only solution, and screw the charges. He figures he has about a half hour before the family convenes for dinner. He heads down to the Grote Markt in his hoody, which only partly protects him from the sweeping rain. The thunderclaps are loud and nearby. He finds a small kiosk that sells phonecards and hands over a ten-Euro note — all the money he has on him.

Next stop: a phone booth. The first he tries is out of order. The second, off the Grote Markt near St. Martin's Cathedral, has a dial tone. He taps in the phonecard access number, then listens to a recorded message in Flemish followed by one in French. Johnny reaches into his pocket for the scrap of paper with January's phone number on it. Only, it's a cellphone number. He knows full well that calling a cellphone internationally on a phonecard will cost the earth, and probably only last a minute. So he decides his first call will be to UK directory enquiries. He remembers the name of the hotel January and her family are staying at — the Ashlington. She may not be in her room when he calls, but it's got to be worth a try. It takes two attempts to finally be connected to directory enquiries, then bingo — he gets the number for the hotel. A thunderclap roars so menacingly, it feels as though the entire town is about to be crushed. It sounds more like Godzilla has just taken a step forward. Johnny has to ask the operator to repeat the last few digits of the number. He reads it back to her to make sure he's got it right. He hasn't. She repeats the number; he writes it down once more. The rainfall intensifies.

Johnny's nerves begin to tingle as he dials the number for the Ashlington. He's anxious in case one of January's parents answers the phone. It will all be worth it, though, just to hear January's voice. To hear her say "Hi, Johnny" in that way she does, which makes him feel so welcome, so wanted. The overwhelming possibility of talking to her obscures the possibility that several things might go wrong (not least of which the phonecard running out of credit).

The hotel phone rings and rings. Johnny's heartbeat picks up pace. He can feel his neck and shoulder muscles tensing up. Finally someone picks up. Johnny *has* got the right hotel. The receptionist connects him to January's room.

The phone starts ringing once more. Will she be in? Will she answer? Sod's Law dictates that she'll be in the shower. On the eighth ring, the phone is answered.

A soft "Hello" pours into Johnny's ear like a river of honey. He's so happy he can't speak. January repeats herself.

"Hey — it's me," he says. He closes his eyes.

"Hi, Johnny," she says. And it's exactly as Johnny had predicted. Her tone is so familiar, so warm, and he knows she's happy to hear his voice. The unconditional acceptance manifests itself in the small things, like the way she's so damn happy to hear from him. Johnny opens his eyes again.

"My God, how did you get my number?" she asks.

"Directory enquiries. I'm on a phonecard, I didn't have enough credit to call your cell — is this okay?"

"Yes, yes it's okay. How are you? How's Belgium?"

"I'm okay and Belgium is kinda boring. Good food and all, but I just really want to be back home. London, I mean."

"God, tell me about it. I'm tearing my hair out. George is driving me crazy. We're sharing a room and he's just giving me attitude every damn minute he's awake."

"Is he there now?" Johnny asks.

"No, no he's not. It's okay."

"I really miss you. I wish you could be here." He has waited so long to say it, it's a big relief to finally be able to.

January's response is not instant. There is a pause of three seconds.

"Cool. I miss you, too," she says.

Johnny is too wrapped up in his own delight to notice that, although she does sound happy to hear from him, there is a slight frost in her voice.

January asks again what he's been up to in Bruges and Brussels, which seems to be far more interesting than what January's been coerced into doing in and around Leeds. Her trip seems to involve visits to relatives and long walks on moors.

"It's a nightmare," she says. "And George, the little brat, is always getting his way. If he screams loud enough Mom and Dad will always change their plans. I'm like the invisible older sister."

"Sounds rough," Johnny says. "I'm lucky; Lydia's being okay."

"It's just . . . after traveling on my own for so long, it's hard to go somewhere with my family now. I've *outgrown* it," January says, a tad pompously. Johnny wonders if she's directing that remark at him — as if to point out that he has not yet outgrown the family vacation.

Johnny begins telling January about the ghostly feel of sodden Ieper, when she interrupts him —

"Oh, I've got to tell you, I saw something you'd absolutely hate. We were walking on Ilkley Moor and we got to this really high point and I looked down and there were like these white domes, this cluster of spooky white balls just in the middle of all this countryside. Turns out they're listening centers for a US Air Force base. Right in the middle of Yorkshire."

"Jesus. I can only apologize," he jokes. January sniggers. "Hey, I don't have long left. I was going to ask — did you tell your parents yet?"

"They know I'm seeing you. George made that very clear."

Johnny doesn't want it to come from George; he wants January to introduce him to them.

"I mean, haven't they asked anything about me? Do they even know where I'm from?"

"Relax, it's fine. We'll sort it all out when you get back. Listen, have a great time. We'll talk when you get back, yeah?"

"When do you go home?"

"Tomorrow night. Can't wait."

"I'll call you as soon as I walk through the door," he assures her.

"You don't have to call me *that* quickly," she says, quite seriously.

"I know I don't have to, but I want to."

January doesn't respond. Johnny continues:

"I can find out the number of the hotel here if you want?"

"No, it's okay, Johnny. I won't be allowed to call long distance, anyway. Don't worry — we'll talk when you get home."

They say their good-byes and, although he's itching to declare it, Johnny cannot find the courage to say that he loves her. Her absence has made him absolutely confident that this is more than just a crush. But communicating that isn't going to be easy.

* * *

Dinner that evening is tasty but tired at a restaurant Siska has been recommended by an old friend. Huddled under their umbrellas, the Hazzards trek across the largely empty Grote Markt to a spot some five minutes north of it. The restaurant is packed full of locals, and the menus don't contain English. This is a good sign. No cut-price fare for the gastronomically naïve English tourists here.

Up to the age of twelve, Johnny would try new food at any opportunity. This sense of culinary adventurism was worthy of a Tintin investigation. Inspired and encouraged by his mother, an excellent cook whose cookbook collection carried recipes from every continent and utilized every ingredient imaginable, Johnny was always keen to try. But at some point in his twelfth year, he lost that interest, that spark of curiosity. Ever since, he's stuck to some reliable staple meals. For a few days this summer, the adventurism has been rekindled by January, but now it's a reversion to type, as Johnny snubs the variety of fish dishes he has never tried (swordfish, crayfish) and asks for a *steak frites* instead. One obvious difference Johnny has noticed among home, England, and the rest of Belgium is the food. In Texas, the restaurant serves portions so large and fatty, several major arteries can be clogged with just one mouthful. In England, the restaurant serves portions so small, you're still hungry two hours later. In the other European countries Johnny has visited, the restaurant serves perfectly sized portions with *taste*.

The meal is not animated. Everybody — even Siska — is tired and untalkative. There are some reflections on Brussels. Lydia waxes lyrical about the Belgian beer. Johnny orders some potent Trappist gold beer that leaves his head feeling like a busy swimming pool. Trappist beers are brewed in monasteries. If that's the way Belgian religion works, Johnny is prepared to start believing. Mr. Hazzard and Siska share a bottle of French red wine. Johnny gobbles down his apple pie dessert, which tastes nothing like the American equivalent. Johnny notices his sister and father giving him occasional peculiar glances. He realizes that they realize he is not his usual self, but he doesn't care. There will be no show to impress, no attempt at suppressing the truth of the situation. Johnny is sad.

However, at least the rain has stopped. After the delicious meal, they finally go for a stroll around town. There is, at long last, a sign of human life; tourists mingle around the square. Johnny notices there are many, many English people. The cars parked in the center of the Grote Markt have mostly Belgian license plates, but there are several British vehicles, too. He hears more English than Flemish in the snippets of conversation he picks up. Most of the visitors have come here to learn and to pay respect. This is not your average tourist town.

Back at the hotel room, Johnny sits by his window and looks out at the view of the cobbled Grote Markt down below. The vast Cloth Hall and Town Hall buildings glow like lighthouses in the middle of a dark night. But once again, it's the architecture that is most noticeable for its detail and numerous bricks. The roofs are all decorated with peaks on their front side. These peaks are like two rows of steps leading up to a minispire. This style is by no means exclusively Belgian, but they sure have it in abundance. The second thing Johnny notices is the lack of chain stores. No fast food, fast clothes, or fast coffee outlets. This is the farthest Johnny has managed to get from America.

But the influence of the US Empire is never too far; running around the square are a group of small kids, most of them dressed from head to toe in sports labels from back home (designed back at home, if not manufactured there).

At least, muses Johnny Hazzard, *there's no chance in hell I'm gonna find American beer here.*

Stubbornly refusing to unpack, Johnny brushes his teeth, examines his face in the mirror, pops a zit on his chin, strips to his boxers, and gets into bed. He does not feel sexy tonight. He flicks through the channels before falling asleep, accompanied by no less a bedfellow than the BBC News.

It is the job of any museum worth its entry price to convert the unenlightened. The In Flanders Fields Museum tells the story of the First World War through the experiences of Ieper (which, at the time of the war, was still known by its French name Ypres), and the battle line around it, known as the Ypres Salient. It is along the Salient that the cemeteries and former battlefields — now cow fields — are located. A potted history of the medieval Ieper, a busy cloth town, kick-starts the exhibition. A history of the background to the war, and details of its origins, follow. Siska and Mr. Hazzard seem, as responsible parents ought to, considerably more interested in this than their children. Johnny attempts to whiz through the displays, but the section detailing the Christmas truce of 1914 stalls his progress. Here, among the details of mustard gas and overzealous young soldiers being manipulated into war by their leaders, among the stories of trench rats, limbless corpses, and rotting horse carcasses, there stands a beacon of hope.

Johnny's imagination is quickly captured — and his curiosity piqued — by the story.

On Christmas Eve 1914, along most of the front line, battle ceased, weapons were dropped, and Germans and Allies came together in no-man's-land in a spirit of togetherness and pure, generous humanity. The peace was apparently prompted by the German troops lighting candles on small Christmas trees, which they placed on the parapets of the trenches for their enemy to see.

The men exchanged gifts. German sausages, British newspapers, buttons, tobacco — any object represented a gift, and any gift represented a tiny molecule of hope toward ending the bloodshed. They shared beer and drank to each other's health. *They drank to each other's health.*

For some, the truce lasted only until Boxing Day. For others, it went on long into January. These impromptu demonstrations of peaceful brotherhood were, of course, against the orders from the top.

Johnny Hazzard rereads the accounts from British and German soldiers two or three times. He cannot understand how opposing forces could spontaneously drop their arms and come together. For Johnny, it's too beautiful and perfect to make any sense. He cannot imagine Americans and Iraqis giving up the fight one afternoon and enjoying some coffee and bread together. But why shouldn't they? By Christmas 1914, the German and British soldiers were all too aware that they were cat and mouse in a game of European power politics. They were pawns, dispensable foot soldiers fighting a battle neither side could truly win. For some days they were brought together by that which they had in common — their humanity. Johnny ponders: Days after singing Christmas carols, swapping gifts, and sharing a drink, they were trying to kill each other again. If they had been the ones making the orders — if the soldiers who fought the administration's wars made the choices — would they have resumed the fight?

Johnny reads Brigadier General Count Gleichen's statement,

"They came out of their trenches and walked across unarmed, with boxes of cigars and seasonable remarks. You could not shoot unarmed men."

Johnny then reads a telling quote from Winston Churchill, who was First Lord of the Admiralty during the war and went on to be British Prime Minister during the Second World War. Johnny doesn't quite understand how anybody has the balls to call himself Lord of anything. Nonetheless, the First Lord's words ring true: "What would happen if the armies suddenly and simultaneously went on strike and said some other method must be found of settling the dispute?"

For one Christmas, that's what they did.

Had the poor bastards had the nerve to go on strike, who knows what might have happened? thinks Johnny.

"It took them one hundred days to fight their way to Passendale. They gave it up in three days," Lydia tells her brother. "How fucked up is that?"

She walks off. Johnny is in the middle of an information overload. He wants to take it all in, remember it, be able to tell his friends and argue back convincingly when he faces a war hawk back home. It's as though he's a pedestrian standing in the middle of a freeway: All the cars whizzing past are snippets of information, feelings of despair and images of war.

Johnny slows right down and ends up reading almost everything the museum has to show. Mr. H, Lydia, and Siska are well ahead. Johnny doesn't care. He's interested. He reads that the American involvement, in July 1918, although late in the war effort, proved a morale booster for the British troops and contributed considerably to the ultimate victory by British and French forces. But Ieper, it becomes agonizingly clear, was the wrong place at the wrong time. On April 9, 1918, the Germans launched an offensive with the aim of capturing the French ports of Calais and Boulogne. In response, the British had to withdraw troops from Ieper, relinquishing all they had fought for and won in the Battle of Passendale in 1917. Three hundred thousand dead and nothing to show for it.

From hidden speakers, a haunting opera singer shrieks over a simple, speedy piano tune. This doom-laden musical accompaniment succeeds in making the quotes on the wall feel all the more vivid, real, and, above all, alive. They are relevant. Johnny doesn't feel as though he's just having a history lesson here. He feels like he's learning about his government, and about everybody else's governments, and about how similar we all actually are.

"There was not a sign of life of any sort. Not a tree . . . not a bird, not even a rat or a blade of grass. Nature was as dead as those Canadians whose bodies remained where they had fallen the previous autumn. Death was written large everywhere. It is not possible to set down the things that could be written of the Salient. They would haunt your dreams." — *Private R. A. Colwell, Passendale, January 1918*

The music continues. Johnny doesn't quite feel a shiver, but there is a definite tingle. And it's not the kind of tingle he experienced on meeting January, or touching her for the first time. January, as it happens, could not be farther from his mind.

> "I have seen the most frightful nightmare of a country more conceived by Dante or Poe than by nature, unspeakable, utterly indescribable. Evil and the incarnate fiend alone can be master of this war, and no glimmer of God's hand is seen anywhere. It is unspeakable, hopeless, godless. I am no longer an artist interested and curious. I am a messenger who will bring back word from the men who are fighting to those who want the war to go on forever." — *Paul Nash, artist*

Sense comes out of the nonsense, clarity out of the confusion, and a powerful reckoning of reality out of the indisputable. Johnny sees the glaring similarities between this account from the start of the twentieth century and the accounts of soldiers at the start of the twenty-first century. Johnny Hazzard has been alive just fifteen years. The men — for it is almost always men — who make the decision that war ought to "go on forever" have been on the planet a lot longer than fifteen years. Why, therefore, is it so blindingly obvious and logical to the teenager, and not the old man, that the "unspeakable, hopeless, godless" horror can and should be avoided?

And so Johnny now begins to form ideas of power. Although he has often disagreed with the things his government has done around the planet, for the first time he decides that injustice only occurs because the masses follow the minority and allow it to be done. For the first time he realizes that there is a way out. He remembers what he has been taught about civil rights, the communist states of Europe, the Vietnam protestors. And just as quickly as he realizes the enormous possibility and hope that is offered by ordinary people coming together, he realizes that, more often than not, the dumbasses will make the decisions, we will follow, and our condition will inevitably worsen. But he does not want to believe this conclusion; he wants to challenge it.

Johnny reaches the final room of the museum. On one wall, a quote from British Prime Minister Lloyd George declares that, "this fateful morning, came to an end all wars."

On the final wall, a television set shows images of conflict, and titles scroll across the screen. They list countries and years. On the wall behind the TV set, in large letters, it reads,

THE INTERNATIONAL RED CROSS AND RED CRESCENT MOVEMENT HAS BEEN OPERATING IN MORE THAN 100 ARMED CONFLICTS SINCE THE END OF THE "WAR TO END ALL WARS."

The number of armed conflicts is updated regularly. The countries and years on the TV set form a list of all these armed conflicts. The hope offered by the Christmas truce is a million miles away. The museum ends with a reality check. Its optimism fades while the fear grows. The In Flanders Fields Museum is not a horror film, but it is terrifying. It is not a library, but it forces you to read and think. Its downbeat conclusion is quite deliberate; people must not leave the building with a shred of complacency. Instead, they must be horrified and adamant. Just like Johnny Hazzard.

Johnny is angry that he has allowed himself to be moved quite so much. He expected boredom and instead feels a frustration and anger that he doesn't recognize, that he hasn't felt before.

Museums aren't supposed to be like this.

Another line remembered:

> "We hold this place for moral effect only. For an ideal. In holding it, men have died for a dream." — *Letter by Private P. H. Jones, August 1915*

* * *

The gift shop sells the usual mementos as well as a vast selection of books and videos about the war and Ieper. Johnny settles on buying the book of the museum and a couple of postcards. One screams out at him.

DESTROY THIS MAD BRUTE

(There is an image of a huge, salivating orangutan clutching a defenseless white woman standing on the shores of America.)

Johnny smiles at the craziness. The orangutan is supposed to represent Germany. The card seems to be saying to Americans that they ought to enlist to prevent America, and all its defenseless white ladies, from being kidnapped and beaten by the barbaric Germans (who look nothing like orangutans, for the record).

Lydia buys *The Penguin Book of First World War Poetry*. She has always been a closet poet. Johnny found a few of her pieces recently, which she is not aware of. She is embarrassed to even talk of her closet poetry skills. But Johnny, being as objective as possible, actually finds the poems rather moving. He cannot be sure, but to him they are about Mrs. Hazzard's loneliness.

Outside the museum, Siska ushers the group on to the convening point for the tour of the cemeteries along the Salient. Lydia is the protestor, not Johnny.

"Haven't we had enough death for one day?"

"No, I have booked it. No arguments now. This is important."

Lydia huffs, Mr. Hazzard carries Siska's sketchbook and a box of pencils, and on they go.

The Hazzards are joined by a couple from Liverpool, who do not say much. The cemetery tour takes place in a minibus, and the thirtysomething male tour guide (blasé, bony, not beautiful) is English. Johnny is a tad startled by the way that, when referring to British soldiers and British strategies of the war, the guide talks of "we" and "us." Is it really "we" so many years later?

The tour takes in cemeteries as well as key spots of the conflict. Despite the odd German or Allied bunker here and there, it is very difficult for Johnny to imagine the rolling crop fields and cow farms ever having been barren mud baths, strewn with dead bodies and horses, crisscrossed with trenches, blanketed by the stench of death. However, one element of the conflict is easy to picture when the guide points out an unexploded shell lying on the roadside, clearly visible, within reach of some curious passersby.

"They found that shell three months ago. The bomb disposal unit still hasn't picked it up," says the guide, as nonchalantly as is humanly possible. Mr. Hazzard laughs and Lydia's jaw drops half open.

"A little child could play with it," says Siska, aghast.

"I know," the guide says with a sigh. "Tons of unexploded ammunition are dug up each and every year. The war is still with us, really. Hasn't gone away."

They visit the Essex Farm Cemetery, the main resting place for Canadian troops. It is sizable, about the same as the one where Johnny's grandfather is buried back home. But here, all the gravestones are the same. Rows and rows of white stones, all the same size, all bearing the crest of the Canadian armed forces. Opposite, a house is being built. Builders listen to pop music on their portable radio, banging nails into wood; construction beside destruction.

But the war comes alive for Johnny here, for this cemetery was once Essex Farm Dressing Station, where, soon after his young friend was pronounced dead, Dr. John McCrae wrote the famous "In Flanders Fields" poem.

> *We are the Dead. Short days ago*
> *We lived, felt dawn, saw sunset glow,*
> *Loved and were loved, and now we lie*
> *In Flanders fields.*

The tour guide does not recite this poem; Johnny looks it up in Lydia's book. He reads it in the same spot where, almost nine decades ago, McCrae wrote his haunting words. Johnny tries to put himself in McCrae's shoes and imagine what it would be like losing a good friend in such a way, but he cannot do it. The thought does not move him. But the poem's "We are the Dead" stays with him.

The next stop is Langemark village. The cemetery is darker, broodier, more intimidating. It feels more like the graveyards of Hollywood horrors. The guide tells the story.

"About three thousand German students, completely untrained in battle, were killed when they were pitted against the trained British troops. This is the only German cemetery in Belgium. Between the nineteen twenties and nineteen fifties, there was a lot of anti-German feeling, and most of the graves were moved to

Germany. Locals wanted the land back for farming. This cemetery was founded in the nineteen fifties. In the middle there, there's a mass grave of twenty-five thousand. Eight thousand of these men are unknown."

Johnny has been formulating a question in his mind.

"Why were kids allowed to fight?"

"That's a good question. In England, certainly, you are supposed to be nineteen years old to fight. But recruiting sergeants were paid more for each new recruit they signed up. And teenagers were often the most enthusiastic about going to fight for King and country."

This is not the kind of place you would want to spend eternity. No endless rows of gleaming white headstones here. No manicured lawns and cute flowers. No other visitors. The first, striking image is of four black figures standing at the back of the cemetery, watching. They are in fact statues of men holding their hats. If it's supposed to be a scary and menacing reminder of war, it is successful. Johnny feels as though these four silhouette-like creatures are watching his every move.

The family split up and walked around, taking their time to examine the stones. Johnny, hands behind his back, stares long at the mass grave. It does not look cared for. Ugly plants and uglier weeds cover the soil. The grave is flanked by large, rectangular gravestones that list, in minuscule letters, the names of thousands. The cemetery is surrounded by tall trees that block the sunlight.

Johnny checks the visitors' book. All the cemeteries have one, along with a folder containing all the names and locations of the dead people. Jenny, age fourteen from Scotland, has signed the visitors' book: *It's a disgrace. The grave is covered with weeds and stuff. They may have lost but they deserve our respect.*

The contrast with the Tyne Cot Cemetery could not be greater. The biggest British Commonwealth cemetery in the world is the minibus's next stop. The guide explains, "The large White Cross of Sacrifice in the middle of this cemetery is built on top of a German bunker. Around the cross are the graves of some twelve thousand soldiers. And at the back, you'll see a wall with the names of some thirty-five thousand soldiers who were never identified and therefore never buried. These are the names they couldn't fit on the Menin Gate. See you at the minibus in half an hour."

The guy has mastered the routine. To him, this is just a job. It must be impossible to be moved when it's the same thing every day. He returns to the minibus, makes himself comfortable, and turns on the radio. The Hazzards, and the English couple, split up and walk around the cemetery, taking their time. Johnny cannot believe what he sees; it is not what he imagined. But then, trying to imagine twelve thousand gravestones is not easy. Row after row after row of gleaming white stones, made even brighter and more obvious by the sunshine. There are so many gravestones, it is hard for Johnny to fathom that each one represents a human being. It is, like so much about Ieper and its war, unreal. Unlike the German cemetery, there is open space, and there is sun, and perfectly kept grass and beautiful plants and flowers in front of each and every gravestone. There is care and detail. The fresh flowers and signed wooden crosses, left by the graves, are evidence of recent visitors. The German teenagers and their comrades have not been visited recently.

There are various other visitors. Some of them obviously tourists like the Hazzards. But others carry flowers for distant, ancient relatives. There is an elderly couple, perhaps in their eighties, standing before one grave. Johnny wonders if it belongs to the old woman's father, or the old man's. They stay still and silent for at least five minutes. The grave belongs to them; it is theirs at this moment in time. The passersby all notice them, all wondering what the old couple's story is. The slight breeze plays with the old woman's short, white curly hair. The man wipes his nose with a handkerchief. He raises an index finger to his face, wiping what must be a tear away from behind his thick spectacles.

Johnny wants to be moved, he wants to find sadness.

Beneath the brilliant and vehement sun there are British soldiers, Australians, Canadians, New Zealanders, and more. There are several unknowns, listed as *A Soldier of the Great War* who is *Known unto God* or *Asleep in Jesus.* Johnny thinks, for a brief moment, of the parents of the numerous soldiers of the Great War who were not even given the dignity of seeing their sons laid to rest. The anonymous graves are, to Johnny Hazzard, more powerful than the known ones.

Then he comes across the grave of Lieutenant F. Ditzell, of the 25th Battalion Australian Infantry. The message at the bottom of

the stone reads, THE ONLY BELOVED SON OF MR. AND MRS. J. DIT-
ZELL OF INVERELL.

Quite suddenly, Johnny thinks of *Fahrenheit 9/11* — the crying
image of Lila Lipscomb, the woman from Flint whose son,
Sergeant Michael Pedersen, died in a Black Hawk downed over
Karbala, races into Johnny's mind. He remembers Lila's visit to
the White House, when she was confronted by a woman dressed
in black, with the cold accusation that "this is all staged." "My
son's death isn't staged," Lila responded. The look of unbridled
anger in her face was intense. It stayed with Johnny long afterward. "Blame al-Qaeda," was the woman-in-black's advice.

Lila walked away. She began crying, uncontrollably. "Al-Qaeda
didn't make a decision to send my son to Iraq," she said. Seeing
the White House, finding a place to project her anger and sense
of injustice, and then being faced with such an unsympathetic
person, had been too much. The cruelty had been too much.
The conflict had been far too much. "I need my son," she said,
crying and crying for the son who was taken away, struggling to
find a noble cause for the loss. Struggling to find sympathy from
the same country whose flag she had proudly displayed in her
front yard each and every day.

Lila Lipscomb makes Tyne Cot Cemetery feel real to Johnny.
He usually forgets so much of so many of the hundreds of movies he has watched. He does not forget much of the Lila Lipscomb
story. Two or three tears drip as Johnny crouches down before the
grave. He recalls Lila telling Michael Moore about the moment
she found out her son had died.

217

Questions race through Johnny's head. Did Lieutenant Ditzell's parents react in the same way when they received the telegram? How does any parent react?

A parent is not supposed to bury their child, thinks Johnny. He has never contemplated this before today. He feels stupid for crying. But it feels right. Johnny Hazzard is not a parent. He is not even an adult. But in his imagination, he sees grief and senses a kind of loss. And the anger continues to strengthen.

"You okay?" comes the voice from behind him.

Johnny turns. He did not hear anyone approaching. It is Lydia.

"Yeah, I'm fine." The red eyes betray the confidence of the words.

"Some of these guys were the same age as you," says Lydia.

Brother and sister continue standing, looking around themselves at the graves. Endless white graves. In the distance, they can see Ieper, the reason for all the carnage. Johnny imagines a uniformed soldier, rifle in hand, standing in place of each and every gravestone. He sees row upon row of soldiers. He wonders what might have been saved if, as the First Lord of the Admiralty had feared, all those men had gone on strike.

In believing that nothing has been learned since 1918, Johnny is properly moved. In acknowledging that the indignity of anonymity these men still suffer is also suffered by thousands today.

Johnny Hazzard begins to think about what it is to be a foot soldier, and what it is to be a First Lord.

"Where have we got to?" muses Johnny Hazzard. Only this time, he says it out loud.

"What?" asks Lydia, who has not heard him.

"Nothing."

"We should get back to the bus," says big sister.

Back in the minibus, Johnny opens his In Flanders Fields Museum book at an opportune page, and finds this quote from Siegfried Sassoon, Lieutenant, Royal Welsh Fusiliers:

> "I am not protesting against the conduct of the War, but against the political errors and insincerities for which the fighting men are being sacrificed. On behalf of those who are suffering now I make this protest against the deception which is being practiced on them; also I believe that I may help to destroy the callous complacency with which the majority of those at home regard the continuance of agonies which they do not share, and which they have not sufficient imagination to realize."

TWENTY

"There died a myriad,
And of the best, among them,
For an old bitch gone in the teeth,
For a botched civilisation."
— Ezra Pound, *Hugh Selwyn Mauberley*

"We wage a war to save civilization itself."
— President George W. Bush

After the tours, the family arranges to meet up again at a quarter to eight for the Last Post at the Menin Gate, just five minutes' walk from the hotel. Johnny has a couple of hours of "alone time." He cannot chill out. Instead, he reflects on the day's events, remembers what he has seen, thinks back to the Michael Moore movie. He has always equated war with badness, and almost always wrongness, too. He has always been brought up to believe that it is avoidable. His parents have taught him this much, and their influence has shaped Johnny's and Lydia's ideas. But just as it is our instinct to put one foot in front of the other in order to walk, opposing warfare has been an obvious and instinctive reaction for Johnny that he has never questioned. He has been horrified to hear the dead and wounded figures of any war, but he's never really thought *why* he opposes it. Walking around the battlefields and cemeteries of the Salient today has awakened an understanding and brought home the reality of what it is he is arguing against. His passion is stronger, his insight sharper, and he hopes his commitment will only grow ever more sturdy after today's sights.

It all comes full circle, back to Ieper, to 1914 and the Christmas truce, and to the three hundred thousand soldiers killed in a town they did not know in a war they did not understand. The similarities between the modern war on terror and the "war to end all wars" seem obvious to Johnny. The most crushing and frustrating thing is the helplessness of the cause; Johnny recalls footage of his secretary of state declaring, in February 2001, that Iraq had no weapons of mass destruction. Then eighteen months later, the same man was attempting to convince the world that the country did possess them. And the helplessness comes from the knowledge that the people in power don't really care what they say, they don't care if they contradict or lie or mislead or deceive, because they will always do what they need to do in order to gain public support for what they want to do. Whether it's "destroy this mad brute" or "smoke him out," what has to be done will be done.

There is an hour and a half until the Last Post. Johnny wants to take his mind off the heavy day, so he picks up his skateboard, tells his dad he's off for a wander, and goes for a skate — or at least, he tries to. There are still many shoppers and tourists mingling about the Grote Markt and surrounding streets. Johnny is struggling to find a smooth surface. The cobbles are everywhere and they're not giving up. He walks off the Grote Markt down a busy road named Boterstraat. Background music plays from loud speakers located above shop windows. Every speaker along the street plays the same music. It reminds Johnny of Austin. Johnny sees boutiques with expensive, designer clothes, and cellphone shops, and hip record stores. Here on the cosmopolitan Boterstraat, the Tyne Cot Cemetery feels like a different country.

Skateboard tucked under arm, Johnny continues ambling. He goes off the beaten track, down a small square (cobbled, naturally). An old man, wearing what resembles a blue janitor's coat, watches the world go by on a stool on the pavement outside his apartment. He has a beret on his head and folded arms across his chest. This particular square does not offer much world going by to watch. Johnny smiles at him. The old man does not respond. Down a side street, two boys play badminton without a net. Some elderly passersby look as though they're still living in the 1940s. Johnny has noticed several people like this; they wear clothes, hats, and hairstyles that seem decades out of joint. This is nothing like Austin.

Johnny goes into the supermarket, opposite St. Martin's Cathedral, to buy some mineral water. As he leaves, he does a double take. A kid, perhaps two or three years younger than him, sits on his skateboard on the pavement. Johnny stops and eyes the board. The kid says something in Flemish.

"Sorry, only English," Johnny replies, awkwardly.

"Ah . . . okay. Tourist," says the boy. He is tall, has rosy cheeks, messy light brown hair, and wears the kinds of expressions more usual on the face of a grown-up. He's dressed in baggy skate clothes and American sneakers.

"Yes, tourist. You live here?"

"Yes. My English is not good."

"That doesn't matter. Where do you skate?"

The boy thinks for a few seconds. He tentatively begins a sentence, then another, but cannot explain.

"I show you," he says, and begins walking. So Johnny follows.

The boy's name is Andy. He is indeed twelve years old. Johnny passes on his age and name, and explains what he's doing in Ieper.

"You are American?"

"Yes, from Texas."

"Cowboys and Indians," replies Andy.

"No. Cowboys and Mexicans," replies Johnny. They both snigger.

And then they arrive at a quiet backstreet, without cobbles but with very little in the way of random objects or ridges or levels to use for tricks. None, in fact.

"This is where I skate," says Andy.

They goof around, without much being said, for about ten minutes. Johnny enjoys himself. He doesn't know the kid, but he doesn't need to know the kid. As on the South Bank, these guys are brought together by a common interest, and that's enough.

"You like Belgium?" asks Andy.

"Yeah, it's cool. I like it. Do you?"

"No. Bullshit. I want to live somewhere else when I become older."

"Where?"

"I don't know. America, maybe."

"No, you don't want to move to America," says Johnny, smiling at the very idea.

"Yeah, I do. Why not?"

"I dunno. It sucks. I want to see more of Europe."

"Spain is nice. Belgium sucks."

"Where else have you been?" asks Johnny.

"France. London. Er . . . Spain and Italy. I like Spain. Maybe I live there."

And the kid pulls off an impressive crooked grind off the curb. But Johnny wishes he could pull off speaking another language. He checks his watch. It's time to head back to family affairs.

"I have to go. Last Post."

"Fucking Last Post," Andy says, smiling.

"Why?" Johnny smiles, too.

"Just every day. Lots of people, always. Boring."

"Did your family take part in the war?" The kid looks bemused. Johnny rephrases:

"Was your family in the Great War?"

"No. We are not from Ieper. My family is from Brussels."

Johnny thanks Andy for showing him this spot.

"See you," says the Texan.

"Yeah. When do you go home?" asks the Belgian.

225

"Saturday."

"Ah, I see you around."

Andy seems very confident in that last assertion. They exchange pleasantries, and Johnny heads back to the hotel.

* * *

Lydia's mouth gives away her boredom. Siska's eyes reveal her exhaustion. Mr. Hazzard's shoulders show he's fed up. This holiday really is on its last legs. Johnny joins the clan, with skateboard, and they head down to the famous Gate.

The Last Post ceremony began on November 11, 1929. It is held at the Menin Gate — actually a large, cream-colored archway — where the troops of Britain and its Empire marched through on their way to the front line. It is surprising that, given its context, the Menin Gate is not a frightening or imposing building in the way the Town Hall/Cloth Hall is. It is quite the opposite. Every evening of every day, the Last Post sounds at eight P.M. in remembrance of all those who died.

Today, it is thousands of tourists and visitors who march to the Gate to pay their respects and hear the haunting notes of the bugle. Sometimes there is a special presentation. Today is such an occasion; a Scottish secondary school has brought a class along. The Hazzards join the considerable crowds that flank either side of the road. The traffic has not yet been stopped. Johnny notices several local teens cycling through, apparently oblivious to the crowds and to the significance of this focal point of Ieper. They have seen it all before and, like Andy, probably think little of it. All it means to them is that the key road into the town center is closed off for ten minutes every evening. Johnny is surprised at how ordinary their lives are, given the extraordinary nature of their hometown. The road is eventually closed off and the ceremony begins. A girl of around fourteen from the Scottish school stands in the middle of the road, addressing both sides of the crowd. Johnny cannot hear her too well, only her final words — "They shall not be forgotten." The girl places a poppy wreath at the foot of the wall, underneath one of the many long columns of names. Names of dead soldiers, denied a burial.

The simple tune of the bugle begins.

As self-serving and gratuitous as it might appear to be, thinking of Iraq brings the tragedy home for Johnny. The hopelessness, the futility, the ineptitude, the torture, the civilians, the heartless and tiresome declarations of the administrations. The legal wordplay to justify the actions, wordplay that does not, will not, cannot bring back a dead soldier or civilian. None of their words mean anything, and yet they mean everything.

Like everybody with a television set everywhere in the world, Johnny Hazzard saw the planes smash into the World Trade Center. He saw it happen approximately one hundred and fifty times, in fact. He saw the first day of "shock and awe" in Baghdad, when the relentless bombing looked more like a fireworks display than a civilian slaughter. He also saw the pictures of American torture and humiliation, of Japanese, Korean, American, Italian hostages, of coffins draped in US flags, and the footage of scream-ing Iraqi mothers, pleading for an explanation as to why their young children had been killed by an apparently misdirected mis-sile. These were shocking, these were astonishing, and these were new images. Johnny Hazzard had not witnessed war before.

But they were distant and unreal. Rolling news turns the most dramatic into the most repeated. And the more you see the foot-age, the less real it becomes. It is a video game, or a DVD you've watched a few times. It is not a war; it is prime-time entertain-ment. Endless analysis by "experts" fails to bring home the reality of the horror. Watching the TV, Johnny knew what he ought to feel, but he couldn't feel it. When he tried to bring on some kind of terrible sadness, he just felt fake. And that made him feel bad, cruel, without a heart. CNN, BBC, Fox — they have all made war more immediate, accessible, graphic, visible, visual, and hor-rific. But they did not make war real in the way the cemeteries or the museum did.

Standing beneath the Menin Gate archway, listening to the haunting notes of the Last Post, watching the faces in the crowd, the unreal abruptly and brutally becomes the real. It is about that fourteen-year-old soldier, it is about that Iraqi wedding destroyed by a US missile, it is about those limbless children, and it is about all the parents whose children died in the name of power politics. It was power politics in 1914 and it was power politics in 2003. It matters.

The remembrance service itself does not move Johnny Hazzard. Rather, it provokes other thoughts and ideas that do. The footage of the Iraq conflict suddenly feels pertinent, powerful, and moving. It feels dangerous and threatening. Johnny can't get a line out of his head —

The land of the free, and home of the brave . . .

The free. The brave.

Johnny thinks again of *Fahrenheit 9/11*. Of the hundreds of senators without a son or daughter in the armed forces, supporting a distant and calamitous war. Johnny thinks of the Patriot Act — to oppose it, they tell him, is to oppose the land of the free. Freedom, after all, is what we are all fighting for.

As the Last Post comes to an end, Johnny looks again at the people packed under the archway. He sees those old enough to remember war on their doorstep, and those young enough to forget. Two old women wipe their noses with handkerchiefs. Johnny begins to cry. He does not want to. He wants to banish those images of exposed bone on an Iraqi toddler's arm, of the screaming infant whose face was covered in stitches, of the anxious relatives looking for their loved ones in the Ground Zero wreckage. The images will not vanish. The haunting melody finishes. The crowd applauds. Lila Lipscomb's voice repeats itself over and over inside Johnny's head.

"*A parent is not supposed to bury their child.*"

Johnny avoids his family and walks up the steps to the top of the archway. From there he sees the moat that surrounds the south side of the town. There is a monument dedicated to the Australian soldiers who died for the British Empire. Australians. Men from the other side of the world, duped into fighting for a honor and cause that did not concern them. They only fought because they had the misfortune of being born in a country that "belonged" to the United Kingdom. The monument states that "Ieper was rebuilt and today acts as a gateway for all those who come in search of the past, and of the generation that perished in Flanders Fields. . . ."

The names are endless. Majors, captains, lieutenants, sergeants, corporals, privates. 54,896 in total, all of whom "fell in Ypres Salient but to whom the fortune of war denied the known and honored burial given to their comrades in death."

TWENTY-ONE

Boredom must have been truly chipping away at Lydia's brain for her to even think about knocking on Johnny's door.

It is ten o'clock. Having endured a relatively low-key, drab, and untalkative meal at one of the restaurants on the Grote Markt, the family retired to the hotel at around nine thirty.

In room number nineteen, Siska has found the inspiration. She sits on her bed sketching what she hopes will later become an oil painting. Mr. Hazzard lies on the other side of the bed, socks off, watching some cable news. Siska rapidly grows impatient.

"Dahling, I need you to go outside."

Mr. Hazzard looks up at Siska. He's heard this routine before. It has caused many a holiday argument.

"No," he replies, standing his ground for the first time.

"I need the space and quiet."

"This is my vacation, too, Siska."

"Dahling, please . . . just tonight. I promise just tonight."

"It's always 'just tonight,'" replies a weary Mr. Hazzard. Minutes ago he was close to nodding off.

"Please?" she asks, softly, one last time.

Mr. Hazzard gives in, as he always does. He puts on his socks and grabs the armchair.

"I still don't see why you can't just draw with me in the room. What's the problem? Do I lack suitable inspiration?"

"No, of course not. It's just one of those things. I know it pisses you."

"Yeah, it pisses me."

And Mr. Hazzard takes the armchair outside into the thin corridor, where the noises from the restaurant and bar below can be heard filtering up the stairwell. He takes a newspaper and sits, watching absolutely nothing or no one go by.

In room number twenty-one, Lydia is seconds away from tearing out her hair. She is not used to staying indoors and whiling the nighttimes away with cable TV and books. She has developed an electrifying social life of late, and this trip to Belgium has interrupted it. Both in Austin and London, Lydia has been painting the town red. She hasn't just been painting the town red, she's been painting it yellow, silver, and gold, too. Lydia is not a pisshead, but she knows how to have a good time.

Perhaps she is motivated by seeing how upset her brother was in Tyne Cot Cemetery. Or perhaps it's the hideous beige walls of room twenty-one. Whatever the reason, Lydia needs out. She approaches room twenty-two, thinks twice, then knocks on the door.

Johnny Hazzard is still dressed when he answers. He holds the Michael Moore book in his hand.

"What's up?" he asks.

"Look, are you bored?"

"I'm reading."

"I'm bored."

Johnny opens the door wide and returns to the bed.

"No, I mean, do you wanna go somewhere? Just for like an hour or something?"

Johnny frowns, and puts down the book.

"I know, I know . . ." she says, embarrassed at her bridge-building. "But come on, you gotta be banging your head by now, don't you?"

"Actually, no. I'm catching up with my reading. But I'll come out, if you want."

"No."

The Hazzard eyebrows raise.

"I mean yeah, okay, let's go. Come on. Hurry up," she says.

Johnny tries to hide the smile from his sister. This is exactly what he wants.

* * *

When it comes to beer, the Belgians have the monopoly on taste.

Choice is all well and good, but it's difficult to know where to begin when faced with a menu of three hundred beers. Ter Posterie is a famous local haunt, which Lydia discovers in her guidebook and figures is worth a visit.

To find it you must first go down a path, which leads to a small courtyard, which in turn leads to the underground bar. Inside it's dark and dingy, and feels more like a log cabin than a Flemish waterhole. There are not many drinkers out; maybe three or four people in the courtyard and a few more inside.

Johnny and Lydia pass a tank of miserable terrapins by the door and head straight to the bar. The woman smiles and passes a menu. Neither Johnny nor his sister have the first idea what they are looking at. Johnny opens a random page, runs his finger along the list without looking, and stops randomly at a beer with eight and a half percent proof. Lydia laughs at his technique, then does the same, finding a lightweight number at six percent. They order, receive the bottles and particular glasses (almost every beer has its own special glass to be served in), and head upstairs to the courtyard. It is not a warm evening, nor is it chilly. It is tepid. The beers, however, are suitably cool.

"Poor Dad," says Lydia, with a smirk.

"Yeah. It's fucking funny, though," says Johnny.

"She better come up with some good art when we get home."

Pause.

Johnny does not feel particularly comfortable. Nor does Lydia. This is one of those awkward social moments nobody tells you about. Going out drinking with your sibling. Soho was made easier because of the crowds and the students. But tonight in Ieper, silence is the word. The pause lasts an age. A dog begins barking next door, and continues intermittently.

"Reminds me of Oscar," says Johnny, referring to a childhood pet. Oscar was the Hazzards' chocolate Labrador. When Johnny was nine and Lydia thirteen, Oscar died of cancer.

"Yeah, he does. But he's gonna piss me off if he carries on."

The dog carries on.

"Do you remember that time Oscar came with us to Zilker, and he got covered in mud, and then came back and rolled on the rug right before Mom and Dad's dinner party? Pissed the hell outta Mom," says Johnny.

Lydia laughs. Her eyes look very pretty when she smiles.

"Jeez, that rug looked worse than him after that."

"Dad could never get angry with Oscar," says Johnny, looking into his beer. "Never."

"That's 'coz Oscar was a smart mutt. He knew how to get what he wanted from Dad. Puppy dog eyes. He had Dad wrapped around his little finger."

"Just like Siska," jokes Johnny. They both laugh.

"How's the beer?" asks Lydia.

"Good. Tastes nice. Try."

Lydia does.

"You can't taste the alcohol," she says.

"Yeah. Dangerous stuff."

And the dog barks on.

"Oscar, shut up," says Lydia. They laugh again.

Johnny says, "I miss him. Poor Oscar."

"Yeah, me, too."

Lydia takes a big gulp of her beer, leaving the glass almost empty.

"What about her? Do you miss her?" she asks him.

"Who?"

Lydia looks at Johnny with droopy, don't-mess-with-me eyes.

"Of course I miss her. Wouldn't you?"

"Yeah, I guess I would."

"So . . . it's all going good," Lydia says, asking a question with a statement. Johnny hates the way she does that.

"Yes, it's all going good. I'm doing great. She's doing fine. We're happy."

"I'm pleased."

"Lydia . . ."

"No, really. I am. It's about time you started."

"Started what?" Johnny feels nervousness starting to drown him. He's not ready to talk about sex with Lydia. No way.

"Seeing people."

"Oh. Yeah. I agree. It's about time."

Pause. The dog has shut up.

"It would be nice if she was here. Doing what we're doing," says Johnny, finally expressing in words what he's been thinking since day one of the holiday. "I mean, it's been good, especially here. But I'd love for her to see it all, too."

"You're into her."

"Of course I'm into her. Wouldn't you want to share stuff with your boyfriend?"

Lydia finishes the glass. Her mouth remains conveniently full of beer so she cannot speak. After a few seconds, she swallows, and looks at the table.

"Sure I would."

"So?"

"So what?"

"You don't tell me shit. Is there somebody back home? Or in England or whatever?"

"No."

"Oh."

"Well —"

"There is?"

"No."

"But . . . ?"

"But there was. Somebody."

"Who?"

"Just somebody. Another?"

Johnny nods, even though the bottle of eight and a half percent is already taking its toll; he feels like there's a track meet going on inside his head. Lydia goes to buy the beer. Johnny calls after her —

"Make it a different one this time. We got three hundred to get through and this place closes in a few hours."

Lydia smiles. He feels good about that — Johnny doesn't make his big sister laugh or smile much. But he's confused about this "somebody." And, judging by her timely disappearance, Johnny isn't sure she's going to spill any beans tonight. But he wants to know. And, with his psycho-sleuth hat on, Johnny wants to help. He really does want to help.

Lydia returns with the drinks a minute or two later.

"Here, try this blonde. She's got a cool name."

"I can't pronounce it," says Johnny.

The dog starts up again.

"Oscar, if I told you once, I've told you a thousand times," says Johnny. Lydia smiles again, although she looks less at ease. Her shoulders have curled inward, her back is curved, and her eyes are sullen.

Johnny thinks about how to say the next question. We have all done this a thousand times in our head, and, on occasion, out loud. How to get the tone just right so it doesn't sound persistent, rude, sleazy, bitchy — whatever. Johnny gets it just right.

"So who was the somebody?"

Pause. A painful pause for Lydia. The dog has heeded Johnny's advice.

"All the time I was at the bar, I knew you were going to ask that. You're damn predictable, bro."

"Maybe I am. But I answer your questions. You bullshit around mine."

"Okay." She breathes in, breathes out, takes a sip, then looks down at the table. "The somebody was a stupid thing. I mean, I was stupid about it. It doesn't really matter anymore."

"Who was it?"

Lydia starts fiddling with the cardboard beer mat. Johnny keeps looking at her, waiting for a crack in the armor.

"Was it Jim, the dude you did photography with in tenth grade who moved to London?"

"No way." Lydia laughs a little. "Jim's gay."

"Oh."

Johnny's psycho-investigations made him sure Jim was JB. He is disappointed and discouraged.

"You can't laugh," says Lydia. The armor finally cracks. It is a hairline fracture, but she is allowing Johnny in.

"Why would I laugh? Of course I won't laugh."

"Jake Blaze."

"Jake Blaze? The singer?" Johnny cannot believe he's heard that right. His sister. Jake Blaze. Impossible.

"Yes, the singer."

"That's awesome!"

"No, it really isn't. He's a cocksucker. Grade A."

Johnny won't let reality get in the way of a cool story just yet.

"Lydia, you went out with Jake Blaze? Jesus! Is that his real name?"

"No, of course not. His real name — and you can laugh at this all you like — his real name is Jake Baggins."

Johnny does not laugh, he smirks, but he understands why Baggins became Blaze overnight.

"How the hell did you end up dating Jake Blaze? Half the girls in my class love the dude."

"That was the problem. We met at South by Southwest. Last year. He picked me out, believe it or not."

This story just gets cooler. Johnny Hazzard feels practically related to a celebrity.

"Jake Blaze picked you out of the crowd? During his concert?"

"No, no. It was another show. The Beat Piece. He was in the crowd. Came up to me, and that's it."

"That's it?" He knows there is more, and he wants to hear it.

"That's how we met."

"How old is the dude?" Johnny wants to ask so many questions, but time is against him. He feels like writing them all down so he doesn't forget.

"Twenty-one. He has too much money for twenty-one."

"Well, he's not huge or anything." Johnny wants to retain *some* perspective. He's Jake Blaze, not a Beastie Boy.

"He is in Austin," says Lydia, almost defensively. Her ex-boyfriend was a celebrity, dammit.

"Yeah, but I mean, he's not really famous, is he?"

"He played two dates in London."

"You're kidding? When?"

"Last month."

"Ah." Johnny begins to piece together the story in his mind. "He jerked you around?"

"You could say that. I was most definitely jerked around."

The initial shock and the subsequent awe have subsided. Johnny senses a prime opportunity to learn about his sister. He wants her to trust him and, above all, respect him. This is his chance.

"How?"

"Johnny, I'm not sure you'd understand."

So much for trust and respect. Johnny flies off the handle.

"I'm old enough, dammit," he says. "I told you about me. You tell me about you."

Lydia sees the anger in her brother's face, and relents. Slowly and certainly, she begins explaining how it all happened.

"We met at the show, and he invited me and Beth for a drink at the after-show. It was a great party — free food, free drink. Who isn't going to be like 'wow'? We were at a huge house with a huge swimming pool drinking champagne. And free champagne always tastes sweeter."

Johnny smiles. He can imagine how easy it was to be seduced by the excitement of it all.

"So Jake asked us back to his place —"

"On the night you met?" asks Johnny.

"Yes, but no — there was no getting naked," she says. "We sat around drinking more champagne and eating cookies, actually. Whenever he left the room, Beth was telling me he was really into me and she told me to go for it. But I wasn't so sure."

Johnny is stuck between feelings of admiration for his sister's honesty and courage in telling him about all this, and sympathy for her story.

"Turns out she was right. He was very interested. And, of course, he is beautiful. And popular. He's not a celebrity, but he has an army of fans — especially in Austin. And he's really sensitive — more sensitive than any guy I've met. I mean, he wasn't a tough guy. He was real. And he had the brownest eyes I'd ever seen on a white man."

There is a lengthy pause. Johnny begins thinking that Lydia is starting to feel self-conscious.

"Go on, its okay," he says, so quietly she struggles to hear him. "It's okay," he repeats.

"I was convinced he was only interested in a quick screw. Hate to be so blunt, but that's what I thought," she says, guiltily.

"It's not your fault. None of it is your fault," says Johnny.

"I know, I know." And Johnny is immediately reminded that he is talking to Lydia here. She's sensible, and perceptive, and two steps ahead of the game. But all of those attributes dissolve when love gets in the way. "Took a while before I agreed to go out with him. I'm kind of pleased my first thoughts were right, but I should have acted on them. You see, I had this hunch that there could be trouble, but he was being so damn sweet. He kept messaging my phone, and he even wrote me a letter. Nobody writes letters anymore. And you won't believe it, but Jake Blaze was a virgin."

Johnny puts his glass down. The shocks are all crawling out of the woodwork tonight.

"That's *awesome*," he says, thinking immediately how cool it is that he — Johnny Hazzard of Olfman Drive — lost his virginity at a younger age than Jake Blaze. And he didn't even have the guitar or adoring fans to help him.

Lydia takes a sip. Johnny switches thought journeys from Jake Blaze to his sister.

"He lost it to *you*, didn't he?"

She half smiles, declining to answer the question directly.

"So I knew he meant it. He wasn't just after a screw."

"So he wasn't just an asshole after a fan."

"I didn't say he wasn't an asshole. And I wasn't a fan. I never bought a record or CD of his. The ones I got he gave me."

"How come Mom didn't know this was going on?" asks Johnny.

"Oh, she did. So did Dad. Actually, Dad was really great about it. It was just you who didn't know."

Johnny is livid. He is fed up with being treated like a juvenile dumbass.

"Why not?"

"Because, Johnny . . . you would have told your friends, who would have told somebody else, and then it would have been everybody's business."

"So?"

"I didn't want that. It was strange and scary enough as it was."

Johnny shrugs. He does not get it. He is so proud of January. He wants everybody to know about their relationship.

"So you went out a whole year?" he asks.

"No. We were in London for the summer. He came over for a few days, we met up."

"This sucks. Why didn't you tell me? Dammit, I wasn't a little kid."

"Yes, you were."

"Fuck you, Lydia. The whole family knew except me. Mom and Dad never keep secrets."

"Don't drop a ball — this was special."

"So what happened? He dump you?" Johnny deliberately cuts to the chase; his anger at the secrecy displays itself through petulance. Lydia rolls her eyes at the childishness.

"He was with somebody else. From before last summer, before we came to London. I found out just after Christmas."

Lydia looks a little embarrassed by her own openness. (She has only shared this information with one best friend before.)

"Yeah. Happy New Year, Lydia. He actually said that, after the showdown. Nine months wiped out."

Johnny wants to seriously harm Jake Blaze.

"How did you find out?"

"You're full of questions tonight."

"Sorry."

Lydia looks at her brother. "It's okay." She pauses again by taking a big sip. "He sent me a text message he meant to send her. Gave the game away in twenty words. It was that simple."

This hits Johnny like a quarterback on ecstasy. The stark reality of relationships has been conveniently concealed by the wonder of his first romance — until now. He is faced with the callous truth of how people can treat each other and he immediately wishes he didn't know. He prefers ignorance.

"So you weren't arranging to meet him that night I came out with you in Soho?"

"A few weeks ago? Hell, no. Those were just some friends I made last year. Jake Blaze is yesterday's news."

Johnny Hazzard suspects this is not the case at all. Even if she has gotten over him — which Johnny doubts — she has obviously not moved on. But moreover, this evening has changed Johnny's perception. Lydia was once the Queen of All Things Sensible. She always did the right thing at the right time. She rarely messed up. She was almost superhuman in her good taste and judgment. Suddenly, she seems fallible, and Johnny finds her far more approachable than ever before.

"So Jake Blaze was your first boyfriend. . . ."

"No!" protests Lydia. "First *real* boyfriend."

"First love, right?"

Lydia nods, but clearly feels awkward; it's that four-letter word. It can inspire confidence, openness, and sheer, unbridled happiness. It can also inspire nervousness, crippling fear, and vulnerability.

"I'm gonna get one last one," says Lydia.

"Make it a blonde. I like blondes."

"Yeah. I bet you do," she says, and disappears down the staircase.

Over the last drink, the onus begins to shift onto Johnny. After his glowing enthusiasm and positivity, Lydia skillfully teases out the insecurities, his fears about the relationship. Lydia has her own fears, undoubtedly linked to the disaster that was the Blaze experience. She is careful not to sound too bleak, but she knows how being head-over-heels cuts out all rational thinking.

"And let me tell you something," she says to her little brother. "Being the dumpee is shit-on-a-stick. Being the dumper, well, at least you've got some control over the situation. And the whole head-over-heels thing — it's stupid. It's more like ass-over-tit. It's shit. Don't let yourself be sucked in like that. You lose reality, you lose yourself, and everything just revolves around this one person. You gotta have your own shit going on. Your life can't just be a part of somebody else's; it has to be your own."

Johnny has to disagree here. The very magic is in allowing your life to be a part of somebody else's. The joy comes in losing yourself, in not caring about anything as much as you care about her.

"But sharing —"

"Yeah, that's it. Sharing. Equal sharing. Keep it equal. If I'm being totally honest, that's why I worry, bro. She's older."

"So was Jake Blaze."

"It's different. For a start we were older than you are now. And it's different when a girl dates an older guy."

"How?"

"Just is. I don't know any friend who's dated a guy more than a grade younger."

"Well, January's different." Johnny is persuading himself as much as Lydia here. He is, however, *fairly* certain that January is different.

"I hope she is."

"She's really great, Lydia. She cares."

That is the first time Johnny Hazzard has told someone the fundamental reason why his girlfriend is special. He does not plan to say it, he just says it, and he feels immediately vulnerable and exposed.

"Then I hope it really works out for you," says Lydia. "But we all do stuff for ourselves. That's it."

"No, I don't wanna only do stuff because it suits me."

"When it comes to personal stuff, we all do what suits us. Nobody else. You'll see."

There is something in her tone that is not entirely convincing. But, as we often do when we hear something we do not want to hear, Johnny Hazzard simply pretends he did not hear it. Instead, he switches back to the infamous Mr. Blaze. He asks Lydia if she went to his recent London concerts.

"I went, yes. I went to one of them. He saw me."

"I thought you said he was yesterday's news," says Johnny.

"He *is* yesterday's news. But I was curious. I didn't really want to go — I just ended up going."

"And?" Johnny sees an excellent learning opportunity for himself in the story of Lydia's botched relationship. What are older siblings for if not learning from their fuck-ups?

"And . . . nothing. I told him I wasn't interested anymore. And I'm not."

"You can't forgive?"

"No. It's one thing to cheat. It's another thing to take advantage of someone because they think they're the only one."

Johnny feels anger toward Jake Blaze. He has never seen his sister quite so honest. Nor has he ever seen her quite so hurt (not since he jumped off the garden slide and landed on her when he was four — the one-inch scar on her right arm is still there today).

Lydia finishes off her beer, Johnny his, and they decide to head back.

* * *

There are a few old men on stools drinking in the hotel bar downstairs. Johnny and Lydia walk up the stairwell and reach the third floor.

Mr. Hazzard sits, arms folded, awake, outside room nineteen.

"Dad!" says Lydia. "What the hell are you still doing here?"

"She won't let me in. She's nuts. She's actually nuts."

Johnny laughs.

"Did you have fun?" Mr. Hazzard asks.

"Yeah," replies Lydia. "Can't you even just go in there and sleep, Dad?"

"I tried that already. She says she's nearly finished."

Johnny and Lydia wish their dad luck, and continue up to the fourth floor. Once safely there, they both disintegrate into laughter. Then they hug and thank each other for the talk. Johnny is contented. Not only is big sis giving him the time of day, but his psycho-predictions had some foundation, after all.

TWENTY-TWO

Weeping angels are almost as dispiriting a sight as weeping children. St. Martin's Cathedral (just behind the Grote Markt) is, like most of the other famous religious buildings in Belgium, a stunning, huge, and rather daunting gothic building, its one-hundred-meter tower particularly eye-catching. There are numerous confession boxes, which make Johnny Hazzard wonder just how sinful the locals were back then, and there are the statues of weeping angels. They are striking in their sadness, all the more disturbing because they are positioned on either side of a skull. This cathedral fits perfectly into its town's history.

After the cathedral, the Hazzards enjoy a hearty lunch of the delicious national specialty *moules-frites* (mussels and fries), followed by the equally special national specialty *gaufres* (waffles) with chocolate sauce.

"How's the painting, Siska?" asks Lydia, shooting a glance at Johnny, who smiles back at his sister.

"Sketches, dahling, not painting. I paint when I get back. And very good, thank you."

"Can we see?" asks Mr. Hazzard, completely aware of the answer that is coming.

"No."

Mr. Hazzard looks at his kids as if to say, *See what I have to put up with? Nights in the corridor and not even a glimpse at the master-piece.*

"You can see when I finish. Does a football coach put a team of five players on the pitch? No. He needs the complete eleven. Patience, dahlings."

Mr. Hazzard rolls his eyes and Johnny smiles.

Lydia and Johnny don't say much to each other over lunch. It's not as if last night never happened, but it's as if all that had to be said was said. Their relationship has changed. Forever? Perhaps. For now? For sure.

Johnny spends the afternoon strolling around the town. He buys some postcards for mementos. He looks at some skate shoes, which are approximately double what they cost in Austin. He browses the record store, dominated by American artists. There is a piece of home everywhere Johnny Hazzard goes. How many people in the world have not heard of the golden arches, the swoosh sneakers, the starry coffee, the vegetable extract soft drink?

Or, for that matter, the Beach Boys, Elvis, John Wayne, Madonna, or Tom Cruise?

Last year, the year before that, and so on, these elements of home made Johnny feel comfortable. Like the reliable Belgian comic books, the reminders of the USA made Johnny feel safe. Almost everywhere in London, the nearest slice of Americana is only a few feet away. You certainly cannot wander down a major shopping district in any British town without finding several examples of America's commercial influence.

This year, however, Johnny doesn't find comfort in this. Whereas once it provided a welcomed attachment to the safety, security, and routine of life with Mom in Austin, now all it does is disrupt Johnny's adventure. This year more than any other, Europe has given Johnny all he could hope for and much more. He doesn't need America, nor does he want it. But the American tentacles keep tapping him on the shoulder, trying to wrap themselves around his arms and legs, and he keeps having to run to get away from them.

As Johnny wanders the aisles of the store, with Michael Jackson on the speakers, he remembers that in Austin he is part of the majority in despising many of the values America has exported. He reads the alternative magazines and flyers at Waterloo Records, he subscribes to the popular belief that America is a great nation run by idiots, and he insists on being liberal and proud. And yet, despite his long-held views, Johnny always felt a little embarrassed at how happy the sight of something American made him when he visited Dad in London and they went on

European vacations. So more often than not, previous trips to London were filled with visits to the bookstores and coffee houses Johnny had seen a hundred times before back home. Adventurism was not on the agenda.

Johnny leaves the record store and returns to the Europeanism of the Grote Markt. The wind picks up, and Johnny walks and walks, his thoughts turning slowly to January. There is now a sense of guilt enveloping — guilt that he has not thought about her as much as he thinks he ought to have. She is still everything, but perhaps "everything" is not quite as large a quantity as it was before the holiday began. That said, she remains the first thing Johnny thinks about in the morning. And he wants her opinion, he wants to know what she would say about all the experiences he has gone through these past twenty-four hours or so.

"Maybe," he says to himself, "this is how January felt in Vietnam and Cambodia and Australia."

Johnny arrives at the Menin Gate. He decides to take a closer look at the names. As usual, there are other visitors. Some with camcorders, some with notebooks, all of them with admiration. Johnny climbs up the steps to the top of the archway, where there are more names, and the view of the moat.

He looks down one column of names. The 1st Battalion London Regiment, Royal Fusiliers.

Under the heading PRIVATE, he finds:

HARRIS L.

HAYTER G.

HAZARD J.W.

Johnny stares. One Z and a W out, but striking all the same. Johnny wonders who the guy was, how old he might have been, how he died. There are numerous questions and, of course, no answers. Johnny speculates that the soldier might have been the same age as he, or a little older. How did Mr. and Mrs. Hazard learn of their son's death? Did they live much longer after they found out? What did they think of their country and its leaders after their son was killed in a war of attrition? Did they really believe the Prime Minister's assertion that this was a war to end them all? Were they alive to see the horrors of the Second World War, the Korean War, Vietnam?

The sheer number of names engraved on the Menin Gate and the wall at the Tyne Cot Cemetery had a profound effect on Johnny. But seeing someone with so similar a name delivers an even more potent body blow. Johnny will not tell anyone about this.

There is a small park behind the archway, running alongside the moat. Johnny decides to take a stroll as he collects his thoughts. The images of *Fahrenheit 9/11* creep back into his mind — it's Lila Lipscomb again. The mother of the dead sergeant. This woman has brought the Great War home to Johnny Hazzard. His face creases up, he desperately fights against his body's instincts, but he loses the battle, and tears begin rolling down. The tall trees of the park darken the atmosphere, as well as the light. There does not appear to be anybody else there. Johnny walks slowly. These feelings are new and, unlike the starry coffee or record store collection, completely unfamiliar and rather frightening. At first, Johnny was angry because he had not been moved. Now he is confused as to how and why he is so moved. He tries to push certain thoughts away. But it is a truism: When you try hard to expel those images and memories, they stick more stubbornly than ever, with more sharpness and clarity. And Lila's hanging in there:

"I need my son."

The metallic, shiny benches are not especially comfortable. They are modern and out-of-joint with the old-looking surroundings. Johnny sits with his back to the moat, composes himself, and thinks of January and Waterloo Bridge. He wants her here now, hugging him. He wants to feel her breath on his arm. He wants the comfort and familiarity she now represents. He wants the misery to end and the tears to dry.

A noise can be heard in the near distance. It is a rickety, rough sound, as though someone is scraping a tree branch along a road. As the source of the noise approaches, Johnny is sure the clatter is in fact four small wheels running along the uneven tarmac of the park's path.

Andy comes into view, struggling hard to gain something resembling consistency in his skating. He keeps having to push himself along with his left foot. Johnny wipes his eyes, making sure he doesn't look as though he's been crying. He takes out a tissue and blows his nose. Andy approaches.

"Hey!" says the Belgian kid.

"Hi, Andy," says Johnny, feeling extremely self-conscious.

"Told you we meet." Andy takes a seat alongside his new pal.

Johnny is happy to see a friendly face, but he's in no mood to chat. Andy, on the other hand, is brimming with enthusiasm.

"What did you do today?" he asks, slowly and definitely, as though he has rehearsed this particular piece of English ad nauseam in school.

"Nothing much. The cathedral. Walking around."

"You like?"

"Sure I like. The Belgians have been very good to us. Better than the Parisians were. I guess there are so many different people in Europe. It's a bit like America — Texas is very different from New York. Florida is very different from California. You've never been to the US, right?"

"To America? No."

"It's huge." Johnny notices Andy doesn't yet know the word. "Big.

And kind of like Belgium, we have very different people all living in the same country. Hell, Texas is bigger than France."

"Good?"

"Sometimes. It sucks, too. I like Belgium."

"I hate Belgium."

"We'll swap. I'll live in Ieper, you live in Austin."

Andy smiles.

"High school particularly sucks," says Johnny Hazzard, remembering Natalie Perez the cheerleader, Mr. Legwinski, the tedium of tests, and the monotony of math.

"School sucks here."

"School sucks everywhere," concludes Johnny.

The wind picks up, the trees sway. The weather takes a sinister turn. Both Johnny and Andy look around. The gust goes on for a good ten seconds.

"Skating in Ieper is shit, huh?" asks Johnny.

Andy nods. Johnny begins feeling sorry for the kid, which he doesn't really want to do. But he can't help feeling that he's been lucky growing up in a city, especially one as chilled out as Austin.

Johnny deduces that small-town life, wherever the hell the small town is, must offer less variety and therefore less experience. Johnny can skate in so many different places. He will get into trouble at many of them, granted, but at least he can do it. Andy is limited. That's it — he's limited. He has little choice.

"But you have good friends, right?"

"I have friends, yes, of course. A few skaters. We are good friends."

Johnny thinks back to Kade, David, and Jack.

"Girlfriend?" asks Johnny.

"No. I had but we . . . how do you say . . ."

"Broke up?"

"Yes, broke up. Like two weeks ago."

Johnny tries to imagine the twelve-year-old's relationship and how it must have been. He struggles.

"Hey, you want to e-mail?" asks Andy.

Johnny is happy to swap addresses. He wants to keep in touch, although he worries that the kid, being three years younger, won't quite be on his level. Then he remembers his own age gap with January. Then he justifies it to himself, telling himself that twelve is nothing like fifteen. Then he finishes writing johnnyhazzard@gmail.com on a scrap of paper and hands it over.

"Cool," says the kid.

"Thanks," says Johnny Hazzard. "And thanks for showing me the skate spot yesterday. I was getting seriously bored."

Andy smiles. Johnny is not entirely sure if the kid has understood what he just said, but it doesn't matter. Andy smiles, stands, waves, and skates off down the tarmac path toward the Menin Gate. Every few seconds, he must again push himself along with his left foot. Johnny watches him go. He is filled with a sudden and odd sense of happiness. He has made friends with this Belgian — Flemish — boy. The boy has been generous and gracious and welcoming, and Johnny feels good about people. In a town that has shown him the worst of what humans are capable of, he suddenly feels upbeat and optimistic. It's the same kind of feeling you might get on New Year's Day. That feeling of moving forward, of freshness, of newness, and, above all, of optimism.

* * *

That evening, all previous records are broken and Johnny and Lydia go out together for a second consecutive time.

Things are more relaxed now. Less has to be said. The air has been cleared, and the four-letter word has finally been confronted and talked about openly. It is time to move on and enjoy each other's company without burden or fear.

So after dinner on their final night in Ieper, brother and sister head to Vismarkt, a pedestrianized road that hosts the town's hot nightspots. There are around five bars in the area, most of them doing a roaring trade on this particular night, filled, it seems, primarily with local teens, twentysomethings, and thirtysomethings out for a good time.

There is something of the time warp about one particular bar. The music is stuck in the last decade, and the one before that. The decor and lights look new and sparkling but woefully corny. There is only one thing worse than too many mirrors, and that's too many mirror balls.

Johnny and Lydia are not in the mood for drinking tonight. They stick to the softies and conversation is thin. The music is too loud, and there is too much going on around to watch. Lydia leans in and talks directly into her brother's ear.

"You were cool last night. Thanks," she says.

"What?" says Johnny, unable to hear her properly. Like a dodgy cellphone conversation, he only caught a few sounds of the sentence.

"I said you were good to talk to."

"I can't hear you."

"Doesn't matter."

Lydia will never repeat this compliment.

A new track begins, and the music gets louder. It's Swedish rock masters Europe, and their seminal "The Final Countdown." This is epic guitar-riffing, drum-thumping, headbanging rock.

More and more people arrive. The chilled-out doorman doesn't question anybody. The pedestrianized road outside is filled with smiling faces and people hopping from bar to bar. The music is blaring. Johnny cannot hear his sister speak; he can only hear the music. The lights flash quicker. There are so many lights, so many colors. The only two black people in the club dance on the stage, watched by the others as though they were objects of display in a museum of people. Cute girls in sexy clothes mill by the bar, chatted up by oafs. Two boys sing lyrics of the song to each other. The club is suddenly tiny, and the music deafening, and Johnny needs to escape. He tells Lydia he's not feeling so good, and that he wants to head back.

The brief night out is ended. Lydia asks Johnny what's wrong, but he just says he's tired. He does not know himself what is wrong. They return to the hotel, but Johnny does not retire to his room. Once Lydia is in hers, Johnny goes for a late-night walk. He does not feel scared, wandering around alone at night in a town he does not know, but he is aware that his father would be furious if he knew. He walks toward the train station and finds a sign for the Lille Gate Ramparts Cemetery.

The cemetery is small and, like all the British Commonwealth cemeteries, well kept and tidy. It looks onto the moat. There are almost two hundred people buried here — British, Canadian, Australian, New Zealanders (including Maori), and five unknown.

The full moon reflects off the moat and the headstones, making it only half-dark. Johnny walks among the gravestones, thinking about the entire trip, thinking about Tyne Cot, about remembering the future, and about his girlfriend.

As he did at the German cemetery, and also at Tyne Cot, Johnny takes a look at the visitors' book. He is curious as to who has been here, what they thought, why they were moved to write.

We will remember, for those who do not are destined to repeat it.

And beneath it —

In memory of the brave lions, led to war by cowardly pillocks — a visitor from Lancashire

Johnny doesn't know where Lancashire is, other than somewhere in England, but he likes the sentiment.

The wind picks up. A cemetery at midnight ought to be frightening, but Johnny Hazzard is at peace. This is not a teen horror movie; these are not haunted graves. They feel too real to Johnny to be scary; they feel like people. He walks up to the edge of the cemetery, looks out at the water, and spots a nocturnal fisherman waiting for his catch of the day. Johnny feels a sense of gratitude toward Belgium, and Ieper in particular. He cannot exactly pinpoint why. He feels lucky, and he feels strong, and he feels different.

TWENTY-THREE

"I have so much to tell you," Johnny Hazzard tells his girlfriend on the telephone. "So much has happened." He calls January within three minutes of walking through the apartment door, taking the cordless phone to his bedroom and lying back on the bed, his eyes closed, savoring January's voice.

"You'd better not have met someone new," she jokes.

Johnny begins to tell January sketchy details about the trip. He tells her about In Flanders Field Museum, and the tour of the cemeteries and battlefields. She seems interested but doesn't say very much. Johnny takes her quietness as a sign of exhaustion rather than apathy. When it comes to the end of the conversation, Johnny is reluctant to hang up. He wants to still hear her voice, every last syllable and sound. He has not heard it for so long, it has been nothing short of torturous. It helps that January's is a particularly sweet and melodic voice. Prior to the most long-winded and stretched good-bye in Johnny's telephonic history, it is agreed that January will come over to Maida Vale first in order to meet, for the very first time, the Hazzard clan. Johnny knows full well that, if she is given any advance warning, Siska would make an enormous fuss, but Johnny doesn't want January's arrival at the flat to turn into a state procession with lavish buffet, bunting, and Shostakovich's *Waltz 2 from Jazz Suite* playing tenderly in the background. January has already told him she will be nervous, especially about meeting Lydia, so Johnny is determined to keep the encounter low-key.

At about eleven thirty, the intercom buzzer goes off. Johnny leaps up and grabs the phone from Siska, almost knocking her off her feet.

"Dahling, where's the fire?"

Johnny buzzes January in.

There is a knock on the door a minute later. Johnny opens it immediately. He is only two steps away from his girlfriend, but he runs into her arms. Standing in the hallway, they embrace for what feels like an eternity, but is actually sixty seconds. January is a little tearful. Johnny is pure happiness. He looks at their reflection in the mirror. It is a wonderful sight. He strokes her hair a little and then they kiss. January keeps her eyes open and sees the snog rebounding off all the mirrors. It makes her feel awkward. She pulls back.

"I missed you so much," he tells her.

"So did I," she tells him.

They hug again.

"You smell good," he tells her. She smiles coyly. This is a new perfume, and it has done the trick.

"Wanna meet the family?"

"They're all in?"

"Yep. All three. Come on."

January winces. Johnny holds her hand and walks into the apartment. For the first time he can remember, it is he who is leading January by the hand, and not the other way around. He guides her into the kitchen, where Siska is reading a newspaper and Mr. Hazzard is making an omelette.

"Dad, Siska, this is January."

Siska looks up from the newspaper, her reading glasses on the verge of sliding off her nose. She looks at January over the glasses, and her face breaks into a broad, enthusiastic smile. If Johnny were sitting down, he'd be on the edge of his seat.

"It is a pleasure to meet you, dahling," she says, standing up and shaking January's hand.

"Nice to meet you, too. Johnny's told me a lot about you."

"It's all lies, dahling, ignore him!"

Johnny is relieved that Siska's opening remarks have avoided the inappropriate or the downright ridiculous. Mr. Hazzard, who has been assessing January during the course of her introduction to Siska, leaves the omelette, and keeps a hold on the wooden spoon as he comes over to shake hands.

"Good to meet you, January. How are you?"

"Good to meet you, Mr. Hazzard. I'm good, thanks."

Johnny wants to tell his father to put the wooden spoon down, but he doesn't want to light any kind of fuse that might kick off a family dispute.

January notices some of Siska's works dotted about the kitchen.

"Oh, what lovely paintings you have," says January. Johnny knows she's pretending not to know they're Siska's.

"Dahling, you don't have to kiss bum in this house."

Johnny feels immediately sorry for his girlfriend. January laughs, partly in shock at the wonderful frankness, partly in embarrassment that her ploy has been thwarted. She sits at the kitchen table, beside Johnny and opposite Siska.

"Johnny, you should have told me January was coming. I would have prepared something for her," says Siska.

"That's why I didn't tell you."

Siska scoffs and embarks on some small talk with January about where she lives, what she'll do at university, and her travels. As Mr. Hazzard goes to make a quick phone call, Lydia walks in.

Standing behind January, she gives her brother's girlfriend a quick once-over. Girls are remarkably quick at the once-over — they can analyze style, color coordination, skin, and general demeanor in less than ten seconds. That is a formidable feat, as commendable as running the one-hundred-meter dash (an achievement that takes around the same time). Straight men are wholly incapable of the quick once-over, and more often than not they will make completely ludicrous judgments based on frivolous factors. Not so the ladies. Once Lydia has deduced that January is a well-dressed and fashion-conscious girl, she makes her presence known.

"Hey, you must be January," she says sweetly. January turns her head around and stands. Lydia has kept the upper hand by forcing January to do the twisting and turning and standing.

A visibly nervous January starts by saying, "Nice to meet you, Johnny's told —"

"— you so much about me? Don't believe him, he's biased," Lydia says, with a smile. January laughs a little, politely. Johnny is pleased with how things are going so far. He is confident Lydia won't let him down.

"So how are you doing?" Lydia asks January.

"Good, thanks. Just got back from a family holiday."

"Ah, that makes two of us. How was yours?"

"Hmm, well, you know. It was okay — typical family holiday. Annoying younger brother . . ."

"How interesting . . . same here," says Lydia, poking Johnny in the arm. He smiles.

Siska watches the whole of this exchange like a birdwatcher waiting for a glimpse of the kestrel. She's doing everything but taking notes, although inside her head there is probably a small army of inspiration sergeants who are furiously scribbling down every detail of this human interaction.

"Johnny tells me you're studying in Austin?" January asks, nerves subsiding a little.

"Yeah. And you're about to go to school, right?"

"University, yep. All a bit nerve-racking," she says, following it with a nervous giggle.

"Sorry, *university*. We call it school back home. *University* is better. I'm sure you'll be cool," says Lydia. Johnny, the silent witness here, is proud of his sister. He would have expected nothing less from the sensible, reasonable Lydia, but he knows that beneath the sweetness, there is still a lingering fear that her brother is being shafted by the older woman.

The polite banter continues. Lydia tells January about the London nightspots she has been to, none of which January has heard of. Lydia, although only a year older than his girlfriend, looks at least three years older. *January is a youthful-looking eighteen,* he decides for the first time.

"Well, I'm not sure I'll come to London for the whole of next summer," Lydia says. "I think I want to check out more of Europe. Scandinavia, Italy, maybe Prague."

"Oh, yeah, if you get the chance, do it. It'll be such an eye-opener," says January, as enthusiastic as ever about traveling.

"Yeah, we've been pretty lucky. We've seen a lot of places," says Lydia, with a hint of "I have seen the world, too, you know" lacing her words.

And then the smoke starts billowing from the frying pan, where Mr. Hazzard's omelette has gone from being cooked, to singed, to downright charred. Siska is disturbed from her observations, and starts flapping.

"Oh, the bas-tard!" she shouts, running over to the stove and turning off the gas.

The blackened omelette sits in the middle of the pan, looking like the remains of a funeral pyre. The deafening smoke alarm starts wailing. Mr. Hazzard rushes in, full of apology.

"Dad, for Christ's sake," says Johnny, embarrassed at the chaos.

"It wasn't my fault, you were supposed to keep an eye on it," he says, pointing at Siska, who is wafting the smoke with a tea towel as the whiny smoke alarm keeps on beeping. Johnny grabs the newspaper and helps waft.

Lydia sits at the kitchen table and, accustomed to the carnage, begins calmly reading the Culture supplement of the newspaper. January doesn't really know where to look or if it's okay to laugh or not, so she just stands and watches, trying not to smile.

"Four eggs ruined," says Siska. "And expensive eggs!"

"Well, I didn't tell you to buy organic, free-range, corn-diet, vitamin goddamned C eggs."

"They are natural. Not the crap you buy when I leave you shopping."

Johnny can sense a weekly tiff coming on. He nods to January to get up, and they exit and seek sanctuary in his bedroom. Siska carries on wafting the smoke, but the alarm won't let up. The omelette is tossed into the trash, smoke still rising from it.

Johnny lies back on his bed. January sits at the desk, turns the chair around, and faces him.

"Well? Fucking lunatics, huh?" says Johnny.

"No more lunatic than my family."

"Yeah, when am *I* gonna meet the parents?"

"Soon."

January breaks eye contact, and looks at Johnny's book collection.

"When, though?" he asks, the urgency blatant.

"Johnny, when I'm ready, I'll tell you. You don't have to keep on asking the whole time. I haven't forgotten."

Johnny is a little taken aback by her abruptness.

"Hey, it's cool," he starts. "I mean, you're worried about what they'll think, I understand that."

"I don't really care what other people think. The older you get, the less you care," she says, still avoiding eye contact with her boyfriend. For the first time since they've been an item, Johnny feels really young.

January goes on. "But sure, they're going to wonder why I don't date someone my own age. That's just parents for you."

"And friends, huh?"

"What do you mean?" She looks at him at last.

"Your friends all think I'm eighteen, don't they? They have no idea I'm three years younger."

"Yeah, I guess they do. We haven't talked much about it. They think you're friendly and clever and fun. That's the important thing."

"But if you're not honest with them, isn't it like you're lying?"

There is a pause. January breathes in deeply. "They wouldn't understand," she says. But right now, Johnny doesn't understand how the age gap is such a huge issue that it would prevent January from telling her friends. *It's only three damn years*, he thinks. He does, however, respect January's wishes and prefers not to push the matter just yet.

"I thought about you all the time," he tells her. "It's the first time that I've done that. Thought about one person so much. You were stuck in my head."

January smirks. "Wow, I've always wanted to be stuck in a boy's head. I thought about you, too. I had some great memories to keep me going, though."

"Same here. It was horrible not having you right there. But I mean a lot of the trip was great. So much cool stuff happened, I got to tell you about it. It taught me so much."

January smiles.

"I bought you some chocolate."

Johnny picks up an expensive-looking store bag from the floor beside his bed and takes out a box of plush Pierre Marcolini, the world champion chocolatiers.

"These are shit hot. Twice world champions. Nothing but the best. Don't eat them all at once," he says, resting the box on her lap. She kisses him on the lips and hugs him. He returns to the bed and feels very proud of himself.

"Well, come on, then," he says, patting the mattress beside him. January comes on over and lies next to him. She opens the box of chocolates and tries one.

"Oh my God!"

"They're good, huh?" Johnny asks.

"They're not good, they're amazing. Have one."

Johnny obliges.

They eat, and there is silence. Johnny strokes his girlfriend's hair, and blows into her ear. She shuffles her head away slightly. It's a diminutive movement, but a definite one nonetheless. Unperturbed, Johnny goes in for some more ear action. He knows this drives her crazy. It's the key; once Johnny does "the ear thing," January melts. It's his party piece, his signature move, a movement of sexual savoir faire that makes Johnny beam — he feels good about making his girlfriend feel good. So he starts to kiss her right ear, still stroking her hair. His tongue makes an appearance, licking the lobe. His hot breath warms her ear. January shuffles her head away — no subtlety this time. Johnny is left, tongue in midair, feeling like a prize chump. The pride of a few moments ago disintegrates.

"What's wrong?" he asks her.

"Nothing — you know I love that. It's just . . . here . . . with your dad and Siska and stuff. It doesn't feel right. I can't relax."

"They won't come in," he says.

"We can't do it here," she says, adamant. She gets up off the bed and returns to the desk. Johnny is embarrassed. He feels like he's just said and done something mind-blowingly stupid — something really *young*. One half of his brain tells him he has been an absolute fool, the other half that he's done nothing bad at all, merely shown his girlfriend some affection. He feels small, and while this is not a new sensation, it's not one January has provoked before.

"I'm sorry," he says. "I just thought we could . . . you know, cuddle up." His face has gone bright red. Johnny feels anything he says is the wrong thing to say. He feels as daft as he did when he had a fit of giggles at a great-aunt's funeral.

"It's okay," she says. She resumes eye contact, and her face is a picture of sympathy. January's face, Johnny fathoms, can jump from one mood to the other in a split second.

"It's just happened to me before," she says. "Someone's walked in and it's just been really embarrassing."

"I'm sorry," he repeats.

"It's okay — I don't expect you to know this kind of thing."

If he felt small before, now he feels microscopic. Just because it hasn't happened to him doesn't mean he is completely ignorant or devoid of imagination. He feels an urge to tell her this, but at the same time, he feels a stronger urge not to rock the boat. Instead, he has an idea:

"Well, why don't we meet at your place when your folks are out?"

"When?"

"Whenever you like," he says.

"Okay, whenever you want to come."

January starts examining the chocolates and slots another into her mouth. Johnny is aggravated by the lack of commitment. She's taking blasé to a whole new dimension.

"What about tomorrow lunch?" Johnny suggests.

"Yeah, okay. Sounds cool," she says.

Johnny smiles quickly but he is awkward, stiff, unrelaxed. Whereas before he could confidently look into January's eyes and feel like Mr. H-O-T, today he steals a glance at them and feels intrusive. The worst thing is that Johnny knows January has a point; he is not experienced in relationships, he does not know which feelings are normal and to-be-expected. He only knows which ones feel right, and which do not. Is it normal for his girlfriend to be sending out such mixed messages on their first encounter after ten days apart? Is it normal for a girl not to feel turned on after being away from her boyfriend for so long? Because it sure as hell doesn't feel right.

TWENTY-FOUR

Girls love flowers.

Even if they cannot tell a lily from a freesia, it's the ancient romance of the gesture that makes it impossible not to smile when a girl is presented with a bouquet or a single red rose. Unless, that is, if the flowers are being used as a tool of appeasement to make up for the man's sins.

Johnny is on his way from Finsbury Park Tube to January's house when he spots a flower stall on the pavement. He decides it would be a very grown-up thing to buy some carnations.

January is home alone when Johnny arrives. Her hair is pulled back into a ponytail. Standing on the doormat, Johnny takes the flowers out from behind his back and offers them with a smile. Sure enough, January seems pleased to see them. She takes the flowers, allows Johnny in, shuts the front door, and gives him a hug.

"Thank you," she says. "No one's ever bought me flowers before."

Johnny is startled, and hugely pleased with himself. He's clearly more of a suave romantic than he thought he was.

January tells Johnny to make himself comfortable in the lounge while she puts the flowers in some water. Johnny sits on the couch and begins to take in his surroundings. The house is as pristine as an art gallery, as spotless as an operating theater, and nothing like either of the Hazzard abodes. There is an expensive-looking painting above the fireplace, and a recent photograph of the family on the mantelpiece. Johnny goes over to the framed picture and notices the resemblance between January and her mother. He immediately thinks how excellent it is that January will still be good-looking when she is in her late forties. This is something that has often worried him about the notion of long-term commitment — the girl losing all attractiveness and, indeed, him losing all attractiveness and proving to be a huge, ugly prune in his fifties. Speaking of which, January's father looks bland, neutral, and, Johnny is relieved to deduce, not remotely intimidating.

January returns with a carton of orange juice and some chunky sandwiches she has bought from a supermarket.

"Hope one of these is okay. Chicken or cheese?"

"Whatever. I don't mind," he says, meekly.

"Well, which do you prefer? Chicken, right?"

"No, I really don't mind. What do you want?"

"Don't worry about me, just make a decision. Chicken or cheese?"

"No, really —"

"I don't care," she says, dismissively.

"What's the cheese?"

"Cheddar."

"Oh. It's up to you," he says, feebly.

"Johnny! Make a decision!" She half shouts this. It's not clear if she's being cross or kidding.

"Chicken, then," he says sheepishly, feeling like the schoolboy who's just been sent to stand in the corner.

She gives him the sandwich and, as she sits next to him, Johnny cannot be sure but he thinks she rolls her eyes to the sky. He spends the next thirty seconds repeating the motion in his mind, trying to decide for sure if she did or didn't express her disdain with a flick of the eyeballs. It drives him crazy. Then the knowledge that he's overanalyzing the situation drives him crazier.

January flicks on the TV and puts a hand on Johnny's knee. So that's alright, then. She can't be irate if she's making bodily contact. For Johnny, this warm hand on this warm knee is all he needs — his hormones start preparing for rush hour. The TV is spewing out turgid daytime crap; January flicks through the channels while Johnny wolfs down his chicken sandwich. He's not all that hungry (the horniness has dealt with that) but he feels he should eat up.

Little is said over the lunch. Johnny is desperate to talk about his trip, but his mind has been overtaken with more urgent thoughts: Is January upset at him for some reason? Has he behaved like an immature, inexperienced fool? Why wouldn't she decide which sandwich to eat? But the horniness eclipses the worry — it always does — as Johnny puts his hand on January's knee and leans over for a kiss. It seems she is enjoying the snog, which puts Johnny's mind at rest. She isn't doing very much with her hands, leaving Johnny to rove her body and come to a neat rest at her breasts. He gives them a good squeeze. She gasps.

"Let's go upstairs," she says.

Johnny cracks a smile. *Fucking A*, he thinks.

January takes his hand and he follows her up the gloomy, dimly lit staircase. Lining the walls are family pictures. There seem to be more snaps of Doll than there are of January. For a brief moment, Johnny wonders if he should read something into the absence of January pictures. He figures they must be somewhere else in the house, wherever those baby pictures she showed him on Waterloo Bridge are.

Johnny enters January's bedroom with some trepidation. This is a significant step into uncharted territory: the first visit to the girlfriend's bedroom. Hell, a visit to any girl's bedroom is a big deal — back home there are some parents who won't allow boys into their daughters' rooms at all.

It is a low-maintenance, minimalist space, its prominent colors being white and sky blue. Johnny was expecting a darker bedroom. There are a couple of posters of bands Johnny hasn't heard of, and one wall is filled top to bottom with pictures. Johnny notices most of them seem to be from January's travels — there are lots of beaches. He sees photos of January in a bikini and loves what he sees — she looks ravishing, her curves in all the right places. The bookshelf is of a modest size and, on a quick scan, Johnny notices some Dickens, Austen, Adrian Mole, and Harry Potter. He realizes they haven't yet spoken seriously about their literary habits.

While Johnny admires the décor, January whips her sweater off. There is nothing arousing about this rapid disrobement. In actuality, there is nothing less sexy than matter-of-fact clothes removal. It should be slow, sensuous, and, ideally, involve the partner. But January is not wearing a bra underneath; Johnny sees his semi-naked girlfriend and gets an almost instant hard-on. He holds her waist and kisses her lips. He can taste remnants of her fruity lip balm, and can smell that wonderful perfume. January seems impetuous today, almost desperate to get on with it. She tugs at his shirt. He gets the hint and removes it.

They stay standing, kissing with more speed. Johnny undoes the top button of his jeans. The elastic of his boxers peeps out of the top of his jeans, and January can now feel his hard-on against her thigh. The topless couple fall back on to the bed. Johnny looks at his girlfriend's face, intensely but warmly studying her eyes, her perfect nose, her fulsome lips. He takes in her gorgeousness, and in so doing almost detaches himself from the situation. It takes January's wandering hand to remind him that the sex is real, and January is his.

Today's sex is more snappy, more urgent. January offers Johnny a condom and he quickly puts it on. The rush is infectious. Maybe it's because they haven't been close for so long. As Johnny begins, January does the ear thing to him. She really goes for it, and Johnny's whole body feels the effects. So high is the voltage that the licking sets off, it feels as though he is about to explode.

But the ear thing is just about January's only contribution. Apart from some kissing, she seems very hands-off today. Johnny keeps on going, but he knows it's not as it was. In an effort to gets things going, he takes her hands but has no idea where to put them. Instead of getting the hint and doing something imaginative, she just returns her hands to her sides. Johnny looks at what he is fucking. It's like she's just *lying* there, doing her duty. She may as well be a blow-up doll for all the input she's giving. Johnny doesn't feel comfortable because it doesn't feel mutual.

Appallingly, shamefully, weakly, he goes soft and has to move off his girlfriend. This is the stuff of nightmares. He has panicked in the past about not being able to perform and here, on only his second go, it's happening. Or, rather, not happening.

"Sorry," he says, looking at anything but her face.

"It's okay. What happened?"

"I mean, you don't seem to be into it?" he half asks, surprising himself with the bluntness and honesty of the reply. He can feel his face going red and very, very warm.

"I'm into it. Of course I am."

"Not like last time," he says.

"Last time was the first time — it was special. Don't worry — I'm into it."

Johnny is far from convinced. He feels as though he's let her down, but he knows it's not his fault. It just wasn't feeling right.

January sits up and begins rubbing Johnny's shoulder, while her other hand strokes his back teasingly. She floats her fingers up and down his spine, half caressing, half tickling. This is more like it. As she sucks and bites on his neck, producing a tiny red love bite, he is overcome at last and turns to kiss her. This sends Johnny's hormones back into the rush hour, and his dick follows suit.

January lies back on the bed and takes her hair out of its ponytail. As Johnny watches her shake her head, the blond falling into place messily, he is turned on some more, and resumes the lovemaking. He is determined not to go soft ever again, so he works hard and fast. As he nears the end, his mouth opens, his eyes close, and his head points to the ceiling. January's hands run across his chest, almost scratching him, and he lets out a quiet, climactic yelp.

Johnny rolls off and, gasping for breath, asks, "Did you . . . ?"

"No," she replies.

He begins to feel in between her legs, a naughty grin forming across his face.

"It's okay," she says sweetly. "I'm just happy that I made you, y'know."

Johnny believes it. *How selfless*, he thinks to himself. *Completely awesome!*

They lie naked in each other's arms without saying a word for a few minutes. There is no corny love song coming from next door this time. There is just the mundane noise of city life — planes overhead, cars nearby, church bells far off.

Johnny closes his eyes. He wants to savor moments like this. He knows the holiday won't last much longer, and he wants to remember forever what January smells like, what her skin feels like. He wants to form a little sensory time capsule in his head to take back to Austin with him.

"This feels good," he says, almost as a whisper.

"Glad you think so," she says.

Johnny opens his eyes and looks about the room. He notices that they kept the curtains open; eagle-eyed perverts in the nearby apartment block could easily have enjoyed the show. This whole situation still does not feel real. It's like a wonderful movie, and Johnny still cannot believe he is the star.

"So you survived Yorkshire, it seems," says Johnny, cheerfully.

"I certainly did. It was a bit touch and go at times, though. I was looking into buying a train ticket and coming home by myself."

"What stopped you?"

"Would have cost me seventy quid. If I had the money I'd have left the brat and Mum and Dad and come back to London, though. No question."

Another lengthy silence follows. Two, maybe three minutes. Johnny feels sympathy for January's gruesome summer break, but he doesn't understand why she still hasn't asked him about Belgium. During the phone call from Ieper and the one he made on his arrival back home he made clear that a lot had happened, and it changed a lot of his opinions. She knows it was a significant holiday, but doesn't seem to care all that much about it. So, encouraged by the invincibility a decent shag bestows upon the shagger, Johnny comes out with, "Aren't you gonna ask me about Belgium?"

"Sorry, babe," she says, looking up at him. "But you told me a lot on the phone, right?"

"Well, yeah, but a lot of shit happened. I mean the war graves. They were . . . they were just out of this world. Completely blew my mind."

"Cool," she says.

Cool, Johnny thinks to himself, *Cool? It wasn't cool! It was much, much more than cool. Just ask me about it.*

"Made me really think about Iraq, you know," is what he says. "The weird similarity between the two wars."

"Yeah, I guess power is the thing. It's always the thing, right?"

"Yeah, yeah exactly," says Johnny, enthusiasm growing. "It's exactly the thing. Those soldiers in the First World War had no fucking idea what they were fighting for. And the Last Post, January — the Last Post was hard. The bugle plays, and all these people are gathered under this archway, and all the names of the unburied dead engraved into the walls, and I cried. I cried. I couldn't help it."

She squeezes his hand.

"It's okay," she says.

Johnny Hazzard knows it's okay. That's not the issue here. He wants to share what he has learned.

"So do you have the travel bug now?" she asks him.

"Kinda. No, not really. I mean I've always traveled, you know? Most my life I've been to a new country each year. I've never had to think about being into travel, it's always just kind of happened." Johnny is proud of this fact, and it's one he hasn't bragged about until now.

"I don't mean holidays. I mean *traveling*," she says.

"Well, what's the difference?"

"The difference is huge. One is something you do to chill out, to get away from it all. The other is something you do to get right into the middle of it all, to learn. That's what traveling is."

"Can't a holiday also be traveling, though? I mean, isn't that what I did in Belgium? Go on a holiday and get right into the middle of it all? Because that's how it felt." Johnny is careful not to sound aggressive, although he has conviction in what he is saying here. Whether it counts as traveling or holidaying, he cannot say, but that he has had new experiences is undeniable.

"It's about the mind-set, I guess. When I went to Yorkshire, it was a family holiday. I knew it was going to be difficult, and annoying, and probably very boring. When I left for Asia I knew I was going to learn."

"Okay, so I thought Belgium was going to be a boring vacation, but it wasn't. I mean, parts of it were. But really, January, it changed me. I know that sounds like corny bullshit but it did. I mean, Ieper did. Or maybe it didn't change me, but it made me realize a few things. And it made me more convinced than ever about war."

January hears what Johnny says, but she doesn't listen. She accepts that he has learned, and that the holiday turned into something more, but to her it's all about the *nature* of the trip. She says nothing. She leaves an uneasy, heavy quiet just hanging in the air. Johnny does not get why she can't just accept that his form of travel is just as worthy as hers. It annoys him, but he won't get into a fight about it. All that a quarrel will do is destroy the equilibrium his relationship has maintained since day one. That balance must not be disturbed, at any cost.

Instead, they fall asleep. This is a scene of perfect stillness. The summer air is dense, the curtains still, the two beautiful, naked bodies on the bed still but for their breathing chests. Johnny awakes a half hour later to see his girlfriend in a heavy slumber, her face a couple of inches from his. It is something quite special to wake up and see your girlfriend's face before you see anything else. It is something very special when it happens for the first time. Johnny bites his lip, and grins, and breathes in deeply. This is as good as it gets.

January does not wake for another hour or so, during which time Johnny is content keeping absolutely still and just watching her sleep. She looks so peaceful. But thoughts bang away at Johnny's head relentlessly. Something about January remains pricklier than before. He is not beginning to regret going away to Belgium, but he is beginning to believe it may have, in some strange way, driven a small wedge between them. Clarity and openness, two facets that drove the relationship before Belgium, are now lacking, and this has become a source of unbridled frustration for Johnny Hazzard.

When January awakes, she is worried about the time. "My dad gets back in half an hour," she says, busily putting her clothes back on. Johnny follows her lead.

"But so what? I mean, can't I just meet him today?"

"It'll be better if it's planned," she says. "You know, like when I met your family."

"We can make it dinner or something," he says, optimistically. A proper, sit-down, three-course dinner. That sounds like a great idea to Johnny.

In the hallway, moments before she opens the front door, January has an idea. "Shall we meet up central again? We've not done that in a while."

"Sure, wanna skate?"

"No, I was thinking more like dinner, maybe? I know a great restaurant."

"Sure, that's cool. With your parents?"

"No, just the two of us."

This sounds romantic. Johnny likes it.

"Okay, great. When?"

"Friday?"

"That's like three days away," he says, hoping she'll change her plans and bring the date forward. January explains that she can't meet before — she's having a "girls' night out," a birthday dinner, and shopping with Mum. Johnny concedes.

"It's a date," he says, before kissing her on the lips. "Call me with the details, okay?"

"I will," she says. Johnny wonders if she really will call. Suddenly matters seem less certain, and it feels as though the lens has gone out of focus.

TWENTY-FIVE

Some evenings, you go to half effort. You spend three minutes deciding what to wear instead of six. You consider a shave, but conclude that the growth isn't *that* bad. You notice that your shoes aren't pristine, but you haven't left enough time for a proper shine, so you leave them as they are. You don't spend quite as long styling your hair. These are the hallmarks of a half-effort evening.

Despite his desperation to pull and to shag, Johnny Hazzard once was a master of the half-effort evening, because:

a) There just did not seem any point — he never got lucky.
b) Skatewear was infinitely more comfortable.

Not anymore. This summer's events have seen him elevate his game to the status of full effort. And this evening is a case of double full effort: no skate clothes tonight, but an ironed black shirt instead — rather a tasty one of smooth, almost velvety texture.

The hair is carefully crafted into the "just got out of bed" look using a little bit of wax and a vatload of patience. The dark brown, thin corduroy pants are new and a tad baggy, but smart nonetheless. The shoes are trendy enough to look like slippers. The aftershave is sharp, but not unsubtle. Johnny Hazzard doesn't know why, but he has to go to extra special effort tonight. It's the sort of inexplicable hunch that hits you without warning in a second and worries you for hours. He needs to impress her tonight; he needs to remind her he's fully capable of behaving beyond his years. And that starts with doubling his effort.

The West End restaurant is heaving. It is nine o'clock and it could be downtown Madrid. In fact, the restaurant proudly claims to have a sister in the Spanish capital. The bar is small and crammed. From there you can see out onto the vast dining area, where round tables are just a few centimeters away from each other. They are all taken.

Waiting at the bar for a free table, Johnny strokes January's arm, an awkward smile on his face. She smiles back at him before taking his hand in hers. Sure, it's a romantic gesture, but it stops the stroking.

A minute or two later, a caricature waiter approaches (beer belly, bulbous nose, bushy mustache, yesterday's clothes). He shows Johnny and January to their table, in the middle of the room, surrounded by diners and, shortly, by dancers, too. The stage is empty, but an assortment of Spanish tunes, most of them containing Spanish guitars, fills the room. In between the tracks, the garbled dialogue of Spanish, English, French, and a few other, unidentifiable languages can be heard, like a shortwave radio station that hasn't quite been tuned in.

"Good choice," says Johnny Hazzard.

"Thanks. I came here a few times before I went traveling. I love it here. My dad loves it, too."

And Johnny Hazzard sips his table water, a niggling sense of frustration creeping over him. *Why does traveling come into everything? Is it to rub it in that I haven't seen the fucking planet?* he thinks.

"Cool," is what he says. *Cool* is what we all say.

Johnny recounts some more stories of the Belgian holiday. January is interested — but not fascinated. Johnny Hazzard is no longer new. He is not a first experience, a breath of fresh air.

The caricature waiter comes to take the order. After asking for an array of tapas, Johnny asks for a bottle of house red to go with them.

"You have proof of age?" comes the reply.

"Actually, no," Johnny admits, sheepishly.

January flashes her International Youth card — the one she uses to buy budget plane tickets while traveling — but the waiter is adamant.

"You *both* have to be over eighteen. No wine, sorry."

"But I *am* eighteen," pleads Johnny, believing it himself for a few seconds. The waiter couldn't give a damn — he's on to the next table.

It's like he could be back in Austin. He is reminded of the life he hoped was a bygone era.

"Don't worry," January says. "He's a jerk. I'm not in the mood for drinking, anyway." She looks at him with precisely the kind of sympathetic smile that makes her so easy to like, so easy to look at. The waiter brings a bottle of sparkling mineral water. Conversation is less verbose than before. Johnny thinks this is just what happens after the initial enthusiasm of the first few weeks. There's no need to be talking nonstop because you feel comfortable in each other's presence. And besides, they know each other so well now that sometimes words are surplus to requirements. A slight change in facial expression, or shift in the chair, will convey everything that needs to be conveyed.

The lights dim. Johnny notices the candle on his and January's table. The room takes on an almost mystical ambience. The little flames flicker on the dozens of round tables and the dark velvet drapes on the walls take on a slightly sinister air. A scene is being set. The crowd quiets down. Large tables of Spanish families belt up with anticipation. Couples turn their gaze from each other to the empty stage. A spotlight switches on and lights an empty circle on the stage. An old man, from one of the families, starts clapping a quick rhythm. Johnny gives January a bemused look. She turns her seat around to

299

face the stage properly. A muffled Spanish guitar begins, somewhere offstage. Clapping accompanies it. Suddenly, a young man — only a little older than January — appears from behind the curtain and takes his place in the spotlight. There's a smattering of applause — regulars who know the score. The dancer is soon joined by the guitarist and a female dancer — the clapper. The musician takes his seat at the back of the stage while the male dancer takes the attention. He's an androgynous sort of pretty that could get him into trouble. He starts slowly, stamping the stage and clapping with a quiet strength. The buildup is slow and calculated, careful and precise. The quiet strength turns to loud, clipped ferocity. Johnny and January are transfixed. Johnny slips a hand underneath the table and tries to find his girlfriend's. He brushes her knee. A shot of human electricity runs up through him. He finds her fingers and grips them tight. Without turning around, January slips her hand into his, resting them both on her knee. Johnny Hazzard doesn't like the casual, laid-back approach. He still wants her to turn around and catch his eye every time she clasps his hand.

The dancer, meanwhile, is approaching a speedy climax. The old Spanish diner who began clapping before stands up and takes to the dance floor. He's all of sixty, giving it as much gusto as the androgynous boy. He's dancing like nobody's looking. Androgynous boy doesn't flinch, though. He's concentrating on his own world of the stamping and clapping, of the bedazzling flamenco. As is Johnny Hazzard, hypnotized by the noise and swirl of the spectacle. The woman dancer, who until now has been accompanying with claps and piercing eyes, joins the androgynous boy in a kind of sexually charged dancing duel.

There's sex, there's sexiness, and there's speed all dissolving into one alluring experience. Johnny and January are gripped. He tightens his hold on her hand as the dancers approach the ultimate climax. The dance has been going on some five minutes. The old Spanish diner is joined by a couple of women in their forties. He carries on dancing like the disco is about to close and the women compete for his attention. Johnny lets January's hand go and opens the sparkling mineral water. The bubbles fire up to the top with the same sense of urgency as the dancers all around. The room feels smaller, more compact, and suddenly oppressive. The dark velvet drapes feel like they're closing in on the fifteen-year-old. Johnny can only see one thing truly clearly, and that's the flamenco.

As he sips his water, Johnny Hazzard begins smiling. He remembers then and there, as the flamenco hits its high-speed and floor-shattering crescendo, that this summer has been the first time he's knowingly been happy. He has known happiness and what it means. And he knows this same happiness, the one he has just gotten acquainted with and begun to understand — that same happiness will soon be pissing off to find another young mind to deceive. Because although he denies it now, he knows January's warmth has chilled. This nugget of knowledge squeezes into Johnny's mind. But this is not the night, and now is not the time. It is only the time to savor not sour, relish not reflect. Johnny reaches under the table and slowly, teasingly touches her fingers, links them with his and squeezes her hand. This lengthens and savors the experience as the diners break into a massive and heartfelt round of applause for the dancers.

The androgynous boy takes a brief bow. Stepping out of his dancing persona, he seems suddenly shy and embarrassed by the attention. The female dancer, on the other hand, is in her element, taking the plaudits like a grande dame of opera. They exit, followed by the guitarist. The show is over.

A selection of small dishes arrives. There's deep-fried calamari, potatoes with creamy garlic sauce, slices of sausage, prawns, tortilla, and bread. Johnny Hazzard has never eaten tapas before, but he doesn't tell January that. He doesn't want to feel inferior and he doesn't want to seem stupid. Perhaps a week or so ago he might have leveled with her, but not now. It would spoil the moment.

January talks about her flamenco lesson, which went badly awry. Seeing her face lit by the tiny candlelight makes him lose himself. His pupils dilate accordingly. Having wolfed down the food, January says she needs the lavatory. Johnny leans across the table and takes her hand. Somewhere inside him he knows it's the last time he'll get that electric shock of excitement rising through him from waistline to hairline. What's confusing is that he doesn't know how he can be so certain this is the final time. But he's never been more sure of anything since he fell in love.

TWENTY-SIX

Falling in love is an odd and, frankly, absurd concept. It might just as well be jumping, or leaping, or slipping. Falling is not a good thing. It breaks bones and hips. A fall from grace, falling asleep, falling foul, the fall guy, nuclear fallout — love is in some pretty dire company there. Johnny recalls some memorable epitaphs from Ieper — *He fell at Passendale* or *Dedicated to those who fell.* Johnny Hazzard is fed up with the term *falling in love.* He never *fell* in love. It was more conscious and deliberate than that. It felt right, and obvious, and inevitable, but it wasn't a fall. It was a calculated — if irrational — jump. And while the love goes on, there is no landing, bumpy or otherwise. Yet, walking back to Tottenham Court Road, Johnny's certainty that this is the last date is beginning to tear him up. He is silent.

"What's wrong? You've hardly said a word for ages," says January. They are holding hands.

Johnny says nothing. But all that he feels rolls down his cheek with speed in the form of a tear January cannot see.

The evening is still warm and muggy. The humidity feels stifling and intimidating, encroaching and suffocating. Johnny cannot understand. No more lip biting. Courage. Clarity. Johnny Hazzard goes for it.

"Is this it?"

"What?"

"Is this it?" repeats Johnny Hazzard.

"What do you mean?"

"Something's changed. Since the trip. Something's different."

"You think?"

"No, I know."

They arrive at the Tottenham Court Road Underground station, at the busy junction where Charing Cross Road, Oxford Street, and Tottenham Court Road all meet. There are an awful lot of drunken people about and they all seem to melt into a moving stream of rat-arsedness, like the long lines of neon and car headlights in London at Night postcards. The background noise is as intrusive as the heavy, sticky atmosphere. Johnny remembers the air feeling the same when he had sex for the first time. But standing on one of the busiest street corners in Europe, with his world collapsing around him, that evening feels like an age ago now.

"Am I wrong?" asks Johnny, the tear now dry.

January takes her time. She looks Johnny in the eye, then looks away, then back in his eye again.

"It's not really you. I mean, you've done nothing wrong. But you're right. I've changed my outlook a bit. I'm going to university soon."

"So? What's that got to do with anything? We said we'd keep it going. I'd be in Austin. I was going to come back to see you. We talked about that."

"Johnny, I'm going to be nineteen in a month. I've got a new life soon. It would be so unfair to you to keep things going when we're living in two different worlds."

"They're not different. Not unless you want them to be."

"Yes, they are."

"And what about the special relationship?"

"What's that got to do with it?"

"Not very much, it seems. You said this was different. You said this wasn't like a fling. It meant something more. You told me that."

305

"I meant it. At the time, anyway. It's just I realize now that I have to be realistic. I'm going to be doing the student thing."

"What's that supposed to mean?"

"It means what it means."

And Johnny is reminded of the several occasions when he hasn't really understood what January has said, but he's gone along with it, out of admiration and awe and respect more than anything. And, of course, the overriding, all-encompassing wish to have a girlfriend.

"Mate, she's not worth it! Plenty more pike in the pond!" shouts a man in a suit, walking with three other men in suits down Oxford Street. Johnny is more focused than ever. He begins the case for the defense:

"Okay, I'm going to sound like a dick, but you need to know. I've never felt like this before. I really, really like you. You know? It's like nothing else is important. You came along and everything is different. You changed me. And this is really ripping me to pieces. I don't know what to do next. I have no idea. But before, I knew that everything would be okay. I felt like I knew all the answers. Or if I didn't know them, then it didn't matter because I was just so sure. I was sure that we really liked each other. And being so sure meant that I didn't have to worry about anything. Haven't you ever felt like nothing else matters anymore, like this one thing takes over and it makes you so happy and all the shit just gets pushed away because you just feel so good about everything? You made me feel like that. Like anything was possible. And after all that, in the space of one evening, it's all different. I don't know what's going on anymore."

"That's the point, Johnny. You don't know. That's the difference. You're fantastic but there's this difference. I've done more. I've seen more. I'm really sorry if that pisses you off, but that's —"

"You've been to more places. That's different."

"I just think I'm going to university, you're going back to America, it's impractical. It would be great to take things further, but let's be realistic about it. It's not going to happen. I just think, with me going off to study, I ought to be honest with you."

"Why don't you do something because you want to instead of because you ought to?"

"I don't get you."

"No."

Johnny looks to the pavement. He's been trying so hard to control himself throughout the exchange, but the tears begin to edge out.

"Johnny, when you've had time to think things over, you'll understand that it's the only real option. If we lived closer maybe it would be different."

"Would it? You sure of that? Wouldn't you just move on to the next guy because you think you ought to? Because you think you should try a new fucking experience? That's what it's all about. Being there and doing that. Being able to tell your friends how much you've experienced —"

"That's not true and you know it's not —"

"What's next on the January axis? A Canadian? A Mexican? A Greek? You gotta get that experience under your belt. Don't let me stop you. I'm just a dumb American. What do I know about living a little? I'm Mr. Fat fucking narrow-minded fucking-loud cowboy Texan, aren't I?"

Tears roll down January's cheeks as her face slowly crumples. "You're just trying to upset me."

"I'm trying to upset *you*? Jesus. And you're the worldly-wise one around here. . . ."

"I never had you down for cruel, Johnny. But you're being a bastard," she says.

"I'm not the one doing the dumping here."

"I'm not dumping you. I'm just facing the reality of the situation."

"That's a new one. I'll remember that. Facing the reality of the —"

"Stop it," she says, raising the volume.

"Why should I?"

"You're making it harder for both of us."

"This wasn't my idea."

"I'm just being sensible, can't you see?"

"I'm just being in love." And Johnny breaks down; his mind has lost all power over his face. Tears stream down like they're racing one another to the chin. The mouth points southward, the nose is running. Johnny Hazzard is more vulnerable than he ever has been and January wants to hug him more than ever before, but she cannot. "I'm just being in love," he repeats. "That's all."

There is a moment, approximately as long as ten seconds, during which Johnny and January just look at each other. They have never looked more similar. Their hair unkempt, their cheeks rosy and tear-streamed, their hands in pockets, their eyes fixed on each other's. They are a strange kind of one. On the outsides, they are strikingly similar. On the insides, they are at polar opposites. Johnny cannot recall feeling so angry for a long time. Real anger. He's been hurt and with no good reason. January, on the other hand, is confused. To her this conclusion is the only logical solution. And yet all Johnny can do is pour contempt, insult, and misunderstanding all over her.

"Nothing I can say will make you change your mind, will it?" she asks.

He shakes his head.

"You'll have to believe me."

"How long you been thinking about calling it off, then?"

"Only since a couple of days ago. This isn't some huge plot. I never wanted to see you like this. Seeing you cry . . . I just, I want to give you a hug and tell you it'll be okay. That's what I really feel like."

Johnny doesn't flinch. He doesn't know what to say to that. Right now, he wants to hug her, too. But it would be a poisoned hug. There is no point.

"Is it because I'm too young?"

"No, you know it isn't. You're way beyond your years."

With an increasing desperation and speed, Johnny questions her further, desperately trying to think of the right question to ask, the right thing to say to find the solution to this devastating conundrum that has unraveled itself before him.

"Tell me what it is . . . what's wrong with me? Am I not good-looking enough for you? What have I done wrong? Is there something specific I've done wrong? I can change things. This doesn't have to end."

"No," she says, "you've done nothing wrong. You're just fine."

"I'd better go," says Johnny Hazzard. He thinks about giving her a kiss on the cheek, then decides not to. Instead, Johnny turns his back to her and heads to the Underground station staircase. As he reaches the second step, he can resist no longer: He turns around and sees the messy January. Her face is full of some kind of regret. Johnny sees that. He waves, turns back, and heads down the stairs.

Johnny keeps his head low, unable to stop the crying. He boards the train and opts to stand, head against the glass of the doors, tears against the cheek. He doesn't stop crying until he falls asleep that night, still dressed in his clothes. Curled up on the bed, shoes still on feet, Johnny Hazzard has never felt so alone. This low beats the darkest days of the first London trips. He thinks of his mother, alone in Austin. This makes him cry more. He thinks of Siska and all the nights she spent consoling him and reading the Belgian comic books. He thinks of Lydia and how she must have felt when she found out Jake had been cheating. And although it doesn't cross his mind, and he is completely unaware of it, in this state of curled-up grief, his body resembling an unborn baby in need of all the care the womb can give, in this baby state he is tasting adulthood. It is a story of suffering. It is not a story to tell the boys, it is not an episode of his summer he will be proud of, but it is the most triumphant. Yes, it's the most triumphant. But that doesn't change the fact that Johnny is fed up of London tears.

The following morning, Johnny awakes bright and early at nine thirty. Mr. Hazzard opens the door and, standing behind it out of view, he says,

"I've been given some free tickets for the opera tonight. If you wanna go with January, they're yours. If you wanna go with me and Siska, then that's a possibility. Anyway, I'll let you decide."

Johnny had, for the first twenty seconds of consciousness this morning, forgotten about the horrors of the night before. He is still fully dressed and his right cheek rests on the pillow, his stare on the wall directly in front of him. He begins crying again and tells his father he needs to be alone, that he and January are no longer together. About ten minutes later, Lydia walks in. She takes some nervous and tentative steps into the room and can clearly see Johnny's reddened face. She moves forward and sits on the end of his bed.

"Lydia, not now."

"Wait."

"Fuck off," he says.

"I know you're feeling like nothing could get worse, like this is the worst day of your life. I know you think you never want to meet another girl as long as you live. You're probably angry with her and yourself and you're definitely pissed at me, and that's cool. But trust me, you will get over her. She doesn't deserve you."

He says nothing. After a while, Lydia stands and leaves. Johnny wishes he could have hugged her. He feels closer to his sister than ever. But how is she right all the time? That is why Johnny cannot face his sister right now.

One o'clock. Johnny stays as he is. The crying is on and off. Like a wheel of misfortune, the feelings fluctuate between anger, embarrassment at being such an idiot to have fallen for her in the first place, and hurt. Most of all, hurt. This morning, love really does feel like a fall. A long and bruising one.

Mr. Hazzard decides to put a lunchtime phone meeting on hold and attempt to get through to his son. His costume doesn't help matters. Dressed in denim dungarees, an ancient white T-shirt, and the glasses that looked out-of-date in the Reagan era, he slowly creaks the door open and heads toward the bed, standing over Johnny. Mr. Hazzard's son is no longer crying, but he is still staring. Blankly. At the wall. The curtains are drawn and the room is stuffy.

"You know, Johnny, I'm really sorry."

Silence.

"Sometimes it helps to talk these things over."

More silence.

"I know where you're at. I mean I've been there. I remember my first split-up, in ninth grade. She was beautiful. Said I wasn't right for her. I can remember the night she broke it off. We were eating hot dogs, walking down East Sixth. It wasn't dark yet. She dumped me and I felt like someone had kicked me right in the stomach. No, I didn't feel like that — I felt like someone had taken my stomach away. It took me a few days to tell my buddies. I was so ashamed. My dad — your granddad — saw me crying in the yard. Told me if I didn't stop that he'd beat the crap out of me. So I stopped. But you know, it's okay to cry. It's good to cry. I have no problem with it at all. A few months after your mother and I divorced, I was driving —"

"Dad. Thanks for talking to me. I appreciate it. But I just want to be alone right now. Okay?"

Johnny can no longer take the pain of stories from yesteryear, told in the inimitable Mr. Hazzard style. But for a few minutes, at least, it numbs the memory of January's excuses.

Another hour passes as Johnny thinks about every single moment he and January had together. He recalls with longing the first time they met in RedHead. The words they shared at their first date. The movie they saw. The cocktails, the baby pictures, the skating. Absolutely everything. Occasionally, the flow of thoughts is interrupted by a quiet sob into the pillow. It's an important part of the exorcising of January to remember every tiny detail. Once they've all been remembered, fathoms Johnny Hazzard, he can move on. Quite suddenly, the prospect of telling his friends all about his summer becomes horrifying. Johnny doesn't want to speak.

At around two o'clock, he stands. The blood rushes to his head and he has to keep still for a few moments to regain his balance. He walks to the kitchen, where Siska is preparing a salad lunch.

"Dahling, are you okay? Would you like some lunch?"

"No, it's cool."

Johnny takes a glass of apple juice and breaks off a mouthful of French bread. He pays a visit to Lydia's bedroom, but she's not there. He returns to his room and sits at his computer desk, eating the bread and gulping the apple juice down in one.

Twenty minutes pass before Johnny realizes he has been staring at a switched-off flat-screen monitor.

The rest of the fallout day is filled in a similar vein. Turning the radio on is a big mistake. The God of Breakups (archenemy of Cupid and Aphrodite, grotesque body shape, halitosis, provider of lines like "It's not you, it's me," a bitter and terrible man) is smiling down on Johnny Hazzard and using his wicked powers to influence the DJ's choice of music. The first station Johnny flicks to plays a Manic Street Preachers song with the lyric "So why so sad? You live and you learn." The second station he tunes in to is in the middle of a commercial break, before returning to the music with Peter Frampton crooning away "Ooh baby I love your way, I wanna be with you night and day. . . ."

Pausing from his stupor only to pick at food or drink, Johnny begins to think the best way to prove January wrong is to get on with things. But it is easier said than done. Siska manages to make a small breakthrough at about four thirty. She knocks on his door. He does not answer, preferring to sit on his bed pretending to read Michael Moore.

"Only me," she says cheerfully.

"Hi," says Johnny, giving the clearest possible "go away, I'm sulking" vibes.

"You have to eat something, Johnny. A piece of bread all day is crap."

"I'm not hungry. I feel fine."

"What about I make the tomato-and-chili soup?"

Siska knows this is a firm favorite. This is the acid test. If Johnny isn't in the mood for her tomato-and-chili soup, it's a cold day in hell.

"Maybe later," comes the hushed reply. The devil is feeling the chilly draft.

"You must eat."

Johnny doesn't speak, preferring to stare at his book.

"You don't want to talk about it?"

"No, thanks."

316

"*Boule et Bill* would be very upset. You've neglected them. They were always there for you before. Why don't you say hello?"

It's hard to feel anger toward a middle-aged woman who is telling you two cartoon characters in a comic book are angry with you because you haven't looked at them in your hour of misery. Against his wishes, Johnny cracks a smile.

"Oh, thank God, dahling. I was beginning to think you'd never smile again. You have a beautiful smile. You and Lydia have beautiful smiles. You must always smile."

"Siska, you're crazy."

"Thank the God," she says, reaching up to Johnny's bookshelf and taking down a couple of *Boule et Bill* books.

"Say hello to them, they miss you."

Johnny accepts the books, puts down the Michael Moore, and promises to take a look.

"I'll start the soup," says Siska.

"No, finish your painting," suggests Johnny.

Siska pauses, twists her mouth in thought, and says, "No. I'm without the inspiration."

She heads to the kitchen. Johnny smiles again. He opens up book number one. He's read it a hundred times before. He knows the story. He remembers what most of the words mean. And, like before, the familiar brings comfort. It's safe, it's good-humored, and it reminds him of all those times he needed a picking up after a falling down.

Johnny does indeed gulp down a warming bowl of tomato-and-chili soup. And then, without planning, he decides he wants to return to Waterloo Bridge. He takes his dad's umbrella, alerts Siska to his intention, and leaves. Siska finds the wave of *the inspiration* is getting a bit tidal. Within minutes of Johnny's departure, she heads into the studio and begins a new, small canvas. Racked with guilt at the exploitation, she puts oldies on the CD player (The Shirelles) and reminds herself that it's all for a higher purpose. In two hours, the canvas is covered in a splish-splosh of orange and red city buildings, old and new. At the foot of one such construction, in front of a large, apparently rusty door, stands a small figure. Is it a boy or a girl? Dwarfed by the buildings around it, the person cuts a pathetic little figure.

TWENTY-SEVEN

While Siska is busy rapidly painting her city, Johnny is standing on the bridge, looking at the same vista that was once his and January's, but which is now only his. And that's the thing about breaking up. What was once a shared experience, a shared object, a shared memory, a shared opinion or feeling or insecurity or doubt, what was once inextricably and exclusively linked to two people, suddenly becomes separate, dislocated, and, ultimately, solitary. Johnny Hazzard realizes this when the sight of the Thames and the buildings that flank it doesn't feel right somehow. It's not just the experience of standing there, stray rain spitting onto his face, fast-flowing pedestrians gliding past, that is solitary. It's the view itself. The memory cells are telling him something isn't quite right. This stunning and frankly romantic view belongs to Johnny and January. And it will take a long time for the dislocation, the separation to remove its sprawling influence from a London full of memories. A London that so quickly has become a city of the shared, not of the solitary. As quickly as

Johnny adapted to the newness of sharing, he is now forced to switch back to the familiar loneliness.

The rain becomes heavier. Johnny opens the black umbrella and rests it on his shoulder. That experience of acceptance and really belonging to someone flicks on in his mind as if he's just turned on the TV to find *The Johnny and January Show* on all channels. That evening on Waterloo Bridge was just about the most special evening in Johnny's short life. He does not know it yet, but it is a night he will never, ever forget. It is a night that once summed up all that was great in the world and now sums up all that is crap. *Perhaps*, muses Johnny Hazzard, *that is what it's all about. Every bit of great has a bit of shit attached to it, somewhere. It doesn't always show, that's all.*

The burst of heavy rain stops. Johnny keeps the umbrella open, too caught up in his own thoughts to muster the effort to close it. He is conscious of what is going on around him, but still very distant from it. He stays in the same position, leaning on the bridge, looking out at the same view across the river. The view becomes secondary as the feelings take over. The feelings of shyness and fear when Johnny first set eyes on her. The feeling of being lost in the speed at which events took place. The feeling of sureness that the bliss could not last. The feeling of inevitability that the whole thing was about to end. And the way all those feelings, and a list of ones he can't quite put into words, come together to be known as the four-letter word, *love*.

Throughout the whole of his Waterloo Bridge return, Johnny Hazzard does not cry.

He decides to defy his parents and take a stroll over the bridge, down The Strand, through Trafalgar Square and into the West End. It is a Saturday night. Johnny encounters fragments of London life as he ambles through Soho and Oxford Street. He doesn't remember noticing these things before. Not with Lydia, nor with January. This time the city feels more vibrant, more alive. He sees the prostitutes, the drag queens walking arm in arm, the crazed man talking to himself at the street corner. They've been there all along. But it's only now that he sees them.

* * *

As much as we try to pretend otherwise, *good-bye* is the hardest word. Unless, of course, you are leaving a restaurant after a lousy meal and lousier wine.

The day of Johnny's and Lydia's departure is as madcap as any day of travel ever is in the Hazzard household. Passports mysteriously disappear, hot shower water is replaced by ice-cold, suitcases refuse to zip shut, flight documents are found in a small pool of orange juice, and smoke alarms sound several times. This summer day is the sort you wish you'd spent on a quiet beach.

The catalyst of chaos is Siska. She is on an artistic journey. "Dahlings, when I have the inspiration, we must all be happy because it means I will make paintings. I make paintings, I sell them. If I sell them it means more money for everyone."

This justification means Siska can lock herself up in the stuffy studio and, on a steady diet of water, tobacco, and beef jerky,

321

crack on with touching up the paintings that Johnny Hazzard has unwittingly inspired. So with a couple of hours to go before Mr. Hazzard must take his children to Gatwick to catch the plane, Siska, who is normally a great help, cuts herself off from the outside world. With The Crewcuts' "Sh-Boom" playing loud on the stereo, she gets busy.

Lydia is running around in a panic because of the dampened flight documents. The orange juice stains have turned her name into *Yoia Hozzaro*. A lethargic Johnny tries so hard to pack his case, but his clothes-folding skills aren't in danger of winning him any prizes. Mr. Hazzard manages to fold trousers, but shirts prove an insurmountable task.

Somehow, the clan makes it into the Hazzard vehicle by two o'clock. Siska says good-bye in the garage. She hugs Johnny tight and says, quietly, so no one else can hear, "You are brave, Johnny. Be strong. Be strong."

Johnny smiles, unsure of what to say, but grateful.

Lydia and Siska share an embrace. Lydia says she'll be back before long — possibly at Christmas.

Siska blows kisses to the kids and waves them off.

As the car pulls out, Johnny feels sad, as he always does, that he's leaving Siska. It's nothing like the feeling he gets when leaving behind his mom in Austin. Siska is more like the dotty aunt, full of sympathy, whose cream cakes are a delight. It's a different kind of sadness, but sadness all the same.

On the drive to the airport, everything feels smaller, grayer, and somehow less precise to Johnny Hazzard. It's a hard feeling for him to describe. But it's a definite feeling. Traditionally, drives to Gatwick were mixed affairs; part of Johnny was excited, another part sad that the summer was all but over. This time feels markedly different from the others. London isn't so imposing, and Johnny isn't so short.

As is the tradition, Mr. Hazzard enters the airport short-stay car park with a complaint about the rates.

"Jesus Christ!" he shouts, as if he's never known the prices to be so expensive. Yet every year it's the same routine. The prices go up, the scream goes out.

"They're going to charge us to take a piss next time," says Mr. Hazzard, outraged.

The check-in is painless and swift. Mr. Hazzard, as usual, begins blubbing as he hugs the kids.

"Stop growing or I'll get angry," he tells Johnny.

Lydia smiles. "Bye, Dad," she says. Johnny wonders if Lydia misses Mr. H more than he does. There's something about their relationship that is different, a little closer than Johnny's and his father's.

"You take care," Mr. Hazzard says. "You'd better come out and see us at Christmas."

"I'll be there," she promises.

Mr. H kisses both kids on the cheek. He still cries as they walk away, taking their first steps back toward their ordinary world.

After their passports and boarding passes are checked, they both turn to wave at their dad. For an ever-so-brief moment, he sees them as they were six years ago, when this whole thing began, Johnny age nine, Lydia age thirteen. The two children waving back at their daddy. He suffers the same vision every year. And every year Mr. Hazzard feels a little bit guiltier that in some way his divorce, his new life in Britain, has had some detrimental effect on his little boy and his little girl. As ever, he ponders this on the lonely drive home and, as ever, he can't come to any conclusions.

Johnny wanders around Duty Free. A woman who smells as though she's been dipped into a bath full of the latest designer fragrance offers him the chance to try out some aftershaves. She follows her suggestion with a "sir." Johnny is quietly contented, but declines. He buys chocolate instead.

The flight is delayed by a half hour due to "catering problems." Johnny can only imagine that the airline's CEO has tried the cuisine, fainted, and that they are busy preparing a new menu, some sort of variation on the theme of edible for a change.

Seated in the departure lounge, it's almost as though Johnny and Lydia never spoke in Ieper. She is paying him little attention, engrossed in her music magazine. There's something he's been thinking about for a while; he deliberates, thinking it would be a step backward, a futile move. Nonetheless, Johnny makes sure he still has January's phone number and e-mail address in his wallet. He only has one picture of them, taken in a photo booth. He steps up and leans over to put it in the ashtray. Lydia, whose eyes do not appear to have moved from the page of the music magazine, reaches out an arm and grabs Johnny tight, bringing him back to his seat. She doesn't say a thing. Johnny puts the photo in his top pocket.

Some twenty minutes later, when Lydia is in the restroom, Johnny takes the picture out, doesn't look at it, and puts it in the ashtray. He sits back down, elated. Then he leans over, takes the picture out, blows the ash off it and puts it in the wallet again.

The gate number flashes up on the monitor. It's time to go home.

Johnny Hazzard is one step away from the plane, one tiny step away from Austin, from Grandma and Uncle James with his dumb home improvement, from Mom and homemade lasagne, from math, history, and science, from jerks pushing him into the lockers, from cheerleaders bouncing up and down and sticking fingers down throats, from long and lonely Friday nights, from hot and doped Saturday afternoons, from the unimportant and the petty, the silly and the childish.

He pauses and looks over his shoulder, as if expecting someone to be there to say something. Then he steps onto the plane. The cheerful flight attendant smiles, her makeup-caked face wrinkling up. She reminds Johnny of a circus clown. He carefully folds his jacket into the overhead compartment, sits down, and buckles his belt. The window seat is his. And moments after take-off, the dreary aerial view of suburban England feels insignificant, tired, and tiresome, and Johnny Hazzard feels a punishing sense of longing, a desire to recapture, to step back, to start something again. And then, slowly and calmly, he slips into a slumber. When he awakes, all he can see is the Atlantic Ocean.

EPILOGUE

The day after his arrival in Austin, Johnny Hazzard arranges to meet with Kade. David is still on vacation in Florida and Jack is grounded. He got caught smoking.

They decide to meet at an old haunt, underneath Congress Bridge, which the famous bat colony — the largest urban one in the US — calls its home.

NEVER HANDLE GROUNDED BATS
NUNCA AGARRE MURCIÉLAGOS TIRADOS EN EL PISO

Under this ominous metal sign, the friends sit on a bench, talking about nothing in particular for an excruciating amount of time. A conversation of no consequence always precedes a conversation of enormous significance. Neither of them can bring themselves to say all the stuff they need to say. They talk relentlessly about skate moves. Johnny says he hasn't learned that many new ones. Kade says he has and shows off the new belt he bought at the Tekgnar store. They talk about some guy who sells cheap vodka. They talk about the weather, for Christ's sake. And then Johnny decides it's time to get serious.

"Met this girl. British girl."

"Yeah? Awesome." Kade's apparent enthusiasm does little to hide the jealousy.

"She was older. Eighteen."

"No shit?" says Kade, leaning back on the bench.

"Yep. And I'm not just saying this. She was the most beautiful girl I've ever seen. And I mean *seen*. Naked and everything."

"No. . . ." Kade goes a little red in the cheeks.

"Yes. Most certainly yes," replies Johnny, proudly.

"You did it? You got laid?" The incredulity in Kade's voice is all too clear.

"Yeah, don't sound so fucking surprised. I got laid. Johnny Hazzard got laid."

Kade relaxes a little more. He takes a big sniff in. He looks at the sky, darkening. He looks dead ahead. Johnny wants more questions. Johnny wants to tell all.

"Me, too," says Kade.

Right now, Johnny would be perfectly happy to drown himself in the river ahead. He looks at the ducks in the water and thinks it would be far better if he joined them. *Why, why, why, Kade?* he thinks. *Why did you have to steal my thunder? Fuck you! It's me who's supposed to have the big news.*

"That's cool. Who to?"

"Everyone's favorite cheerleader. Miss Perez. She's like totally uncontrollable. It wasn't even my idea. She's got it bad." Kade's newfound cockiness is partly unattractive and wholly annoying.

"When did you do it?"

"After we went to Barton Springs. Romantic walk, all that stuff. You know, you and your English girl must have done that shit, too."

"No, I mean, when? Last week?"

"No, no, a while ago. I was going to e-mail you, but I thought I'd wait till I saw you."

"But how long ago?" asks Johnny, urgently.

"Geez . . . it was soon after you went. Like the second week of June or something. The ninth. Why?"

329

And Johnny is deflated, spent, and so, so livid. He wears these expressions in quick succession. Kade knows exactly why.

"So when did you . . . ?"

"Er . . ."

Johnny hesitates and shuffles around in his seat.

"I beat you, didn't I?" says Kade, smiling.

"It's not a competition, Kade. It's more than that."

"I beat you, and you're jealous!"

Kade starts laughing. If only he knew the hurtful truth about what happened with the relationship. The truth that Johnny is keeping from him. The truth he might never be able to get off his chest. The same truth the boys would probably laugh about.

"I beat you. I lost it first!"

"You motherfucker, Kade. It doesn't matter. It was the experience that mattered. I got it on with an eighteen-year-old."

"Yeah, so what? We've been talking about who's gonna do it first since fifth grade. And I did. And I'm the Boss Man."

Kade ruffles Johnny's hair. Johnny jerks his head away, before punching Kade on the arm. Kade puts him in a headlock. The bats begin to fly away en masse. The sight is spectacular and scary. It is just before sunset, and one million Mexican free-tailed bats emerge with menacing speed. A chorus of *ohhh*s is heard from some nearby place where tourists and locals have gathered to watch the spectacle. The boys are transfixed for a few moments, before Kade resumes his assault. Johnny bursts into laughter. A passing group of middle-aged tourists tut disapprovingly.

That feeling of comfort, that he has craved and loathed in equal measure this summer, returns once more. And, seeing the damn bats fly for the thousandth time, Johnny Hazzard accepts that the familiar is just as exciting as the new.

ACKNOWLEDGMENTS

This book is the result of collaborations with many people, and they all deserve a special mention.

David Levithan asked for an idea. A few weeks later, during a Saturday afternoon game of park football in London, I met my first Austinite, and the Hazzard adventure began. Thanks to David for helping me give shape to the story, and thanks to Josef, the muse, wherever the hell you are.

Big thanks to Mark B for criticism, proofreading, telling me to get on with it, flamenco dancing at the Spanish bar, wild geese, and Hurricanes. Once again, without Mark B, this wouldn't have happened. So blame him.

Thank you, Fletcher Berndt, who I met in the finest skate store in all of Texas. He has answered dozens of questions, taught me a lot about Austin and what it's like growing up there, and introduced me to some of the tightest bands.

It was Ben Hillman's idea, in June of 2003, to go to Ieper. Thank you for all the driving, and the tireless encouragement. In August of 2004, Ben became my pan-Europe chauffeur once more. Special gratitude for the Menin Gate discovery.

Thanks to Jan and Christian, my Brussels tour guides as well as comic book and chocolate advisors. Your hospitality is second to none.

Linda and Hannah, the Brits abroad, were invaluable help to me as I learned about life in Texas. Thanks for the pancake party. Thanks to Dave Wilson for great Tex Mex and greater conversation, and sharp insight into the "special relationship."

Thank you, Eula Sharp and Georgetown High School. The teachers of the English department and my day trip from Austin taught me a great deal. Gratitude to Denise at Another Chapter for arranging it.

Talking to Austin Gunter, the unicyclist, was also very helpful and I'm grateful for your time.

It's marvelous to have parents who are not disappointed in me for not having chosen a proper job. They found a way to come to NYC and, quite simply, their support is everything. *Gracias, obrigado.*

Cheers to the vice presidents of the fan club, whose care is just the best.

Special thanks also to Peter and Jenny Skellen for encouragement through the Greenwich era.

Almost everybody I met in Austin gave me an idea, suggestion, or just that famous Southern hospitality, all of which contributed to *Johnny Hazzard*. Ryan at The Hideout was generous and helpful, and it was his idea that I visit the place that ended up being the most wonderful spot of all . . .

Griffin High (the School of Cool). Thanks to everybody there, particularly Rebekah Jongewaard and all the students I spoke with. You were inspiring, and your mark is left on me and this book. Please, would you all consider running for the presidency?

Vamos!